THE
VAMPIRE
COURT

ALI WINTERS

THE VAMPIRE COURT

THE VAMPIRE DEBT: BOOK THREE

Published by Rising Flame Press
Edited by Nicole Zoltack
Cover design & Formatting by Red Umbrella Graphic Designs

ISBN-13: 978-1-945238-16-1

www.aliwinters.com

More by Ali Winters

The Hunted series
The Reapers
The Exodus
The Moirai
The Fallen
Flirting with Death

In The End duology
Sound of Silence
Light in Darkness

Shadow World
The Vampire Debt
The Vampire Curse
The Vampire Court
The Vampire Oath
The Vampire Crown
The Vampire Betrayal

Stand Alone
Cast In Moonlight
Favor of the Gods
A Sky of Shattered Stars
Army of the Winter Court

Shadow World

S U N . . .

Nightwich
CASTLE

Progsdale

Durford

Littlemire

Valeburn

Sangate

Gloamfarrow

Windbury

Galeport

Murhelm

Stormvale

Crescent
Isle

MOUNTAINS

For Schmuckles,
Thanks, kid.

CHAPTER ONE

CLARA

"Bite me." The words crack in my throat, coming out louder than intended and breaking the silence that settled between us over the past several hours. Cherno startles awake from his perch on the back of the bench and flops down on the seat at Alaric's side.

He lets the curtain covering the carriage window slide from his fingers and leans back to look at me.

"Clara?" he asks, raising a single dark brow.

"Bite me," I say again, my voice normal this time.

Alaric's gaze lowers to my hands in my lap. I force my fingers to release my skirt, allowing the blood to flow back into my whitened knuckles, but he's already seen the way I clutched the material until my fingers ached.

Cherno crawls to the corner of the bench seat and curls up in a bat-shaped ball, wrapping a leathery wing over their head, blocking us out.

Alaric blows out a soft breath then says, "No."

I blink, my lips parting. Then I snap my mouth shut. Did he really deny me the final mark—this man who wanted me to accept it for *my safety*?

"Why in the Otherworld not?" I demand. "You said it was up to me to ask for each mark." I press my hands to my chest. "I am asking for the final one now."

Alaric cants his head then runs a hand through the dark strands, messing them in a way that's all the more fitting to his handsome features.

"Clara, you are only asking because you are nervous. I would rather you didn't bind yourself to me over something so... trivial and temporary." His lip curls as if the thought leaves a sour taste in his mouth.

I clench my jaw and temper my irritation. "Temporary? I'll die without it." My chest feels tight, my tongue heavy and dry. "You said it was my choice," I whisper.

He frowns and leans forward, resting his elbows on his knees then reaches out to take one of my hands in his. "My dear, Clara, it *is* your choice. It will always be your choice." Alaric dips his head and blows out a breath before raising his eyes to meet mine again. "But not like this."

2

I open my mouth to protest, but he holds up a hand, silencing me.

"Victor compelled you, and that is the only reason why Cassius, Della, and Lawrence found out that you were not marked," he adds as if knowing what I was about to say.

I bite down on my bottom lip.

Alaric brushes his knuckles across my cheek. The glove encasing his hand is soft against my skin. "No one will dare attempt anything of the sort at Nightwich. Not to you."

"How can you be so sure?" I am baffled by his confidence. It happened in his territory, and now, we are heading to new ground where the rules will undoubtedly be different.

He's silent for a long moment, but in the end, he only says, "I just am."

I pull my hand from his grasp and sit back. "And what if the other three say something? It's not like you can watch them every second to make sure they keep quiet."

Alaric's gaze darkens. "They won't—not if they wish to continue living." The promise of violence is in his voice, and brutality etches the sharp edges of his features. He lifts his chin a fraction, relaxing back against his seat, completely and utterly confident. "I ordered them not to."

Demons and saints... He ordered them? What kind of assurance is that? I hold back further argument. He's right. I am nervous, but his reasoning is hardly comforting. He believes his order will carry weight even when I'd been attacked in his home.

3

Shifting in my seat, I work over his words again and again, trying to decipher his meaning. Is it possible for vampires to compel each other?

"Besides," he says quietly, his voice thick and dark, "the carriage is far from the ideal place to mark you for the last time." His gaze pins me to the spot, chasing every other thought away until I forget them all. Until the only thing left is the heat in his eyes and the unspoken words—the ones that promise things to come after the bite and the promise he had made after the second mark. *"Next time, my dear, Clara, I will take my time with you."*

My skin heats at the memory and the way his words still have the power to illicit warmth low in my belly.

"And then there's the fact that we both know you would regret it afterward." His voice brings me crashing back to the present, though if he notices the obvious reactions to my thoughts, he doesn't let on. Alaric's expression softens. "You don't want the final mark. We both know that. It's okay to be nervous about what's to come, but don't let the possibility of what may be give you the illusion that you no longer have a choice."

I open my mouth to protest and say that I *do* want the mark, but I clamp it shut, pressing my lips into a thin line when I realize he's right. I don't want the mark. I'm not ready, at least... not yet.

We sit in silence for the next several hours. The wheels of the carriage bounce over the bumps and grooves in the road, making my already aching posterior more uncomfortable, but eventually, even that can't keep me awake. The thin gilding of light that edges the curtains fades, and the rocking of the carriage urges me to rest. A yawn forces its way from me.

Alaric holds out a white-gloved hand. I take it and maneuver to sit next to him and rest my head on his shoulder. He tucks me into his side, wrapping an arm around me, and entwines our fingers.

"Rest," he says. "We still have several more hours before we arrive."

I rest my head against his shoulder and close my eyes. Already nearly asleep, I feel Cherno's small feet as the demon clambers into my lap and settles into the crook of my arm.

"Wake up, Clara." Alaric's deep voice whispers near my ear.

I sit up, blinking blearily, and stretch out as much as I can in the cramped space. On one side of the carriage, the curtains have been drawn back, allowing the rosy glow of dawn to enter. I lean across Alaric and take in the view.

After three days and three nights, there is finally more to see than distant mountains, vast expanses of fields, and groups of trees too small to be considered forests.

Mountains rear up alongside the road, stretching for as far as the eye can see. Built into the side is a castle, larger than any I could have ever imagined. Surrounding the castle is a town that must be at least five times the size of Littlemire and Durford combined.

I'd expected a dark, haunted castle with broken spires, but this one gleams as though it were made of polished, white marble trimmed with gold.

The carriage slows as we enter the edge of town to avoid tramping the people going about their business. *Humans*. I shouldn't be surprised. It makes sense that the vampires at the castle would need a vast human population to sustain them throughout the year after the claiming.

We pull through the gates of town and continue down the short road leading to the castle. We come to a stop at the edge of a moat. A bridge lowers with a heavy thud, and the carriage jerks forward once more. I lean forward, pressing my face closer to the glass window and gulp.

Unholy demon shit. That is not a moat, but a vast chasm that nearly reaches into the Otherworld itself. Massive stone spikes rise from below, jutting up like jagged and razor-sharp teeth.

The depth sends a wave of vertigo through me, and I drop back down to my seat. Alaric gives me a knowing look but says nothing. Outward, he is the picture of calm except for the tell-tale twitch of muscle along his jaw.

He pulls the curtain closed again. Tension builds in the air, nearly crackling like a lightning storm. It's a few more minutes before we come to another stop. From the way Alaric scoots forward, I know this is our destination.

We have arrived at Nightwich.

My stomach bottoms out, and I'm not sure if I will be able to get out of this carriage by my own ability.

The door opens, letting in a chilly blast of winter air. I shiver, telling myself that it's from the cold and not because I am about to walk into a castle filled with vampires.

The footman steps aside, his gaze facing forward as he holds the door open. His uniform is crisp. Red threads glint in the morning light against the black cloth, contrasting with the castle's bright exterior.

Alaric climbs out first then turns and offers me a hand. I take it, holding a little too tight as I step down beside him.

"Your luggage will be brought to your respective rooms immediately," the footman says.

Alaric's head whips around to face him. "You will bring her things to my rooms. She is to stay with me."

"Of course, Sire," the footman says with a bow. He closes the door and walks to the back of the carriage.

I stare after him. Something about the few words he spoke snag in my mind like a splintering piece of wood.

"Come, my dear, Clara," Alaric says, guiding me with a hand at the small of my back. His eyes never leave the castle until the second we are inside. Something akin to dread hardens his expression.

We pass through the antechamber. The walls are a dull, pale stone, but paintings, statues, and expertly placed fabric bring a touch of color. Alaric hurries us through the halls, without a second's hesitation. He knows exactly where he's going. After a few turns, we end up in a cramped corridor lacking any decor. These must be the servants' passages, though I'm not sure why we are taking them.

The soft beating of Cherno's wings against the air trails behind us.

A woman clears her throat behind us, stopping us in our tracks. Alaric's fingers flex against my back. Taking my hand in his, he turns, partially hiding me with his body.

I list my head to the side and look past his shoulder to the woman dressed in a soldier's uniform. The gold metal of her spaulders and bracers is polished impeccably and set against the dark black of her clothes.

"Her majesty requests your presence in the throne room," she says.

Alaric's hand tightens slightly over mine. "We will come as soon as we have settled."

The guard frowns then says, "The queen has requested your presence the moment you arrived, not a minute later."

Alaric is silent for several beats then gives her a curt nod.

8

"Very well."

The guard spins on her heel and walks back the way we came.

Alaric lifts a hand and motions to Cherno. The demon bat nods their head then flutters off down the hall in the direction we were headed in. I briefly wonder if sending his demon away is a good or bad sign.

He turns to me with worry written across his face. "Are you ready?"

I nod. Then together, we follow the guard back down the hall toward the throne room where the queen awaits.

CHAPTER
TWO
CLARA

"I will inform the queen that you have arrived." The guard turns to me and narrows her eyes. There's a distinct curl to her upper lip as she says, "She will be taken to the human quarters—"

Alaric bares his fangs. "She stays with me."

The guard bristles. I'm surprised when she doesn't object further but instead dips her chin and strides through a side door nearly hidden in the shadows of the corner.

Before us is a stone archway over two massive doors that narrow to a point at the top. The sun-bleached wood is gilded along the edges and embossed with the crescent moon with a feather cutting down through the center.

I swipe my clammy palms down over the hips, hoping the

gesture isn't noticeable. We are alone, yet I can't shake the feeling that hundreds of eyes are watching us.

"It's about time the two of you arrived," Cassius's voice booms, sounding too loud for the previously quiet space.

Lawrence walks a half step behind him. I can't help but notice that Della is not with them.

Alaric says nothing as the two men join us, but he squeezes my hand reassuringly before letting go.

The two vampires turn toward me in unison. Their stony expressions only reinforce the fact that I should not be here.

What protocol is he breaking to keep me by his side?

I reach for Alaric to question him, but before my hand is halfway to his arm, one of the ornate doors swing open. The room is crowded. Men and women are dressed in elegant suits and gowns. All heads turn toward us, and I am left feeling more than underdressed for the occasion.

Then, as if by some unseen cue, the crowd parts down the center, revealing the vampire queen upon her throne.

A white dress accented with obsidian beading hugs her body. Her honey-blonde hair cascades down her back loose, and upon her head sits a bone-white crown with thick points jutting up. Rubies decorate the tips and along the base.

A man leans closer to her and whispers something in her ear. The queen throws her head back and laughs, her voice carrying throughout the room. She is slight and delicate like Kitty, but that is where the similarities end. She holds a power that seems to radiate off her in waves. Where my sister is soft and warm, she is harsh and cold. Her eyes cut through the room toward our small group. Even from this distance I can feel the scrutiny of her gaze like sharp claws tracing every vein over my skin.

A large raven sits on the high back of her throne. Their red eyes are so bright they throw off a soft glow within the brightly lit room. Even her demon has a presence.

Alaric strides forward, and I move to follow, but a hand grabs my wrist and holds me back. I tug on my arm, and when I'm not freed, I turn to glare at the vampire holding me.

"Stay with us," Lawrence says. He slowly pries his fingers off my upper arm, dropping his hand when I remain where I am.

The door slams shut behind us. Cassius and Lawrence stop as if that were a cue. Together, we wait at the edge of the room, away from the crowd.

"What a waste of time," Cassius mutters under his breath. "All to prove to Alaric that she has him under her pretty little thumb."

Alaric continues until he stands at the foot of the dais before the queen. He kneels down on one knee. The queen shifts her attention to him, her face somber. The demon bird above lets out a caw that echoes through the room, silencing the barely audible whispers.

"Stand and come to me, my prince," the queen purrs.

"Prince?" I nearly choke on the words.

12

"You truly did not know?" Cassius asks, his voice filled with amusement. "Our dear Alaric didn't tell you..." He feigns a scandalized gasp then murmurs, "This is fantastic..."

Lawrence shoots him a warning glance.

Things that have been said and done start to piece themselves together. How Alaric ordered the three vampires, the footman calling him Sire and the guard not arguing with him...

I pry my gaze from Alaric and look at Lawrence from the corner of my eye. I'm embarrassed that it has taken this moment for me to learn the truth.

Lawrence's expression changes, taking me in as though seeing me for the first time. His features soften to something akin to kindness. I swallow thickly. That can't be right—he hates me.

"Who did you think he was?" he asks under his breath.

Alaric stands and walks up the dais and into the open arms of the queen. She wraps herself around him. He doesn't return the embrace, but he doesn't fight it. My heart squeezes painfully in my chest.

"I... I don't know. I suppose I thought he was just a vampire," I say. I probably shouldn't admit anything to him, but I don't think he's asking out of malice or trickery.

"Just a vampire?" he scoffs.

I cringe.

He shakes his head, genuinely shocked that I never had a clue—as if who and what Alaric is was common knowledge among humans.

As the queen releases Alaric, the crowd resumes movement and sound. Conversations pick up, but the path leading to the queen remains clear.

"You had no idea he was the first of Elizabeth's creations and the most powerful of us all and fated to be the vampire queen's consort? You didn't want him for his money or the things he could do for you?"

His questions rip the air from my lungs—painful realizations. My face heats with every word that comes out of his mouth because I naively believed everything was simple. I believed Alaric was an ordinary man.

"How could I?" I ask, voice cracking. "I've never seen him until he claimed me."

He looks at me for a single heartbeat then throws his head back and lets out a sharp laugh. I cross my arms and wait for him to finish.

"Look," I say, attempting to keep my temper in check. "I never wanted anything from him. Not his money, or that manor, or..." I trail off shaking my head, feeling foolish. I wrap my arms around my middle. Then in a small voice, I add, "I still don't want anything of his."

"Then what is it you *do* want?" he asks.

Then I understand. When he questioned me about where I would want to be if I could choose, his cold demeanor, trying to scare me off in the library the day he arrived at the manor, and all the accusations that I might want what Alaric has... Lawrence was worried about my intentions. He must be a good friend to worry for Alaric like that. Even from someone with such a limited lifespan, such limited strength... someone powerless.

"I want—" I shake my head. "I don't want anything," I say.

Lawrence's eyes narrow on me.

I only want him.

I don't dare speak the words aloud. How can I admit that to Lawrence when I haven't even admitted it to Alaric, let alone to myself?

I can't.

It would only complicate things, but knowing that doesn't stop the words from building and bubbling up to the surface. I lo—

I close my eyes for a brief moment and push the thoughts back down, locking them away.

The rest of our conversation dies on the air as Cassius pushes off the wall, clearing his throat. He moves across the floor toward the queen. Lawrence grabs my arm and drags me along.

The queen and Alaric descend the steps of the dais and walk toward us. He avoids looking at me as if I don't exist, but I can't help but frown at her arm linked with his.

Our two groups meet in the center of the room. The crowd closes in behind us but spreads out, giving us privacy.

I study Alaric's face.

A prince…

And he's fated to be with the vampire queen — to be with this unearthly woman standing among us.

It's hard to believe. Not because I think it's impossible, but because he looks every inch the part in the way he holds himself and I never noticed before. He knew it and never saw fit to tell me.

I feel as though I don't know him. Have I ever known him? If he hid this from me, what else is he hiding? It stings. He didn't trust me enough over the past three days and nights alone in the carriage to tell me this. He had to have known that I would find out once we reached Nightwich.

"Cassius, Lawrence, I am glad to see you both here as well," the queen croons. Her voice is saccharine sweet and dripping with false joy. "I don't see Victor. Where is he?"

There's something dangerous in the way she asks the question, and her voice sends a shiver down my spine.

My stomach knots, and I'm grateful she has chosen to ignore my existence.

Lawrence pales, but before he or Cassius can speak, Alaric waves a hand dismissively and says, "Elizabeth, my queen."

She smiles at the way he says her name and title.

"We have traveled a long way over the past few days. I am tired, and there is no reason we cannot discuss these things another time."

She looks as though she might refuse, but when Alaric gives

her a sultry smile, Elizabeth returns the look, victory glinting in her eyes.

"Very well," she says, reaching her arms up around his neck.

Cassius grabs my arm and spins me around, leading me away. Lawrence follows closely, blocking my view of them, but not before I see the queen place a kiss on his mouth.

The second we leave the throne room, I jerk my arm out of Cassius's grip. My breath hitches. They all knew what we were walking into, but no one warned me about any of it.

I walk over to a window on the far side of the hall and rest my forehead against the chilled glass. The outside view looks inward to the palace grounds. I grip the ledge and focus on my breathing. A slimy feeling blooms inside me. I hate how it feels. It's ugly, dark, and twisted.

I feel betrayed. I feel lied to, and—

I swallow down the thought, not ready to face it. I focus on the anger and hurt, holding on to them and willing them to grow until they drown out anything else.

Soft footfalls sound behind me. Alaric's hand lands softly on my shoulder but I don't turn to face him. If I do, I'll give in to whatever comfort and accept any reason he might give for what happened.

"Come, Clara." His hand slides down my arm to take my hand.

I don't fight or resist as he leads me down through the halls. I'm too angry with him to pay attention to my surroundings as we

17

meander toward his room.

The queen kissed him. Not a chaste kiss on each cheek, but on the mouth. I could brush it off if she had greeted Cassius and Lawrence in the same manner, but she didn't.

I sneak a glance at Alaric, but nothing in his expression gives away his thoughts.

We climb two flights of stairs before we reach a landing and continue walking until we reach the only door halfway down the hall.

Alaric drops my hand and places his on my lower back, guiding me inside. I walk a few paces into the room and stop, focusing my unseeing gaze on the floor.

A prince... fated to be the queen's consort.

The door closes with a soft click.

"Clara?"

I don't respond.

Alaric turns me around and cups my face, tilting my head up and forcing me to look him in the eye.

I push away, and he lets go. I stumble back a few steps before catching myself. Warm pressure builds behind my eyes, blurring my vision. I blink, and hot, angry tears slide down my face.

"Why didn't *you* tell me?" My words are sharp and cutting.

At my outburst, Cherno startles somewhere across the room. Leathery wings flutter erratically until the demon settles above us on one of the thick beams.

"Because it doesn't matter."

I suck in a breath. "How can you say that? You're fated to be with the queen."

He goes deathly still. "Who told you that?" he asks sharply.

"It doesn't matter." I throw his words back at him. "Why didn't you tell me?"

He takes a tentative step closer and, when I don't back away, another and another. Alaric reaches out and takes me by the shoulders. He swallows hard, the knot in his throat bobbing. "Because of the way you're looking at me now. I never wanted you to see me as the others do, but to see me for who I am."

That strikes me like a physical blow. In the short time since learning who he was, I put up walls, blocking him out. If I had known all along, I never would have accepted his deal. I never would have allowed him to give me any of the marks, and I never would have returned to Windbury after Kathrine's wedding.

When I don't speak, he continues, "Being a prince means nothing. It's an empty title that I hold only because I had the misfortune of being her second victim."

"Second?" I frown. "Lawrence said you were her first."

Pain darkens his eyes. "Her first *creation*." Alaric turns his face away, glowering at a distant place I can't see. "She nearly killed Rosalie. I had no choice but to submit to Elizabeth's will so I could keep her from dying—" His voice breaks.

My hurt and anger melt away. Forgotten. I move closer and take his hand. His fingers squeeze mine—the only physical sign of his pain he allows himself to show.

"I turned my own sister because of her. I robbed Rosalie of the future she should have had... but I couldn't let her die."

"I understand," I say.

And I do. I would have done the same if I had been in his place. I am thankful now that he refused to give me the final mark on the way here, but I don't think I can ever allow him to mark me when he is essentially betrothed to the queen. I can't allow myself to be tied to a man who can never be mine.

Alaric wraps me up in a hug, but I don't fully relax into him as I would have in the past.

"Thank you," he whispers, and I can feel the relief in his posture.

After a long moment, he pulls back and lets me go.

"You're still upset," he says.

I want to deny it, but I can't. "Yes."

"Why? How do I fix it?"

"It's not your title. You are fated to be with the queen." I spit the words. The ugly feeling from earlier returns with a vengeance, roiling in my gut.

Alaric flinches.

He is not mine. Knowing this—seeing him stand with the queen on the dais, watching her kiss him—forms a hollow shell out of my heart. I'm afraid that he'll slip through my fingers. I have lost everyone else I've ever loved in my life, and now I am afraid I will lose him, too.

It's selfish, but I wonder what will become of me when he is hers.

"Fate is what will come to pass, but we can control it by deciding for ourselves what we want. We can forge our own path. I will not have Elizabeth or anyone else choose for me... for us."

I pull in a breath and hope he's right.

CHAPTER
THREE
CLARA

Strong hands grip my shoulders, pinning me down. A heavy form settled on top of my body keeps me immobile. My eyes fly open, and all I see are bared fangs. I blink at dark sapphire eyes ringed with a thick, red line. Morning sun gilds Alaric's tousled black hair and thick eyelashes.

He's beautiful, even as my mind struggles to understand what's happening.

My heart hammers in my chest. I'm frozen to the spot, too shocked to remember how to move.

"Defend yourself," he snarls, bringing his face within a hair's breadth of mine. "Defend yourself or die."

The air whooshes out of me in a single breath. "A-Alaric?"

A growl issues up from deep within his chest. I flinch.

He's going to kill me.

The space between heartbeats stretches on as time seems to slow to a stop.

I don't understand. Sleep clings to my mind as I struggle to come up with an explanation for his mood change.

An ache forms in my chest. Somewhere in the time that I had fallen asleep, he changed from my friend into a monster that is seconds from ripping my throat out. I squeeze my eyes shut against the burning that rises. A single traitorous tear slips out of the corner of one eye.

Alaric's weight is gone as he shifts to the side. "Clara?"

I don't move.

Alaric's thumb brushes across my temple, wiping away the tear. Then his arms are around me, pulling me into him. "I'm sorry. That was obviously the wrong way to do things."

My eyes snap open. I press my hands against his chest and shove backward. He releases me without a fight.

I flop back onto the pillows. "The wrong way to... what?" I snap.

He ducks his head. "You need to learn to defend yourself. I should have been adamant about it long before now."

I rise to sit, glaring down on him. "And you thought attacking me as a wakeup call, without warning, was a good way to go about that?"

"You must always be prepared. You can trust no one here—and even if you think you can, you must treat them as if they will turn on you when you least expect it." He reaches his hand up, but I push it away.

I set my jaw, teeth clenched, and ask, "And you? Can I trust you, Alaric?"

He takes me in as my heart continues to drum against my chest. I tell myself that it's from the way he woke me and not because of the way his messy hair falls across his forehead, half obscuring one eye... or the way he seems to look through me to who I am... as if he knows me even when I don't.

Slowly, he rises and leans forward. "I will do everything I can to keep you safe while we are here, but no, my dear, Clara, you should not even trust me."

Exiting the bathing room, I pause to take in the opulent main room. Brocade curtains and a wall-to-ceiling double door leading to a rotund balcony. The four-poster bed is large enough to fit several people. Drapes hang from each post, tied back with thick, braided, golden ropes. The bed is situated on the opposite wall of the black stone fireplace. A large painting above it has been turned around to display only the back of the canvas.

I forget about the oddly positioned painting when movement

catches my attention. Alaric leans against the bed, straightening out the cuff of a sleeve. Cherno is perched on his shoulder, quiet and barely moving. The demon's entire demeanor has changed since arriving.

Alaric looks up and smiles, uncertainty lingering in his expression. "I really hope you can forgive me for this morning. There's no excuse for my actions, regardless of my intentions."

He lifts Cherno off his shoulder and whispers something to him before setting him down on the bed.

"It's all right," I say, waving off his apology. I don't want to dwell on it, I don't want to examine how betrayed I feel or how my chest aches as if a fissure has ripped its ways across the surface of my heart, threatening to rent it in two. "I was startled, that's all."

I don't meet his gaze as I cross to the mirror and run my fingers through my hair to keep my hands busy.

"I will teach you how to defend yourself," he says.

The words glide across my cheek. He takes my hair and lays it over one shoulder. I watch his reflection in the mirror. His gaze is locked on the bare skin of the crook of my neck.

"I don't trust anyone here."

I feel the urge to lean back into him and have his arms wrap around me. I want the subtle scent of him to envelop me...

It's only the mark, I tell myself.

"I would appreciate that," I say. Stepping off to the side, I turn to look at him. "But the next time you want to do something for my benefit, talk to me first."

He agrees and leads me out of the room and down the halls.

I notice my surroundings for the first time, having been too tired and hurt to care last night. The outside of the castle was polished and gleamed, but inside, the walls and floors are made of gray, unpolished stone.

The windows are spaced so far apart there is a need for torches and sconces even during the day. It is dreary inside, and it reminds me of an impending thunderstorm. Swaths of material draped along the walls, and framed art pieces of landscapes hang in places where one would expect to find a window. It's as if whoever decorated this castle closed everyone inside off from the real world while attempting to create the illusion of wide, open spaces.

I follow Alaric down two flights of stairs then once more through the servants' halls until we reach a hidden staircase that leads to the dark underground of the castle. He grabs a torch off the wall and heads lower into the shadowy abyss.

A shiver of unease crawls down my spine, but I shove it away and follow Alaric down the narrow stairs. Following him blindly, with my complete and utter trust, I don't question him for a second. I doubt it will ever matter how often he urges me not to trust him. I do.

The air is sticky and damp and smells of soured wood. We walk through several more halls with twists and turns until I think I'd be lost in this labyrinth without his guidance.

"How do you know about this place?"

He stops walking but doesn't turn around. The torch light flickers and dances on the walls, making his shadow waver, and the steady drip, drip, drip, of water in the distance echoes all around us. Gossamer silk webs cling to everything.

"I lived in this castle a long time ago for many years," he says by way of explanation then continues walking.

I don't press for more information. Being here again is bringing his past back up, forcing him to relive things he would rather not remember.

Finally, we stop before an old wooden door. He pushes it open, and a wave of thick, musty air washes over us.

"What is this place?" I ask.

"It's the old training room and armory."

We step inside, and he closes us in. Alaric sets the torch against the wall igniting another. Seconds later, another ignites then another and another until the entire room is lit. On the far side, long wood and metal poles are displayed in a stand.

Through an open passage is another room. I can only make out the glinting of metal. That must be the armory.

Finally, Alaric turns to me and says, "Attack me."

I reach down to my boot and frown as I straighten back up. "I forgot the dagger."

He stalks toward me closing the distance between us with lightning fast strides. Unable to help myself, I concede a step. He twitches his wrist and the dagger appears in his hand. With another flick, it flips through the air. He catches it by the blade then holds the hilt out to me. Not a single cut marks the skin of his palm or fingers.

"*Never* go anywhere without this on your person."

I don't break eye contact with him as I reach out for the hilt, but before I can take it, Alaric pulls back his hand and flings the dagger. It imbeds into the door with a thunk.

"You can get it *after* you learn how to defend yourself without it," he says. The man I know has transformed into someone strict and ruthless.

I look from him to the dagger and back. "If I'm always going to have the dagger with me, then —"

"You can always be disarmed," he says. Then he positions himself into a stance I'm unfamiliar with. "Now, defend yourself."

I open my mouth to speak, but in the space of a breath, I'm on the ground with the wind knocked out of me as Alaric pins me down, snarling. His hand rests behind my head, keeping it from smacking against the stone floor. The caring gesture takes away from the effect he intends by baring his fangs.

"Ouch. That hurts, you ass. I wasn't ready," I grumble, reaching down to rub my sore posterior.

Alaric smirks. "You should always be ready."

Pushing off, he leaps up and holds out a hand. I eye him warily before accepting his help.

"Again," he says.

I blink and land hard on my ass once more.

Again and again, this goes on until I'm sure I'm covered in bruises. Alaric stands over me, hand outstretched. I swat at it... and miss.

"No thank you," I say. "I don't see how bruising my ass is helping me at all. If I'm going to get knocked down, I might as well save us both time and just stay where I'm at." At any rate, it will save me a few bruises.

Alaric laughs and squats down next to me. It's a laugh I haven't heard in... I don't actually remember how long it's been. I also haven't seen that smile, the one where the slightest bit of fang peeks out because he can't help himself. It's only now I realize how hard he works to keep his fangs hidden most of the time.

"We will need to work on your reaction time, but for now, we will move on to something different. Come." He reaches for me, and I clasp his forearm and let him pull me up. "I want you to deflect my attack."

He demonstrates the attack he used slow enough for me to see every move of every muscle. It's straight forward and uncomplicated.

I glower. In the hour or so that we've been practicing, *this* is the move that has taken me down time and time again.

"Now mimic this," he says, coming to stand at my side. Alaric sidesteps, sweeping his arms in an effortless-looking arc.

I watch him a few times before attempting it. He corrects me as I go, having me practice until I can go through the motions correctly ten times in a row.

Once he's satisfied with my progress, Alaric has me attempt it while he attacks—at what he calls *human speed*—except I can't even manage to stop him once. My movements, compared to his natural grace, are clumsy and ill-timed. We go through the drill until I'm out of breath and too weak to hold my arms up properly, barely able to swing them in his general direction.

I step back and rest my hands on my knees. "I don't see how this will help me. I can't even stop you when you're slow. There's no way I'll survive against a vampire bent on killing me."

"It will. This is only your first lesson, Clara. You cannot expect to be an expert on your first day. As long as we keep practicing, then you will improve." He returns to his stance. "Again."

Before I can right myself, he lunges. I follow through, but my foot catches on an uneven notch on the floor. I stumble and try to catch myself, but my muscles are too weak and don't respond fast enough.

I catch him off guard, and we fall in a tangle of limbs. The skin along my elbow stings as it scrapes along the rough, stone floor.

Alaric shifts and holds himself up by his arms. His eyes darken, and I can't help but react. I shift underneath him. He groans and drops his forehead to my shoulder.

"Clara..." My name comes out as a pained plea on his lips.

30

After several heartbeats, he lifts his head. "I think that's enough for today."

In a rush of air, he stands, reaching to help me up for the thousandth time. As I steady on my feet, my stomach grumbles from hunger.

"Let's get you something to eat," he says. Alaric's gaze dips to my neck. I can almost feel his fangs pierce my skin again. He, too, needs to feed.

After removing the dagger from the door, he hands it to me. I slip it into my boot as he grabs the torch from the wall. He takes my hand and pulls me close, leading me silently back down the labyrinthian halls.

Tired and weak, I appreciate the peace that has returned between us over the training session. Even the dank underground tunnels don't bother me.

As we reach the top of the stairs that lead to the servants' halls, he stops. I look up at him, wondering what could be wrong.

"Would you like it if we went somewhere this evening?" he asks.

I blink. I had expected him to say a number of things, but this is a surprise.

"Where?" I ask, hoping it won't be more training. My muscles need a full night to recover.

"To the theater."

I can't help but smile at the simple question. "Yes, I would like that."

As long as it is out of this castle, which I can only assume it is. I think it will be nice to spend some time away from this place while we can because there's no telling what tomorrow will bring.

Alaric takes a step then pauses, turning back to me, his lips pressed into a thin line. "If anyone threatens you while you're here, do not hesitate to defend yourself. Kill them if you must, but keep in mind that there will be consequences, so do not act rashly."

"Consequences. You mean I will die?"

Alaric shakes his head. "No. Not you."

"What about the laws? They would still kill me for..." I don't need to finish. We both know my crime. He doesn't need me to remind him of what I've done.

"I have claimed you," he says as if that answers everything.

Though, I know so little about the way things work here, maybe it does.

CHAPTER
FOUR
CLARA

I run my fingers down my dark red, silken skirt. The front is short, only covering my upper thighs but lengthens in the back, trailing down my legs. Underneath, I wear soft doeskin leggings with black boots that lace up to my knees. The corset forms to my body over a dark red shirt with capped sleeves and a strip of material that ties around my neck. It both manages to simultaneously cover my shoulders and neck while leaving the top of my chest exposed. Every scrap of material is either black or blood red. I list my head to the side. It's a style I've never seen before.

The servant who delivered my clothes three hours ago offered to stay and style my hair. I appreciated the offer but I prefer to wear it loose.

A knock on the door brings a smile to my face. Alaric insisted that he get ready in another part of the castle, promising to come for me when it's time to leave.

I pull open the door to see him standing, fist still raised to knock. He doesn't speak as he takes me in. As the silence stretches on, I squirm under his inspection, wondering if I put the outfit on incorrectly or if I'm missing a key part of it.

Cherno leaps from his shoulder and swoops into the air. Their wing glances off the top of my head as they pass into the room.

"You look beautiful," he says, extending his arm toward me.

My face warms from the compliment, even if it was a reflex. Words catch in my throat, and I lick my suddenly dry lips. "Thank you," I say, dipping my chin and looping my arm through his.

Part of me wonders if this is what being courted is like for everyone else—except I know that is not what we are doing. Alaric wants space from the queen and his memories. I'm going with him because he doesn't trust anyone here to not kill me while he's gone.

I watch him out of the corner of my eye. But that doesn't mean we can't enjoy each other's company. We are... friends.

Out in the hall, he turns us toward the left. Our soft footsteps are the only sound around us as the firelight flickers in the sconces, making shadows dance along the walls. Every several yards, there are shallow alcoves along the inner wall. Within each one, a white stone bust sits atop a gray podium. They are all different, but each face is beautifully carved and stoic.

Only a few sconces along the wall light the way, in contrast to the other way where all are lit. I frown.

Alaric's gaze flicks to me as though he could sense me my eyes on him. His fingers squeeze my arm gently before relaxing again. "I would like to avoid being stopped unnecessarily by any court members who happen to be in the main halls tonight."

I sense there's more to it than that, but I don't push the issue.

We reach the top of a narrow staircase. I take one step and pause. My eye is drawn to yet another bust, this one is of a young woman. The detail of each line and groove stands out. There is a lifelike quality to this one. Unlike the others, the corners of her lips are turned down into a slight frown and her eyes are closed. The sorrow of her expression is heartbreaking.

Her eyes snap open. I stumble back several steps, bumping into Alaric. He clutches my shoulders, steadying me.

"Is everything all right?"

I look from him back to the bust. The face is unchanged.

"Ye-Yeah," I breathe the word. "I thought I saw something, but it was just the shadows."

This creepy castle has me seeing things. I shake my head and descend with Alaric, leaning into his side.

My jaw drops when we step out of the carriage. I've never seen anything like this before. Gas lamps line the sidewalks, lighting the streets and buildings, and even more lights glow from within shops, turning the night into day. There's no sign of a single demon anywhere, not even in the shadows of alleyways.

I'm dressed similarly to the other women out tonight. A mix of old and new styles.

A woman dressed in brightly colored silks brushes her knuckles over her lover's cheek. He smiles down on her and rolls his sleeve up to his elbow before, offering his wrist to her. She kisses his palm just before her mouth clamps down, teeth sinking into his flesh.

My mouth goes dry.

Demon shit. This is a town of vampires, and Alaric has dressed me up as one of them. A shiver crawls down my spine.

"Alaric," I say barely above a whisper.

He takes my arm and tucks me into his side, placing a kiss on my cheek. "You do not have to hide here."

Inside the theater, the crowd gathers in the corners and along the walls. Alaric leads us to our seats. I sit on the inside next to a man who looks a few years older than Alaric.

We take our seats. I ignore the man on my other side, but the weight of his stare is intense, demanding my attention. I swivel my head and meet his gaze. He watches me with unabashed curiosity, grinning and showing his fangs. He scents the air, probably to gauge if I am human or not.

A low growl issues from my other side. Alaric covers my hand with his and squeezes. The vampire's eyes widen, and he dips his chin then looks straight ahead.

I lean into Alaric angling my body toward him just as the lights dim. The curtain raises, and the music starts. A single woman enters onto the stage, twirling and dancing. When the music picks up, more performers join her.

I find it hard to concentrate and keep looking to Alaric.

"Relax, my dear Clara, enjoy the show," he whispers into my ear.

I startle, turning my face toward him. He's leaning in so close that our noses nearly touch. I inhale sharply as his warm breath tickles over my cheek.

He smiles then returns to watch the dancers. His thumb draws circles on the inside of my wrist. It's a simple touch, almost as if he doesn't realize he's doing it, but it feels intimate. I pull my hand from his without resistance and tuck a strand of hair behind my ear. His hand remains in place, landing on my upper thigh, his thumb never ceasing the slow movements, sending my mind to dark and delicious places.

Pretend... pretend the mark is complete. I close my eyes and swallow thickly. We are more than allies—we are friends.

But the absentminded way he touches me distracts me from the performance. All I can think about is his touch and how I want to feel his hands and lips on my heated skin.

Light fills the auditorium, and clapping replaces the sound of music. Some remain in their seats while others rise to make their way to the aisles.

My mouth is dry. I suddenly feel claustrophobic. It's too crowded in here. I jump to my feet.

"What's wrong?" Alaric cants his head.

"I just need some air," I say quickly and make my way past him and hurry toward the lobby.

It's no better out here. Theatergoers crowd the space. I have to push past several people to reach the back. I make my way down the dim, back hall to the room with the open door and close it behind me.

My heart gallops against my ribs. The damned mark is demanding, urging me to seek out the final one. And the casual way Alaric touched my thigh and caressed my hand isn't helping matters.

I inhale deeply and push away from the door, crossing toward the sink. Turning on the water, I let it run over my hands then press them to my cheeks and neck to cool my skin.

I grab a small hand towel to pat my face dry.

I'm getting worked up over something so small. Alaric is good, almost too good. No one would doubt his part in this charade. I know this is all an act, and yet, a simple touch of his hand has me flustered.

38

I lean on the counter, glaring at my reflection, then hang my head. My hair slips over my shoulders and forms a curtain around my face. I have to do better.

Demons and saints, Clara, you signed up for this. Get over yourself and play your part, I scold inwardly.

With that, I straighten my spine and lift my chin, determined. I walk out of the room, ready to return to Alaric.

Nearing the corner to the lobby, I pass a group of four vampires. I keep my chin down, not meeting their gaze. The last thing I need right now is to piss off a random vampire. They could kill me before he could reach me, even with his ability to move inhumanly fast.

The closest vampire clips my shoulder with hers. I hit the wall hard enough to bruise. My arm aches. I clamp a hand over the spot where she collided with me and turn to glare back at the group. Two women, a blonde and a redhead accompanied by three men. The redhead pauses briefly but doesn't look over her shoulder.

The stinging on my arm hasn't lessened. Something warm and sticky seeps between my fingers. Slowly, I peel my hand back, revealing a deep cut.

Well, fuck.

I barely have time to contemplate what this means before a snarl jerks my attention up. A vampire stands inches before me, seeming to have come from thin air.

He licks his pale lips, and then in a blink, a woman appears at his side. Their eyes are ringed in red circles. Behind them, all heads have turned toward me, though no others approach.

Slowly I back up into the hallway the way I came. After a few steps, I turn and run.

Demon shit.

This is a dead end, but I would die in seconds if I was stupid enough to run through the lobby. I can only hope I'm able to fend off these vampires until Alaric notices something is off and comes looking for me.

The breath is punched from my lungs as I'm slammed up against the wall, my cheek stinging from the impact. An arm presses down on the back of my neck.

The vampire brings his mouth to my ear. "Why are you running?"

"Let me go," I snap.

He spins me to face him, his hand at the base of my throat, pinning me in place. He bares his fangs. "If you didn't want to be feasted on, then you shouldn't have been so temping."

He runs a finger along my cut, keeping his eyes on me, watching every flicker of emotion that crosses my face. He presses down. Spots form across my vision. Bringing his finger to his mouth, he licks the blood. His eyes slide closed as he makes a show of moaning.

I press my hands against his chest and shove. Spinning out of his hold, I put some distance between us, not daring to turn my back on him again. The vampire's eyes widen in surprise then a dangerous smirk forms on his mouth.

I push back the material of my half skirt and pull out my dagger.

"Look, Jonathan. The human wants to play," the woman croons, humor in her words. She twirls a finger around a lock of ebony hair.

"Stay back," I say. "I will kill you if you even think about feeding on me."

The man laughs. "Foolish human."

He takes a step forward then another and another. I lift my arm and swipe the blade through the air to warn him.

Hot, sticky warmth flows over my hand and sprays over my chest and face. I blink. The vampire clasps both hands over his neck. Shock widens his eyes, his face paling. Blood gushes between his fingers. I drag my gaze from him to my hand, coated in blood.

His blood.

The vampire crumples to the ground—dead.

Demon shit. My warning had turned into a killing blow.

"You killed him... *How?*" the woman asks, voice trembling. She hasn't moved.

From her reaction, it's obvious these vampires aren't used to humans fighting back. But I won't be the docile prey they are looking for.

Horror flickers over her features, and I let it bolster the confidence I don't possess. Adrenaline floods my veins. I feel a little stronger, more determined.

"It's a night-forged dagger," I say. "Now, back off—or do you want to die too?"

Her head snaps up and looks from the dead vampire to me. "I-I…" she stammers. "Who would dare give a filthy human night-forged metal?"

The vampire blood that splatters my arm and chest must make me look like a strange nightmare.

"Clara?" Alaric's voice comes from the far end of the hall. He stares open-mouthed.

I don't respond, too busy watching the female for any sign that she might attack.

Alaric rushes to my side, and only then do I drop my arm, but I don't sheath the dagger. My hand is shaking so hard I'd probably end up stabbing myself in the leg if I tried.

More vampires fill the hall. Hushed words of a dozen voices mingle into a din of unintelligible words.

"She will die!" the woman snarls even as she backs up.

Alaric stands at my side but makes no move to comfort or protect me.

Then, in a low, deadly calm voice, he says, "She is not yours to feed upon or punish. If any vampire dare lay a finger on her, she has my permission to end them as well."

CHAPTER FIVE

CLARA

We walk through the empty, back halls of the castle in silence. I shiver, my clothes damp from our efforts at removing as much blood as we could. Alaric had healed my arm on the way back. The skin is smooth. Not even the faint line of a scar remains. I don't know what that vampire had cut me with, but it wasn't night-forged silver, and she wasn't one of Elizabeth's, only a lesser vampire.

I pull Alaric's jacket tighter around my shoulders. He's hardly said more than a handful of words since we left the theater.

"Why aren't there other vampires in these halls?" I ask, breaking the silence.

He looks at me from the corner of his eye. "Most in the castle wish to be seen, so they stick to the main areas." He turns to face me fully. "If you go anywhere on your own, stick to these back passages as much as possible."

"So, I don't have to stay locked in the room?"

Alaric's mouth quirks up on one side. "Why would you think that?"

"Because of what I did."

"No. Just stay aware of your surroundings at all times."

I nod. "Will I be punished for…" My question trails off.

"No," he says shortly. "I gave you permission."

Neither of us needs to go into detail. They will not defy him because he is the crowned prince to the throne. That thought that churns my stomach.

We stop before our room. He opens the door but doesn't follow me inside.

"Are you disappointed in me… for tonight?"

Alaric smiles and presses his lips to mine. The kiss is quick, and when he pulls back, his deep sapphire eyes search mine. "No, I am proud of you. I must leave you now to feed."

Without thinking, I extend my wrist toward his mouth. "Then feed," I say.

Alaric wraps his fingers around my hand and places a searing kiss to the inside of my wrist. "No, Clara," he says. I open my mouth to protest, but he cuts me off. "We both know why."

The mark. The *final* mark.

Cherno flits past my head and lands on Alaric's shoulder. The little demon watches me. The intelligence in their eyes and their personality is far more advanced than any greater or lesser demon I've crossed paths with.

Alaric takes my shoulders and says, "Get cleaned up and get some rest."

Then he closes the door between us.

I remove my now ruined outfit and wash the blood off me, scrubbing until my skin is raw. Even when the water is dark pink, I still can't erase the touch of that vampire. My neck is healed of the bruises from his crushing grip, but the memory his hands around my throat squeezing is a physical echo.

While I hadn't intended to kill the vampire—at least not at that moment—I don't feel remorse for my actions. I don't know if I should or what it means that I don't. It was only supposed to be a threat. How could I know he'd speed up?

I dress in fresh clothes. Familiar dark brown pants, fitted perfectly to my shape, glide easily over my legs. Then I slip a loose cream blouse over my head. The gently worn outfit is comforting against my skin. I inhale Alaric's faint musky scent clinging to the material. It's a relief to know I can wander freely here. The sun will rise in a few hours but I am too wound up with excess energy to sleep.

After closing the door behind me, I turn and crash into a solid form, bouncing off and stumbling back several steps. I rub my nose and tilt my head back to see what—or rather *who*—I ran into.

Lawrence looks down his nose at me, a single, thick, golden brow raised. "Is Alaric in there?"

Suddenly, all the moisture in my mouth is gone. Should he be back by now?

"No."

He bobs his head once and turns. I reach out and grab his arm, stopping him. I don't think better of it until his gaze locks onto my hand and doesn't move. Slowly, I let go.

"Could something have happened to him?"

Lawrence heaves a sigh. "That depends."

I wait for him to continue, but he doesn't.

"On what?" I prompt. The question comes out harsher than intended.

"On when he left," he pauses, mulling over his next words. "And if... Elizabeth required an audience with him."

I swallow the lump forming in my throat. "He left to feed about an hour ago."

He nods. "Then you have nothing to worry about yet."

Before I can question him further, he is down the hall in a blink, heading toward the stairs.

The mention of the vampire queen twists my insides into knots. I hate the idea of Elizabeth requiring anything of Alaric, mostly because I know she wants him, and that alone is enough to make me jealous. It's an ugly feeling. She is a powerful vampire, like he is, and I am only a human—a temporary fixture in his life.

One day I will die, and he will continue on, unchanging and unending. It doesn't matter what I feel for him because he can never be mine.

Swallowing down the thoughts that will lead nowhere, I debate whether to follow Lawrence and ask him for more information or to wait to the room for Alaric to return.

But I have too much pent up energy, and I doubt Lawrence would be willing to entertain my questions.

In the end, I do neither, opting to go left toward the less populated halls through the servants' quarters. Looking for the library would give me something to do. I don't know if I'm allowed there, but who would miss a few tomes, especially if I return them when I finish?

I only make it to the top of the stairs before I pause, turning to look at the bust that caught my attention earlier. I approach slowly, as if she would come alive, which is ridiculous. It's only a carving. Leaning forward, I bring my face close.

The figure's eyes are closed, and there isn't a single imperfection visible. It's so lifelike. Each strand of hair, each eyelash, and curve of her features is carved in minute detail. She looks as if she were once a living and breathing person turned to stone.

I reach out and brush my fingers over her cheek, almost expecting it to be warm.

Two voices sound from the far end of the hall, startling me. I straighten, accidentally tipping the bust. I lunge, managing to catch it before it topples off its pedestal, and settle it back into place.

The voices draw nearer. I don't recognize them. Stone grinds. Then the back of the alcove gives way revealing a dark passage. I inch toward the dark opening.

I have two choices: stay here and find out who the voices belong to or go into the hidden tunnel. I'm not overly fond of meeting new vampires, so I duck my head and head into the passage.

The door slides closed behind me as I stand in place, waiting for my eyes to adjust. It takes several minutes, but eventually, the faint outline of stairs comes into focus.

I press a hand to the wall. It's damp, almost slimy to the touch, but I don't pull away as I descend.

The stairs are narrow and steep. I make my way down. Every once in a while, a sliver of the wall is cut out, allowing in fresh air and the thinnest beam of light. It wends in a tight circle, continuing far deeper than it should to reach the ground level.

After a while, the slits in the wall stop, bathing the stairs in pitch darkness. I take two more steps, unable to see anything at all anymore. Just when I'm about to give up and turn back, an orange glow flickers from the depths, barely noticeable, but it's there.

I glance back up the stairs. I have already come this far. I might as well see what is at the bottom.

It's not a doorway but a narrow passage about seven feet deep. A torch, lit on the wall, flickers on the other side. I turn sideways and squeeze through. It's tight. Not many could fit in such a small place.

I inch to the end, stopping before I leave the shadows, and listen. Time ticks by, but there's no sign of anyone or anything else.

Then I hear it—the soft sound of chains moving and a quiet, pitiful moan. I wait for guards to make their rounds, but the area remains empty and quiet.

Slowly, I lean my head out and look from side to side. There's not much there. A door, thick and heavy, is reinforced with two polished metal bands across the width. On the other side are three cells with identical doors. Each is made of dry, splintered wood with a small barred window near the top. The pristine locks and hinges glint. They are about the only thing in this dank place that isn't covered in dirt or grime.

I wriggle out of the tight space. Once in the dungeon, I press my back to the wall, keeping to the shadows as I make my way farther inside.

Chains shift, rattling again. Then a moan, so familiar my blood freezes in my veins, rises from the near silence. I retreat a step. My foot hits a pebble sending it skittering across the floor.

"Is... someone there?" a dry, cracked voice asks.

I move closer as quietly as I can and press my palms on the

warped, splintering wood.

"Hello?" I whisper against the door. I strain to listen. When there's no answer, I ask, "Is someone in there?"

I push up on my toes and peek through the small window. The air shifts around me.

"A visitor? After all this time?" the voice rasps, so dry and papery that I can't tell if they are young or old.

At first, all I see is the inky dark then the slightest movement. I struggle to make out the shape of the chains, the person, the room.

Demons and saints... Who could be so dangerous that they are shoved in a hidden dungeon below a castle belonging to the most powerful being in the world... and why?

The dark figure shifts. Pale light flickers within their eyes. —*red eyes*.

Fuck.

"Clara," they whisper my name.

I stumble back, covering my mouth to hold in the scream that works its way up my throat. My heel catches on the uneven stone floor, and I land hard on my ass.

Otherworld take me... I stumbled into a demon's prison cell.

The demon slams against the door. A dark tendril stretches out, curling against my cheek, smoky soft and icy cold, sending a weird burst of their power zinging through my body. I scramble backward, unable to look away as the demon slams against the wood again and again. The door rattles, creating thick clouds of dust.

Turning, I push up off the floor and run to the crevice, squeezing myself through the tight space. I claw at the stone, struggling to move faster. My breathing becomes shallow. I can't get enough air. Panic surges up, making me light-headed.

Then I burst through to the dark stairwell, panting and gasping as I rest my hands on my knees.

Voices shout on the other side where I was moments ago, their figures blotting out the light of the torch as they pass.

As soon as I can breathe again, I race up the stairs, taking them two and three at a time until I reach the top.

I grope the wall for a way to open the door again. After what feels like several minutes of searching, my finger finally snags on a depression in the stone wall. I press down. After several seconds, the door slides open, and I hurry through. The scrape of stone sounds loud in my ears as it closes.

I race back to the room and stand with my back against the door until my breathing returns to normal, and my heartbeat slows. I wait and wait for the demon to break through the cell and make their way up here.

But they never do.

After my initial fear has faded, I strip down and pull one of Alaric's shirts from a drawer and slip it over my head, needing the comfort of his scent. Then I crawl into bed.

Now that I am calm again, rational thought returns. Of course, the demon wouldn't break out to chase me. It's silly to think they would sit in the dark underground, allowing themselves to be imprisoned until they found a human stupid enough to venture into the forgotten depths of the castle.

I lie on my side and stare out the window as the sky gradually lightens. Eventually, my eyelids grow heavy. The pull of sleep tugs on me, and I fall into unconsciousness.

CHAPTER SIX

CLARA

Cool fingers brush against my face, the soft touch calling me from the recesses of sleep. It takes effort, but eventually, I manage to open my eyes, blinking groggily up at Alaric. He takes my hand and holds it between both of his.

My head swims, and a quiet ache pulses in time with my heartbeat, like I've been asleep for too long. The dark edges of a dream linger in my mind, but the details are hazy. I don't remember any of it, but I know it felt real.

"Are you feeling okay?" he asks.

My muscles resist movement, but I force them to obey, managing to sit up.

"I'm fine," I say with a weak smile.

"You've been asleep all day. You should get some food in you," he says, rising from the edge of the bed. "We have a long night ahead of us."

With those words, I'm wide awake. *This is it.*

I throw the blankets off and stand, swaying slightly. Alaric grips my upper arms and steadies me. The back of my legs press against the mattress, my front pressed against him. My nerves chill the blood in my veins.

"Already?" This is the moment we have to pretend perfectly. There will be no room to allow even the tiniest bit of doubt in anyone's mind. They must believe that I am fully his.

He nods.

I lick my suddenly dry lips. "I don't know if I can do this."

Alaric hooks a knuckle under my chin and lifts my head. "You will do fine. You are stronger than they know."

My brows pinch together.

"Let them underestimate you," he says, his voice thick.

"And let them live to regret it," I finish. It's clear by my tone that I don't believe it.

The ghost of a smile touches his lips, then he places a quick kiss on my mouth before releasing me. He turns and strides to the door.

I'm not sure if he'd meant to kiss me or if it was a reflex.

Alaric's hand hovers over the doorknob as he looks back. "I won't be able to see you until the masquerade tonight."

I say nothing because what can I say to that in this situation?

"Someone will be by later to help you get ready."

And then he's gone, leaving me alone. Again.

This visit isn't exactly how I imagined it would be. I thought we'd be with each other until we grew sick of it, but the truth is I've hardly seen him in the short time we've been here.

"No." I back away from the woman advancing on me. "I can do my own hair."

The older human woman who was sent up here to help me get ready frowns, her hands fisted on her hips. Her displeasure seeps through as she takes me in. As if allowing her to spend the last half hour stuffing me into a corset and dress wasn't enough. I can barely breathe in this wretched thing. I don't need my hair pulled tight and pinned uncomfortably, giving me headaches.

"I can't allow you to show up looking like a feral demon."

I stop retreating and narrow my eyes at her, folding my arms over my chest. "I can brush my own hair. Believe it or not, I'm capable of that much, despite what you may think."

She rolls her eyes and drops the brush onto the dresser. "All right then, I'll leave you be, but at least wear the jewelry set out for you." She turns to leave, muttering under her breath about how vampires are never this difficult.

I'm relieved when she's gone, allowing me to finish getting ready in silence without the pressure of being told I'm not good enough.

The dress is all red with a full skirt of layer upon layer of tulle. The corset is low, covered with intricate beading that drips down over the skirt. Delicate sleeves start just below the shoulder and widen slightly, extending just past my wrist. There's a brace strapped to my left arm for the dagger. I slide it into the sheath. With the loose fabric, it's not even noticeable. I practice drawing the blade several times until I can do it without almost cutting my arm or slicing the dress.

I clasp the necklace, a simple, delicate chain accented with three rubies on the left trailing down from my collarbone. It looks like drops of blood. Tracing a finger over the slender piece, I scrunch my nose at it. Three rubies, three drops of blood... three marks.

There's a knock at the door just before it opens.

"Are you ready?" the same woman from before asks.

"Yes."

She jerks her head. "Then follow me, and keep up."

She doesn't wait to see if I follow or not before walking away. I hurry after her, closing the door behind me. I have to run to keep up, which is no easy task in this heavy, demon-cursed dress. Gasping, I struggle to catch my breath.

After following her down several flights of stairs and hallways,

I lag behind. This dress was not made for running.

Finally, we come to a stop before halfway down the hall. Music drifts out of the room's two open doors, along with many voices.

"Enter through those doors," she says, leaving me alone in the hall.

Eyeing the open doors, I swallow my nerves. Throngs of people crowd the outer edge of the room. Those dancing take up the center, and on the far side sits the queen with Alaric standing close at her side, his body angled toward her.

My throat feels tight.

The two of them talk. She laughs at something he says and leans into him, holding tight to his arm, and he smiles down at her.

I turn away and find a spot near the wall to stand until... I'm not sure what will happen. If Alaric is with the queen and doesn't even know I'm here, then how am I to play the part of a fully marked human? What is the point of my presence?

I press tighter against the wall, wanting to disappear. Every human in the room is with the vampire who claimed them... except for me. By being alone, I stand out, drawing the eye of anyone who passes.

I lower my chin, doing my best to appear submissive as I watch Alaric across the room through my lashes. He turns, surveying the room, pausing when he faces my direction. I hold my breath, waiting for a sign that he sees me.

But there's nothing as he returns his full attention back to the queen again. Not a raised brow or a dip of his head.

I slump my shoulders as much as I can in this too-tight dress and rub my temples.

"Hello again, Clara."

I jump at the voice, spinning to find Oliver grinning down over my shoulder.

"Would you care to dance?" he asks.

"No," I say, angling my body away.

"Why not? This is a ball after all. It's what people do."

I narrow my eyes. "Because I'm not in the mood for any more of your stunts."

Oliver pouts, though his eyes glitter with amusement. "Come now. I didn't mean any harm." He brings his face closer to mine and inhales. "It worked, didn't it?"

My face warms. "What worked?"

"Getting him to want to mark you again."

My hands twitch, ready to push him away... But is that something a marked human would do? I'm not sure, so I keep my arms pinned to my sides.

"I asked for the second mark," I murmur after a group of vampires passes out of earshot.

Oliver hums. "That *is* unexpected."

"Can we please drop this?" I plead quietly. The last thing I want right now is to talk about why I wanted Alaric's mark.

"Only if you dance with me."

"Fine, but only one dance," I agree, instantly regretting it the second he takes my hand and drags me out onto the dance floor.

If I thought he would lead me in a quiet dance around the outer edge, I was wrong. He twirls us and spins me with flare until we are in the center of the room.

"Oliver," I hiss his name as the song draws to an end. I pull my hand from his, backing away, but he catches me, leading me into the beginning of another dance. "I'd rather not stick out like a sore thumb."

"Oli."

"What?"

"Call me Oli, and I promise to behave."

I clench my jaw and grind out his name through my teeth, "Oli, we agreed on *one* dance."

He grins triumphantly but edges us away from the center to blend in with the other dancers.

I look to where Alaric stands beside the queen. He glowers at us, making me want to shrink away. I've never seen that look on him before.

As soon as the music slows, I rip my hand from Oliver's and head to resume standing against the wall. I've already messed up by agreeing to the dance. At the last second, I alter my trajectory and exit through the nearest door.

In the hallway, I feel like I can breathe again, but I don't slow until I round the corner.

"Clara, I wanted to talk to you," Oliver says, his tone serious.

I spin on my heel and face him, spearing a finger at his chest. "Stop whatever it is you're doing. It's not helping."

"Isn't it?" he asks. He takes my hand in both of his and lowers it. "Alaric would never have marked you otherwise, even if you'd asked. Tonight, he didn't even know you were in the room—too busy being the queen's lapdog."

I snap my mouth shut. I don't know how true it is, but his intentions don't seem devious.

"Well, stop it." I shake my head then blow out a puff of air. "I don't know what I'm doing," I admit quietly.

Oliver grabs the back of my neck and pulls me forward, pressing his forehead to mine. He smells of warm pine and earth after a spring rain.

"I wanted to thank you."

"Thank me?" I pull back, looking into his amber eyes. My annoyance dissipates into air at the sudden change in his demeanor. "For what?"

"You saved a cub of the Shade pack."

I stare blankly, not understanding fully.

Oliver continues despite my confusion. "I hadn't heard of what you did until a week before coming here." He cups my face, squishing my cheeks. "You saved the future Alpha's mate. That is no small thing."

Oh. Oooh. The morning of Kitty's wedding.

"I am sorry if I have caused you any trouble, Clara." The corners of his mouth tug down. "I can't protect you from these monsters here, but I can break the bond and take you away. They wouldn't be able to reclaim you."

I try to pull away, but his hold is too strong. "Why? How?" I step back, shaking my head. "I don't need to be saved or protected, Oliver."

"Become my mate. It will sever the mark, and you will be protected by the pack." Oliver lifts my hand and places a kiss on my wrist.

"Mate?" The word comes out choked and strained.

He's nice, sweet even, but to be his mate? I have no idea what the full extent of that entails. I don't understand his world—I've barely scratched the surface of this one—but even so, I know accepting his offer would leaving Alaric behind. It would mean severing whatever it is we have. And I can't. *I won't do that.*

"Well, well, isn't this a sweet little moment," a voice croons.

Oliver retreats several steps as a vampire approaches. His disheveled hair looks like someone had been running their hands through it. He swerves slightly as he walks.

The vampire sniffs the air. "A human and a ... *wolf.*" He wrinkles his nose. "What would the two of you be doing out here—alone. Where are your masters?"

Oliver growls. "I have no master."

"Stand down, dog."

61

Oliver's posture shifts. Though he does as ordered, the tension ratchets up, leaving every muscle in his body trembling with the strain from holding back.

I blink, and the vampire stands before me. Without looking away from me, he throws out a hand and slams it against Oliver's chest, sending him stumbling back.

I wait for Oliver to make a move, to retaliate, but he only shakes his head and averts his eyes. He has no more power here than I do.

A clammy hand grips my shoulder, thumb pressing against my windpipe, applying more and more pressure. The vampire's other hand reaches up and tangles in my hair, tilting my head back painfully.

I swallow. Ice blue eyes ringed in a thin line of red follow the movement.

"Let me go," I say.

"I don't think so, little snack. You don't have a master. If you did, they would be here now. You are just a foolish human who thought you could get away with crashing the masquerade, and now, you will pay for it." His sharp nail drags along my skin, and I feel the warm trickle of blood slide down. He licks his lips.

"I do," I say. "Alaric Devereaux is my master."

He barks a laugh.

"I will kill you if you don't let me go."

The vampire snarls and brings his mouth to my neck. I lift my arms up between us, ready to draw my dagger.

"Step away from the girl, Kerin," a woman commands. Her words are soft but forceful as they echo through the hallway.

The vampire's breath fans out across my shoulder, turning my blood to ice in my veins. Her voice is hauntingly familiar, reminding me of a time so distant it might as well have been a dream.

It is a voice I never thought I would ever hear again.

CHAPTER
SEVEN
CLARA

The vampire snarls. He releases me and turns on the woman. There's a split second where he crouches, ready to lunge. Kerin blocks my view of the woman. There's a pause then a sharp intake of his breath. The woman growls. The sound is somehow both fierce and feminine. He straightens, pressing his shoulders back.

"Yes, my Lady." There is a slight tremble to his voice. Kerin looks over his shoulder at me, wearing an expression of understanding and hate.

He disappears with the speed only a vampire can manage. Oliver grabs my hand and pulls me into a protective hug. I bury my face in his chest, not ready to see the specter behind me.

Her soft footfalls draw nearer, but I don't move.

"Thank you, Lady," Oliver says.

"You should know better than to bring a claimed human out here."

With every word spoken, chills race along my skin. At the same time, her words annoy me. Oliver didn't bring me here, nor is he responsible for anything that happened.

Oliver takes my hand and turns me to face her. The retort on my tongue dies when I take her in.

The woman looks like me, even more so than Kitty does. I know exactly who she is, but my mind struggles to wrap around the truth. She should be older—*she should be dead*.

Instead, she appears to be my age. Her hair is the exact shade of dark brown. Her eyes, her nose, and even her mouth are the same features I see every time I look in the mirror.

"Mother?" I ask, but the sound of that word leaving my lips has me stumbling back several steps. It's heavy... awkward... wrong.

She smiles. I blink, and she has me wrapped up in her arms, holding me in an embrace I haven't felt since I was eight years old. I sink into her arms. The reaction is automatic and impossible to avoid as her familiar scent of sweet vanilla brings back a wave of memories.

"It's wonderful to see you after all this time, my darling girl."

There's a flash of red, followed by stinging pain on my neck as she heals the cut. I jerk back as if I've been slapped. She releases me without protest.

"You're dead," I snap. A million thoughts race through my head.

Mother is alive. She's been alive this entire time... *and a vampire*. Pressure builds behind my eyes, blurring my vision. Kitty, Father, and I mourned her. *She could have returned, but she didn't.* She had been our mother. Though she was never overly affectionate, she seemed to love us.

But you don't abandon the ones you love.

The betrayal stings. My throat is thick with a myriad of emotions threatening to choke me.

She takes a step closer.

"Stay back," I say.

Mother tips her head to the side and smirks. It makes me feel like a child throwing a fit over something small. "Come now, Darling. We can be together again. Everything will be all right."

"No. We thought you were dead. Everyone thought you were dead. But you've been here the whole time." I shake my head. "Why would you become one of them?"

"Honestly, Darling, why dwell on the past when you can see I am alive? Let's just be happy and—"

I shake my head. *How can she act as though she's only been gone for a few hours?*

"That's not how this works. Father destroyed himself drinking after you were taken. Losing you nearly killed him. Our lives were ruined. He gambled away all our money and—"

66

She grabs my shoulders and gives me a gentle shake, cutting off any further words. "It's all over now. You and I are both here. Kitty is married."

"How could you possibly know that?" I ask.

"I know more than you realize."

I wait for more, but it seems that's all she's willing to give me.

I look past her to Oliver. His mouth hangs open. I send him a pleading look, but he seems to be stuck looking back and forth between the two of us.

"You *were* my mother," I manage to whisper.

She sighs. "I am *still* your mother."

"No, you're not. If you were, you would have been there to protect us. Instead, you were alive this whole time, but you never cared enough to come back." I shrug off her hands and spin on my heel, walking back to the masquerade.

"Just give her time," I hear Oliver say as I turn the corner.

I don't need time. I don't need her in my life.

If she wanted a relationship, then she should have returned years ago. It's too late now. She seemed to know enough about us as if she's been watching us all these years, but she didn't care enough to help Kitty and me.

As far as I'm concerned, she can go back to whatever hole she crawled out of.

The din of the ballroom seems louder now, voices mingling and mixing with the music to make an ugly sound.

As I reach halfway across the room along the back wall, Alaric leaves his place at the queen's side and strides toward me. His smile warms my heart, and I don't care about the reason for this sudden shift in his demeanor. I only want to be by his side.

He halts before me. His smile falls, taking my heart with it, but when he holds out his hand, I don't hesitate.

Alaric leads me onto the dance floor. We meld into the throng of other dancers seamlessly, mid-song. His posture is stiff, and he doesn't speak a single word.

I want to tell him what happened. I want to ask if he has any idea about my mother and who she is, but I keep my mouth shut.

Once the song ends, Alaric takes my hand and leads me out to the terrace. The moon is bright and hangs heavy in the sky. But out here, the stars seem to shine brighter than usual against the solid wall of black made by the Sunfall mountains. The cold night air sends a shiver racing over my skin.

He drops my hand and turns on me, lowering his face to mine. His lips twist into a sneer. "What have you been doing? You smell like wolf."

I blink at the harshness of his accusing words. He's acting as if I did something wrong. These are his first words since he left me in his rooms and ignored me for the past hour. I take the hurt and turn it into anger.

"How dare you," I bite out. "You spent the last few hours at the queen's side, pretending I don't exist. And I was supposed to do what? Stand by myself, alone, in a room full of creatures that would kill me if given half a chance?" My words hitch in my throat. "Oliver was there for me when…" I trail off, at a loss for words. I don't even know where to start.

I glance inside the ballroom. Vampires dance, their humans doting over them like faithful pets.

Alaric's knuckles graze the side of my face. "You're right. I'm sorry."

I pull in a breath. His deep blue irises threaten to drown me in their unending depths. He leans in. My heart hammers against my ribs as I wait for the feel of his lips on mine.

"Dance with me," he says.

My eyes snap open. Alaric waits expectantly for my reply. My mouth is dry, my tongue heavy. Unable to form words, I nod. He smiles and takes my hand, entwining his fingers with mine.

"Am I interrupting something?" Oliver asks, appearing in the doorway.

Alaric and I draw back but don't let go of each other. Still, the space between us feels cold. Empty.

He snarls at the shifter. Reflexively, I squeeze his hand. Oliver's gaze drops, observing the gesture.

"I have traveled here to talk to you about the demon problem."

Alaric cuts a hand through the air. "I can do nothing for you until we return to Windbury. You know that."

He tugs on my hand and moves to walk past Oliver.

"That's just it, Mr. Devereaux. Once you and your guests left, the demon issue vanished. It's as if it never happened."

We still, taking in the meaning of his words.

"Whatever—*whoever*—was responsible for the demon destroying the lands was staying with you."

"Impossible," Alaric says. "It was a problem before they arrived."

Oliver shrugs. "It was. The attacks were weak and sloppy. It wasn't until they arrived that the demon grew in strength. Do with that information as you will." Oliver turns to me and nods. "My offer still stands. I'll be here one more day before I leave. You have until then."

"I don't need time to think," I say. "I'm sorry, but no."

Oliver bows to me then turns on his heel and leaves us.

"What offer?" Alaric asks.

I shake my head. "Nothing."

"That didn't sound like nothing."

I glance up at him from the corner of my eyes. "It was ridiculous, and I would never accept."

The muscle in his jaw ticks. Then his eyes darken, and he goes perfectly still as understanding dawns on him.

"I'm not interested in his offer," I reiterate more firmly this time.

After a long moment, the tension eases from his shoulders, and to my relief, he leads me back inside.

CHAPTER
EIGHT
ALARIC

Light streams through the window from the small opening of the curtains as a tentative knock rouses me from sleep. Clara snuggles deeper into my side, grumbling. I close my eyes, allowing myself to sink back into the moment when the knock comes again.

I already know what it is before I slide out of bed. It's been the same every day since the masquerade, for a week straight. A summons from the queen bitch, demanding an audience of me, monopolizing every spare minute that she can while we're here. As if that will change my mind about finally accepting her "offer."

But today, she has sent her messenger hours earlier than usual.

One more week, then we will be free of her and this place.

I amble to the door, still groggy from too little sleep. A human servant awaits on the other side with impeccable posture, chin up, and eyes downcast.

"Pardon the intrusion, my prince," he says.

I wait for him to continue, but when he doesn't, I snap, "What is it?"

Without so much as a twitch, he takes a deep breath and says, "Her majesty, the queen, wishes to have breakfast with you."

"No. Tell her I am still sleeping. She can demand my time later." I move to close the door in his face.

He clears his throat. "Her majesty says that if you do not, then the human will die."

My heartbeat stutters. I immediately look over my shoulder to Clara, still sleeping peacefully, limbs tangled in the blankets. An image flashes in my mind's eye of her dismembered and covered in blood, the sheets and blankets soaked through. Elizabeth would do it without blinking. She would do anything to get what she wants.

"Fine," I growl. "Wait here."

I let Clara sleep as I dress quickly, planning to return before she wakes. This has to stop. I will take Clara and leave early if I have to.

Cherno's head pops up from the spot they claimed on the ceiling beam. I motion for them to remain here. This meeting won't take long. It's the same thing for the last seven days. Elizabeth will ask me to take my place as her prince, and I will refuse.

The demon gives a questioning chirp but makes no move to defy my order. Their power is noticeably weaker since arriving. Yet another reason to leave as soon as possible. Cherno has spent the majority of their time hiding in the shadows, no longer even speaking, to provide me to draw the maximum amount of their power.

The drain on Cherno's power is steady. Otherworld damn Kharis... Elizabeth's demon is targeting Cherno more and more each day. Elizabeth is a fool if she thinks I don't notice.

I follow the servant, and we make our way down the hall. My eyes narrow at the back of the human's head as he places his foot on the first step leading up rather than down the stairwell.

"I thought you said the queen wanted to have breakfast."

He doesn't falter. "Breakfast will be held in the queen's chambers."

I clench my teeth so hard my jaw aches and follow him up wordlessly, dreading the next hour.

We stop before an ornate door. It is one I know all too well, one I had hoped to never see again once I left this place for good all those years ago.

Carved into the wood is a large oak tree with leaves covering the branches and roots stretching out below, as deep as they are high.

The servant steps off to the side, bowing as he backs away.

I continue to stare at the door, remembering everything from my time here in perfect, excruciating detail. The seemingly endless days and nights, the months that lasted an eternity. The cloying scent of lilacs and sugar.

"My prince?" the man asks tentatively, jarring me from my memories.

I glower but push open the door and enter the massive antechamber larger than my own room. A fire roars in a hearth so big a tall man could walk into it without ducking his head. Across from me is a set of bleached wood doors leading to her bedroom.

Elizabeth lounges across the settee, drinking blood. Her demon, Kharis, perches near her head, watching me. Red clings to the glass as Elizabeth slowly lowers it, revealing a sultry curl of her lips.

Once that smile would have moved me, I used to think it was crafted especially for me. Now, I know it was only one more weapon in her arsenal. I never loved her, never felt anything close to it. She could make anyone believe she loved them, and only them.

But there had always been something missing in her. Hollow and broken. She was too manipulative, too demanding and selfish to ever be loved by anyone.

The raven spreads their wings and flaps them twice, stirring the loose strands of Elizabeth's hair before taking to the air. The demon glides around the room, their eyes remaining locked on me the entire time. Finally, they settle near a hanging, gilded cage too

74

small for the large bird.

"What do you want at this demon-cursed hour of the day?" I snap.

Elizabeth flutters her eyelashes as she lowers her feet to the floor and rises gracefully. Every move, every breath is designed to be attractive and accentuate her lithe body. She drains the last of her cup and sets it down on a glass table while giving me a carefully constructed pout. All of the acting and posturing yet her expressions still lack genuine emotion.

She has learned nothing in our time apart.

The thin black dress clings to her form. A slit runs up from the hem to her hips on each side, so her legs show with each step.

Elizabeth saunters over to me, hips swaying, and presses her chest against mine. She slides her hands over my shoulders and locks her fingers behind my neck. She sighs, relaxing into me.

"I have missed you all these years, my prince. You've been away from home for far too long."

Home? My lip curls in disgust at the thought of calling this place *home*. It had never been home—will never be home. It was my prison once but never anything more.

I take her shoulders and hold her at arm's length. "This is not my home. You know that."

Elizabeth juts a hip out and crosses her arms under her breasts. "Don't be like that, my prince. This will always be your home."

I swallow down further argument. We could talk this point to death and never get anywhere. "Elizabeth, I have been here for over a week, and you have summoned me at least once a day. Why do you insist on acting as if this is the first meeting in over a hundred years?"

She trails a finger up my lapel. "But, this time we are truly alone."

I sidestep and cross to the fireplace. Above the mantle hangs her portrait. "Let's get on with this. Tell me why you called me here this time."

Elizabeth drops her arms to her sides and blows out a puff of air, and just like that. All of her attempts to be seductive are gone.

She straightens and pours herself a drink from the bar—wine mixed with blood. She takes a long draw, eyeing me up and down. "It is time for you to stop this foolishness and come to live here again. For good."

I freeze, not even drawing so much as a breath. "I told you no."

"You are the crown prince, and I have given you more than sufficient leeway in entertaining your whims. It's time you take your rightful place at my side." She drags a finger along the wood bar then examines it, rubbing her finger and thumb together as if she was checking for dust.

"How many times must we have this conversation?"

"As many times as we have to for you to make the correct decision."

"I'm not interested. I have a home in Windbury."

Elizabeth hums. "Yes... You do."

My gaze narrows. Simple words, yet they are laced with more meaning than they should be. A thought occurs to me. "You sent Victor to my home knowing he was demon cursed, didn't you?"

She brings her drink to her lips and bats her eyes at me over the rim, her brows rising in mock surprise. When she finishes, she sets the empty glass down and says, "So, I suppose you killed him then, and that is why he never returned with the rest of you."

I mull over my next words carefully. She could sense a lie if I dared, but I will not damn Clara. "He has been dealt with."

Elizabeth sticks out her bottom lip. "You owe me for killing my newest prince. Now you have to stay here to make up for it."

"Otherworld damn you, Elizabeth. You can't use people like that to manipulate me. Victor's fate is on your shoulders. You turned him and sent him. You know those who are cursed must die. It is *your* law."

She closes the distance and latches on to my arm, tugging me toward the bedroom on the other side of the white doors. She may possess a slight build, but she has the strength of her demon.

She bumps the twin doors, pushing them open with her hips, and drags me through. At the sight of her oversized bed, my blood runs cold. I tug on her grip, halting in the threshold.

"Come now, Alaric. Don't be like that. Let's catch up and get to know each other like we used to," she purrs.

"No." I tug on my arm, but her fingers clamp down tighter.

"Alaric, you killed one of my princes, the first in over a hundred years. You owe me."

I grab her wrist and pry it off my arm then twist her around to face me. "Elizabeth, stop this at once. You may have turned me, but do not think I have forgotten the circumstances you forced me into." I lower my face and speak low and calm. "I owe you nothing." I release her and back up, putting much-needed space between us. "I will not touch you, and things will never be as they used to be. You need to understand that. Now if there is no business for us to discuss, then I must be going."

I turn my back on her. Already I can feel the fiery rage of her anger searing against my back, but I calmly close the doors to her bedroom, separating us, and walk out of her room.

It's not until I am down the stairs and down the hall that I can finally breathe a sigh of relief. That was too close. Elizabeth is becoming more demanding and aggressive.

I don't know how much longer it will be before this becomes a battle between our demons. I must be gone before then, or I fear neither Cherno nor I will make it through.

CHAPTER
NINE
CLARA

The warm scent of cinnamon and butter pulls me from sleep. The mouthwatering spices mix with the light smell of fire burning in the hearth. My mouth waters before I peel open my eyes. I roll over and discover Alaric's side of the bed empty. I splay my fingers over the sheets. They're cool to the touch.

Disappointment sits bitter on my tongue. If I had any preconceived notions about what it would be like here, they have been doused by the second day after the masquerade. I have spent the majority of my time cooped up in this room, my thoughts alternating between three things: Alaric, my mother, and the demon deep underground layer.

As the moon rises high in the night sky, thoughts of the demon take over, drowning out even the constant loneliness that plagues me. In my dreams, no matter how they start, I always find my way back down there, seeking the demon out, talking to them, trying to free them. I shudder.

Shaking my head, I chase away the images of glowing red eyes and black smoke held captive by silver that shines even in the dark. I drag myself out of bed, slipping into my worn, fitted doeskin pants, a clean shirt, and my knee-high boots. Out of habit, I slide the night-forged dagger into the hidden sheath strapped to my left arm.

I don't want to spend another day waiting, waiting, waiting, waiting for Alaric to return. I want to see more of this place, to step outside and be wrapped in the crisp, winter air.

Hoarfrost coats the edges of the windows, glittering against the bright, vibrant blue of the afternoon sky. Here on the side of the mountains, the days are even shorter than I'm used to, lasting only a handful of hours.

I take a seat at the small, round table in the adjoining room. There's a tray of fruit and a steaming pot of floral tea. Most importantly, there is a plate stacked with sticky buns. I grab one and take a large bite. The warm bread is light and fluffy. I moan as the flavors hit my tongue—sugar, cinnamon, butter, and something else I can't identify. They are far superior to the patisserie back in Littlemire. Still chewing, cheeks stuffed to capacity, I pour myself a cup of tea.

After three cups and four sticky buns, I lean back in my chair and pat my full belly. It's tempting to finish the plate, but if I do, there is no way I'll be able to get up from this spot.

I stand. The sweetness of the pastries buzzes through my veins. A walk will do me good.

Poking my head out into the hallway, I make sure no one else is around before closing the door behind me.

I haven't seen Mother since the masquerade. It is both a relief and a disappointment. She hasn't tried to find me since that night... if she's even here anymore at all.

She left her entire family once without a word. It wouldn't surprise me that she would leave again without attempting to say goodbye.

Squaring my shoulders, I push her from my thoughts. I don't want to spend another moment thinking about the woman who probably never thought about me, Kitty, or Father since the day she was claimed.

I turn toward the stairs that will take me to the main halls. It's not long before a group of vampires round a corner. Pressing my back to the wall, I lower my chin, watching them through my lashes. As long as I appear subservient, I'll be safe, and the vampires leave me alone with little more than the occasional curious glance.

After wandering down a few more passages, the bite of the air calls to me. I rub my hand over a frosted pane of glass and look out. Below, in the courtyard, is a garden surrounded by maze-like stonewalls that appear to be seven- or eight-feet high. There is no one anywhere near the garden. It's exactly what I was hoping to find: solitude and the cloudless sky.

I make my way down. Gravel crunches underfoot as I step outside. I shiver against the cold, but it feels good to breathe in the crisp, wintery air. I walk along the main path, not quite entering the maze.

So much has happened since we arrived, and most of it within the first three days. Alaric and I share a bed when we sleep, but somehow, there is still no time to talk. He or I are too tired or I want to enjoy what few moments of peace we have together.

There is never enough time.

A dry, gray stone fountain sits in the center of the open court. Vines twist and knot around the base and over the lip to partially fill the basin. Over the entrance to the maze is a latticework arch with flowers that seemed to have frozen overnight, their delicate petals bruising from the cold. I venture further in admiring the beauty of the late afternoon sun shining through the dying plants.

"Clara?"

I spin, stumbling back a step to catch my balance.

Alaric stands an arm's length away. Consumed with my own thoughts as I wandered around the garden, I hadn't heard him approach. Seeing his beautiful face takes my breath away. I've missed him, but it surprises me just how much.

"What are you doing out here alone, and without your cloak?" he asks. He closes the distance between us, moving like the predator he is. My pulse kicks up slightly, and I lick my dry lips.

I lift a shoulder and offer a half-shrug. "I'm fine without it. I just wanted some air," I say. Of course, this would be the moment a shiver skates over my body.

Alaric wraps me up in his arms. "You're cold. We should go inside."

I melt into his embrace and shake my head, cheek press to his chest. "I want to stay here a little longer."

"All right," he says, holding me a little tighter.

Neither of us speaks or moves for a long moment.

"I feel like I never see you anymore. You're always... busy," I murmur.

I wrinkle my nose. I don't know where Alaric goes or what he does when he's away, and he never wants to talk about it. Even now, he stiffens as I skirt the issue. I pull back, staring at the ground, fighting the unreasonable hurt that wants to bubble up. I kick at a pebble. It skitters away, getting lost in the thousands of others.

"I know," he says flatly.

And with that admission, he's closed off again, pulling up his walls to keep me away from whatever he's been dealing with. I swallow delicately and chew on my bottom lip.

"Every time you leave, part of me wonders if it will be the last time," I admit quietly. Alaric frowns, but I continue before he can interrupt me and promise me that everything will be fine. "You're fated to be at *her* side, and I can't help but wonder if one of these times, she will take you from me."

Alaric cups my face, his long fingers tangling into my hair at the nape of my neck. "*We* alone will decide our fate. No prophecy, witch, demon, or queen can take that from us." He brings his face closer until our noses touch. I let my eyelids slide closed. "You are the human I claimed, and I will never regret that."

My fingers tighten on his arms as he lowers his mouth to mine. It starts sweet, promising that he won't leave me here alone. Then his lips part mine, and I open myself to him. The kiss transforms into something wild and unnamed.

He crushes me to his chest, and my back bumps against something solid and cold. The chill seeps through my clothes immediately, but I don't care. My skin is hot, and every nerve in my body comes alive everywhere he touches me. My blood ignites in my veins. All I want is him.

Alaric slides his hands down my waist and over my hips to grab my ass. He lifts me up, pinning me between the wall and his body. I wrap my legs around his waist. I can feel him harden against me.

A voice, muffled and far away, calls out.

Alaric groans against my mouth and pulls away. I'm not ready to let him go yet, but he releases me, his hands gliding up as my feet slowly lower to the ground. We're both panting. Our hot breaths plume in the air between us. We share a smile at almost getting carried away.

"Alaric?" Lawrence calls.

I glower in the direction of his voice as we smooth the wrinkles from our clothes. Alaric leans forward and places a chaise kiss on my cheek, pulling away just as Lawrence enters the maze with us.

"There you are," he says flatly. "I've been looking for you everywhere. You have been summoned."

Alaric pulls away from me, snarling at the man. "I refuse to go to another *private meeting*. She can rot in the Otherworld for all I care."

My gaze darts from one man to the other.

"It isn't that," Lawrence says, his expression stony.

Silence falls like the first flake of snow before a storm. There seems to be an unspoken message that passes between them.

Alaric turns to me, eyes pleading for me not to ask. "I meant what I said, my dear Clara."

I can only nod, trusting his word. Then I watch the two of them walk off in silence.

With the loss of Alaric's company, I suddenly feel the chill of the winter air more acutely. I remain with my back against the stone wall, remembering the feel of his touch and the way he tasted. I don't know how much time has passed, but after a while, the cold seeps into my bones, prickling at my skin like tiny needles. Pushing away, I head inside.

CHAPTER
TEN
ALARIC

Irritation prickles at my nerves as I walk beside Lawrence. He presses his mouth into a tight line, refusing to speak a word until we reach the second floor. I glance out a window to the garden below and see Clara's faint outline through the lattice arch where I left her. It had been a rare moment together only for something to pull me away.

I place a hand on Lawrence's forearm, halting him. He turns to face me, jaw clenched.

He's hiding something.

"What is so important that you had to drag me halfway across the castle?" I narrow my gaze at the man, taking him in from head to foot. His nostrils flare. I hold up a hand, recognizing the tell.

"And don't lie. You never knew how."

He presses the pads of his fingers against his forehead and blows out an exasperated sigh. Dropping his arm back to his side, he looks me in the eye again. His mouth opens and shuts a few times. Then finally, he says, "It is complicated... You need to see this for yourself. I wouldn't know where to begin. It's better if she explains it to you herself."

She. The word instantly raises my hackles. "You said this wasn't about Elizabeth."

He clamps his mouth shut, and after a few seconds, he says, "It's not." A pause. "Elise is here. In the castle."

My brows pull together. I don't understand.

"Wasn't she one of your staff?"

She's lucky another vampire hasn't found her and made a meal of her yet. It is a death sentence for a human to come to Nightwich without a vampire escort. Demons and saints, how could she be so stupid to come here?

"Yes," I say, "but I let her go for her indiscretions."

Lawrence raises a single brow, his expression suddenly intrigued. "Oh? Do tell."

I glower as I push past him. "Don't be a gossip. It is below your station."

He snorts. We both know I don't give two demon shits about my station.

Lawrence hurries ahead, walking backward. "She said you

were expecting her. It was a lie of course. I knew better than to believe you would send for a servant."

His gaze travels back toward the garden as if he could see Clara through the stonewalls. I pick up my pace.

"I just couldn't figure out why she would lie about that... or about everything else." He rubs his chin as he turns to walk at my side again. "Do you have any idea why she's here?"

"None," I say. "She tried to kill Clara the night before you showed up while I was out hunting."

Lawrence's jaw drops. "And... she still lives?" A thoughtful expression passes over his face.

"Clara begged for her life," I explain.

We turn down the hall that houses each member of the court—all except for me. Elizabeth has always kept me separated from the others as a way to isolate me. It tells the others that I am above them, both literally and figuratively, effectively preventing me from allying with anyone.

And it had worked for decades until I finally left Elizabeth and her endless games, behind.

"Meet me in my chambers," Lawrence says.

"Why all the secrecy?"

"You will understand shortly," he says. Then he turns down the narrow servants' hallway.

When I enter his quarters, I go no farther than the small antechamber that doubles as a drawing room. There is a sofa and one chair in front of a desk with a porcelain teapot and a single cup resting atop the silver serving tray.

Like every other court member's room, this one is built for a single occupant, discouraging any from entering into a relationship. Elizabeth has never expressly forbidden it, but it was made clear in the death of two of the newer members one hundred years ago. They disappeared after the winter solstice of their first year and found impaled on spikes in front of the castle the next morning. I shake my head, ridding myself of those morbid thoughts.

A fire burns in the hearth, snapping and popping. It warms the room a degree or two above comfortable. I pace back and forth, waiting for Lawrence to return. When he does, he is alone.

I look past him into the hall before the door closes. He keeps his hand on the doorknob.

"What in the Otherworld is going on?" I demand.

He inclines his head toward the sofa. "You should have a seat." When I don't move, he huffs, exasperated, and says, "Fine. Have it your way."

Opening the door, he reaches out. A woman swaggers in, head bowed and hands clasped in front of her. The emerald hat she wears partially obscures her face and makes her red hair more vibrant. Her silk dress is a deep green that wraps around her thin form. She looks as though she belongs in court.

I don't understand why he brought a strange woman to see

me, or what she has to do with Elise. Then, slowly, she raises her eyes to meet mine. A thin red line encircles her gray irises. She is a vampire.

I gape, having difficulty comprehending what I am seeing. She is so different from the girl I used to know.

"Elise?" I ask.

Elise is human... She was human. Who would have turned her, and when?

She breaks out in a wide grin. "It's good to see you again, Alaric."

My name sounds strange coming from her mouth.

"I-I don't understand."

Her smile turns sheepish, which makes me frown, though this explains how she made it inside Nightwich alive.

Lawrence clears his throat. "I will leave you two alone. You have a lot to catch up on."

Elise turns to him, tilting her head. "No," she says. "These are your rooms. I wouldn't dream of kicking you out."

She is different from the meek girl I knew, more confident.

"Elise... How?"

Her attention returns to me. "The same as anyone else here. It's the winter solstice. All vampires are welcome here this month. You know that."

"You know what I mean," I snap.

"I'm leaving to feed," Lawrence murmurs.

Neither of us pays him any attention as he slips out. The soft click of the door seems loud in the silence that hangs between us.

"How did this happen?" I ask more softly this time. My heart aches at what her mother would think if she were still alive. I feel responsible for this. If only I hadn't dismissed her like I had... I cut off that line of thought.

"Alaric, please," she says tiredly, as if this is just another banal conversation about some trivial matter. "Let's not talk of the past. We are both here now."

The fool acts as if this is some small matter, something to be dismissed.

I close the distance between us in two strides and grip her by the shoulders, giving her a light shake. "Who turned you?"

Elise smiles uneasily. "Does it matter?"

"Yes, it does. If your mother were still alive, she would be heartbroken to know you turned into *this*." I motion with my hand.

Elise jerks back as if I'd slapped her, pulling free. "She worked for you almost her entire life. She would have wanted this for me," she snaps. For the first time, the calm, demure facade falls away.

That she believes what she says makes my heart ache for her because she does not remember her mother. Charlotte hated what Rosalie and I were, but she respected our philosophies.

"Anyway, I didn't come here to talk about that. I've come so we could make amends."

"Who turned—"

"It doesn't matter who my sire is," she shrugs one shoulder. "He was a means to an end." Her hands ball into fists at her side. Her skin becomes blotchy with anger.

"What end, Elise?" I narrow my eyes.

Her chest heaves with her breathing. After a strained moment, she pulls in a deep breath and releases it as she smoothes nonexistent wrinkles from her dress. "If you didn't want this fate for me," she says with deadly calm, "then you should have treated me better and not dismissed me in favor of someone who hates your very essence. That human would gladly kill you. No matter what she says or does, she will always hate you."

The words are cold. Cruel. They echo doubts I've had in my mind since the day I claimed Clara. Despite what Elise did to her, it was easier to let Elise live when the heat of the moment had dissipated, and I knew Clara was safe.

With as much trouble as she has been, I am glad that I spared her. I watched her grow up. She was always like a niece to me. Her mother had been a valuable employee, and Rosalie had cherished Elise.

"What do you want, Elise?"

"This. I've always wanted this. I wanted you to see me."

My brows draw together. "I've always seen you. You were Charlotte's daughter, but you were still an employee."

Elise recoils at the last word. "Is that all you ever saw?" her voice breaks. "I loved you," she says accusingly.

I bow my head. "I'm sorry. I never have, and I never will see you as anything more. I do not, nor will I ever have feelings for you. I watched you grow up. It would be impossible to see you any other way."

"Loved," she all but yells the word. "I had loved you once. When you sent me away, you killed that part of me, but now, I am here asking you to see me as your equal."

The fire snaps in the hearth as if punctuating her words.

"That's not how this works." I shake my head. "I never thought you would need to understand the intricacies of vampire hierarchy... But, Elise, you will never be my equal. You are a lesser vampire, turned by a member of the court, not the queen."

Elise goes deathly still for several heartbeats. When she moves, her upper lip curls in a snarl. Her eyes are hard as steel as red seeps in, swallowing up the pale color.

"That's not true! You are a liar, Alaric," she hisses through her teeth "I see my sire was right about you."

"Elise..." I lift a hand, beseeching her to end this fight.

"You will regret this, Alaric Devereaux," she hisses, then spins on her heel and storms out of the room.

I rub my forehead. Who the fuck could have sired her? It must be someone I know, at least in part, to have said something to her.

I sigh, regretting that I hurt her but refusing to play into her games, refusing to be manipulated by guilt. Her threat is empty, of course. She is a lesser vampire with weak powers at most, and depending on her sire's power, she could be little more than a human, and I am the crown prince.

The title is a bitter taste coating my tongue, but I am more powerful than all the others, save for Elizabeth.

Elise will heal in time. She will forget about me.

I stride from the room, heading for my own. Clara should have returned there by now.

CHAPTER
ELEVEN
CLARA

I only managed a few minutes alone with Alaric before he was pulled away for demons only know what reason. It feels like we've been here for an eternity, and I have been waiting the entire time—waiting for him to open up, waiting to learn why he brought me here… and waiting for him to see him again.

Doubt seeps in.

Was coming here a mistake? Should I have just disappeared and changed my name? I cringe at my selfish thoughts.

Before we left Windbury, Alaric admitted that if I hadn't come, he would have remained indefinitely. His disdain for this place shows in the tick of his jaw and the sharpness of his words when he speaks of the queen. He means something to me, and I couldn't leave him to that fate.

Knowing that he won't end up trapped here makes this worth it. It doesn't matter that we will hardly see each other for now. There are only a few days left before we leave, and then... then we can talk, and I can decide where to go from there.

Knots form in my belly, twisting painfully at the thought of never seeing his face again, because... because...

My world shifts.

My heart thumps in my chest as the toe of my boot catches, and I stumble.

*I care for him. As m*ore than a friend... Far more than I should. I want him, and I can't deny the connection between us, but this is so much more than that.

It's not just the mark.

The feeling squeezes my heart in a way I don't understand. Swallowing thickly, I brace against a wall for support. I can't name what it is I do feel. Part of me is afraid to, but what I felt for Xander for years pales in comparison.

I press a clammy hand to my forehead to slow my racing thoughts. The urge to find Alaric is overwhelming. I want to look him in the eye so I know if it's real or a product of loneliness. I want to see if he feels even a fraction of this, and if he doesn't, then I'll never have admitted it, not even to myself. I can push whatever *this* is down and lock it away for good.

For the first time, I look around. Too lost in my thoughts, I wandered into a part of the castle I've never been before. The halls are empty. Paintings and tapestries decorating the walls lend warmth and opulence to the interior that is lacking in most other areas. Tall, decorative stands hold lit beeswax candles in the spaces between sconces, and thick, heavy drapes are pulled to the side of the windows. Iron crisscrosses create small, diamond-shaped panes of frosted glass.

With all of the yards and yards of material, the area feels overly indulgent. Even where Alaric and I are staying isn't this nice.

He is the crown prince... above all except the queen.

Fuck.

I take a step back as understanding dawns on me. I should head back and wait in the room for Alaric.

My pulse kicks up in warning. I turn to go back and barely avoid crashing into someone. I blink, my vision focusing on a shiny, black button too close to my face. I back up, mumbling an apology, keeping my head down.

"I didn't see you there," I say again. "Please excuse me. I must get back."

I keep my eyes downcast, staring at the ground. I don't trust him. I move to the wall to skirt around him, watching his feet rotate as I walk past. I bring my hand to my left wrist, wrap my fingers around the hilt, and unsheathe it, pressing the blade flat against my forearm.

"I know you," he says.

My head jolts up as he's suddenly before me, red power glinting in his eyes. I recognize him too. *Kerin.*

"You're that snack Vivian was protecting." He hums thoughtfully to himself. He still hasn't made the connection between Mother and me. "But why would she protect another vampire's human?"

Pretty sure he's talking to himself at this point, I retreat a step then another and another.

"Why would anyone protect *you*? You're nothing extraordinary." Kerin frowns then shrugs. "It doesn't matter. We are alone, and there is no one around to interrupt us."

I hold up a hand, using the other to hide the dagger behind my back. "Stay away."

He doesn't listen, of course. Kerin grins and advances slowly as I continue to back up.

"I've already been claimed by the crowned prince." My eyes widen. I realize my mistake the second the words are out of my mouth.

Kerin smirks as if I said something funny. "That bastard hasn't been part of the court in over a hundred years. His title is an empty one to flaunt around. It gives him the delusion that he holds any power at all, but don't worry," he says, stalking forward. "I will try not to kill you."

"Alaric will kill you if you touch me."

He laughs, a nearly uncontrollable belly laugh. He wraps his arms around his waist, nearly doubling over from his amusement.

I take my chance and bolt down the hallway, but a human outrunning a vampire is near impossible. I don't make it far before his fingers tangle in my hair and pull me to a stop. I cry out, my scalp burning from the vicious treatment. He spins me, and my back slams hard against the wall, forcing the air painfully out of my lungs from the impact.

"Don't touch me," I snarl.

He pulls down on my hair, wrenching my head back. I bite back a whimper of pain as I pry at his fingers with one hand, squeezing the hilt of the dagger with my other. I could cut him right now, but if I did, it would have to be a killing blow. Both options carry undesirable consequences.

He lets go, placing one hand against the wall next to my head. The other snakes up to my neck, splayed fingers curling around my throat. His thumb tilts my chin up and to the side.

He tsks. "Shame, there is already a scar."

The sharp edge of his nail scratches over the area.

"This is your last chance." My voice is barely audible. I want him to release me, to stop whatever game he's playing, though a small part of me knows that this isn't a game.

He moves too fast for me to see, sinking his fangs into my neck. I can feel each draw of blood he takes—the pressure, the searing heat and freezing cold racing through my veins with it. My fingers grow icy cold, prickling with an onset of numbness. Black spots form before my eyes.

"T-that's enough," I manage to say.

I can feel him chuckle against my skin as he continues to drink. Faster and faster, I can feel him draining me. Tingles spread through my body, weakening my muscles. My legs tremble.

Otherworld save me—he's killing me.

Shifting the dagger in my hand, I whisper, "I warned you."

He pauses and starts to pull back just as I bury the blade in his throat. Kerin stares at me in shock as I jerk the dagger then pull it out. Blood gushes from the wound. I can see his thoughts skitter across his face—confusion that his immortal body isn't healing and then understanding as he his eyes drift to the night-forged silver weapon in my hand, and linger there.

He falls to his knees, collapsing to his side. His hands reach up to his throat as if that could stop what is happening.

I slide down, crouching. There's the faint clatter of metal on stone as I drop the dagger.

Kerin stills, his hands going limp and falling away. I watch for the slight rise and fall of his breath, but it's not there, not anymore.

I wait for guilt to hit, for sorrow at taking another life, but I feel nothing.

A piercing scream rents the air.

I slowly lift my head, dragging my gaze up to a group of vampires on the other end of the hall. Their faces move in and out of focus. Then one pushes forward. Blond. Familiar.

I'm too tired to think.

My feet slide out from under me, and I land hard on my butt. Black spots continue to dance, blocking out parts of my vision, growing in size.

If I pass out, I know I will never wake up again. I cling to the edges of consciousness, willing myself to stay awake. I'm quickly losing the battle.

A smile forms on my dry lips. *At least I took this bastard out first.*

"Clara."

The name sounds familiar.

My name.

And the voice…

I try lifting my head but can only manage to lull it to the side, looking up at the man at an angle. I squint. Slowly, his features sharpen.

"Cassius?" I murmur. Or at least I think I do. I can't feel my mouth anymore.

I think that should worry me.

He plucks up the dagger from the floor and wipes it off on his sleeve then sheaths it in my boot. I want to tell him that's wrong, but I can't seem to form words.

He hooks an arm around my waist, draping mine over his shoulders, then hauls me to my feet. I try to push away from him and walk on my own. My feet trip over nothing, and I almost fall.

"Stop fighting me," he growls under his breath as he leads me away from the crowd of onlookers.

I try to get my limbs to cooperate, but they are loose and uncoordinated.

"Stop right there," a woman's voice commands.

Cassius obeys. I glare from the corner of my eye, willing him to keep going and ignore her. Instead, he turns us to face her.

The crowd parts down the middle, and a small figure emerges. The vampire queen storms toward us, furry twisting her features.

"What in the Otherworld happened here?"

I open my mouth to tell her exactly what I did, but Cassius cuts me off. "He drank from Clara when he knew that she was already claimed and marked."

I wrinkle my forehead but keep my mouth shut tight to avoid saying things I shouldn't. My head swims. I can't keep my thoughts straight.

A shrill voice yells from down the hall, "She did it! She killed Kerin!"

Cassius's fingers tighten, pressing into my ribs, a low growl rumbling from deep within his chest.

The feeling in my limbs gradually returns but not fast enough, but I am thankful for the warmth that accompanies it.

The queen snarls, drawing closer. She lowers her face to mine. "The sentence for murder is instant death."

"Slayer," Cassius mumbles.

My body goes cold, and I can feel what little blood remains draining from my face. His head snaps toward me, eyes wide with fear.

Elizabeth's hand shoots out grabbing Cassius by the shirt and pulls his face within an inch of hers. The movement throws us off balance, and I barely avoid falling into her.

"What did you say?" Her words are whisper soft and deadly. There is a mix of rage and fear in her words.

"One more kill... and she will be a slayer."

Licking my lips, Lawrence's words from the day we left come back to me. "*A third kill will make you a slayer.*" I had pushed it from my mind, dismissing it as ridiculous.

I killed my third vampire that night at the theater. Too preoccupied with everything else happening, I never stopped to think about it. I don't know what it means to be a slayer, other than the fact that I have killed several vampires. Kerin was my fourth.

Elizabeth releases him and turns her gaze on me.

I pull my arm from Cassius and stand on my own. I am weak, but I don't want to appear helpless. She fears something in me. I can see it in her soft bright blue, almost violet eyes.

Blood trickles down my neck, warm and sticky.

Her pale skin grows blotchy with her rising anger, moving up from her chest to her neck and face.

"You will not get the chance to become a full-fledged slayer," she says, and I almost admire the calm in her voice when there is a storm clearly raging inside. "It will not be a quick death for you, girl."

Cassius is wrong, though. They both are.

I am already a slayer.

The queen snaps her fingers. There's a blur followed by the whoosh of air as two guards, baring their fangs, appear at her side.

"Take her down to the lower levels," she commands. Her words are barely audible but are coated in venom.

I am ripped from Cassius and dragged down the hall at blinding speed. The toe of my boot trails along the floor as they move too fast for me to keep up. The speed makes my stomach churn, and the ground seems to drop from under me as I'm taken to a lower level.

Metal doors screech open then slam closed behind us. The air turns stale and damp, smelling of mildew and rot.

I open my mouth to protest, but no sound comes out.

The guards come to a sudden halt. The world spins, and I wretch the entirety of my stomach's contents at their feet.

They drop me. I barely manage to catch myself before my face connects with the stone floor. A boot collides with my ribs, knocking me to my side then again, rolling me onto my back.

Straw pokes through my clothing, but I don't care. I pant though I don't attempt to get up. I don't have the energy. I can still feel the warm trickle of blood down my neck.

"Should we kill her?" one guard asks.

"No, our queen will make an example of her."

Their footsteps echo in my ears. Then, a door slams, followed by the click of a heavy metal lock rattling into place.

I take a deep breath and instantly regret it. My head pounds, so I lay still until the world stops moving.

Closing my eyes, I take several deep breaths then roll onto my belly. I inch my way up to my hands and knees then sit back on my heels and take in my prison.

A thin layer of straw is scattered across the floor. In the far corner is a bucket I assume is for waste. And from the smell, I don't think it has been emptied since before the last prisoner stayed here.

I stumble to my feet and make my way to the nearest wall. It's not far, but even that exertion has winded me. I use the damp stone and lower myself, bringing my knees up to my chest.

There's nothing to do but wait for Alaric to come.

CHAPTER
TWELVE
ALARIC

Rubbing my head, I step inside my room. "Clara, I—"

My head whips to the side as a resounding slap echoes through the quiet room. Snarling, I turn on the offender. Elizabeth stands before me, nearly panting with anger, face both pale and flushed.

"Be the prince you are meant to be and stand at my side." She grinds the command out between gritted teeth. "*Give me your power.*"

The pretense of seduction has dropped entirely. This may be the first time in one hundred and seventy-four years that she is honest with herself and me. It was my power she craved, a truth I have always known. When I rejected the throne she offered, she somehow got it into her head that I would fall for someone who pretended to love me and that I wouldn't notice there was nothing real about it.

But she was wrong about that, too. Elizabeth had dismissed the one thing I cared about—keeping Rosalie safe. I never even wanted to be a vampire, something she could never understand and refused to believe.

"No," I say simply then walk around her, ready to enter the bedroom and close the doors on this conversation. I am tired of being used for what someone else might gain.

"You brought a potential slayer into my domain," She snarls. "You're lucky I didn't rip her head off and leave it as a present for you on the bed."

I freeze, my hand hovering over the door handle as her words sink in. *Potential slayer?*

She doesn't know.

I spin to face her. Elizabeth crosses her arms over her chest and offers me a smirk. Her eyes flick to the closed door at my back. For a heart stopping second, I expect Clara's head to be waiting for me on the bed. The longer Elizabeth looks at me like that, the more I believe it.

Turning from her, I throw open the door, heart in my throat.

For several seconds, I stand unmoving and staring at the sight before me. It takes several heartbeats to understand what I'm seeing.

No head.

But the bed has been remade. The sheets, blankets, and pillows have all been replaced with pristine white versions.

Elizabeth stands by my side, quiet and amused.

"What have you done with her?" I ask.

Instead of answering, Elizabeth takes my hand and unfurls my fingers, holding it up to her face. Her long nail slices across my palm. I hold back a hiss at the unexpected cut. Her nail feels like acid. A thin line of blood wells up. Smiling, she watches me as she brings her mouth down and licks the blood off.

The shallow wound is already healed. Pulling my hand from hers, I wipe it down the side of my leg.

"The better question," she purrs, her voice soft yet deadly, "is how the fuck can she be one kill from being a slayer when she's only killed one vampire while she's been here? How, when you have complete control over her, has she managed to commit such an atrocity, not once... but twice?"

I press my mouth into a thin line and say nothing.

"She *is* marked?"

I don't even dare to breathe. Finally I say, "I am in the process of marking her. It is nearly complete."

On the outside, Elizabeth is calm, and to the world, she would appear so, but it's when she's as still as death, with her face pleasant, that she is most volatile. Raging anger courses through her like wildfire. It's in the tightening of her hands clenched at her sides and in the slightest narrowing of her eyes.

After ten heartbeats, she lets out a sigh, the tension releasing from her muscles. "We were lovers once, you and I," she says. "We shared a life, a bed... We had no secrets. You lived to please only me. You loved and worshiped me."

I refrain from showing any emotion. She obviously remembers our time here together differently than I do.

"You were nothing to me," I say flatly. "It was nothing more than sex. You could have been anyone else, and it wouldn't have mattered to me."

Elizabeth doesn't acknowledge my words. They have lost their effect on her long ago.

"What happened between us?" she asks.

I glower. "You know exactly what happened. Now, enough of this—what have you done with Clara?"

She blinks rapidly several times as if coming out of a reverie. Elizabeth's head snaps up and purses her lips.

I have every right to know, yet she debates if she will tell me or not.

The door bursts open before she can answer. My glower at the interruption morphs into a frown as I see the worry on Lawrence's face. He skids to a stop as his eyes land on Elizabeth. He looks between us, taking us in to decipher the energy between us.

She gives him a passing glance before returning her full attention back on me, heaving a sigh. Elizabeth's lavender jewel eyes are flat and lack the depth emotion brings. It only furthers my suspicion that she is incapable of feeling anything at all, and everything she does is a careful calculation of getting what she wants. I can't imagine what happened to strip her of the ability to feel more than an endless lust for power.

"The two of you will be separated from here on out."

I open my mouth to protest, but she cuts me off.

"You are forbidden from seeing her again. However, you will be present at her interrogation. You will stand at my side—not at the side of a would-be *slayer*," she spits the final word.

I swallow down a growl. According to her laws, I am permitted access to the human I claimed. However, no human who's ever killed a vampire has ever been claimed before, and I have no doubt that she would use that as the reason to break the rules she created.

"And make no mistake, Alaric, when you judge her with the rest of my court, you *will* vote exactly how you are expected to. You will not go against me in this."

Pushing my protests down, I keep my face in a neutral mask. There is no use arguing with her.

The corners of Elizabeth's mouth quirks up. She has me exactly where she wants me—uncertain and unable to do anything about it. The trial could be hours or days or even weeks from now.

Or never.

Clara is alive and in the dungeon. All the vampires in the castle will know of her crimes by now. Clara's chances of making it to the trial alive are slim.

"When is the trial?"

She regards me with a soft hum, tilting her head and pressing the tip of her tongue to a pointed fang.

"When I am ready to deal with the filth you brought into my domain." With that, Elizabeth saunters out of the room.

How hypocritical of her, to find Clara's presence here so offensive when she sent Victor to my house knowing he was cursed. Whether he knew it or not, his mission was to kill my claimed human or be killed by her. Either way, Elizabeth's motives were to place Clara in this very situation.

Lawrence closes the door quietly.

I grab a decanter of fresh blood, sitting on the table at my side, and hurl it into the fire. The glass shatters, and the scent of hot blood fills the room before it is burned away. For decades, she urged me to claim a human, and when I do, she sets out to destroy her.

He turns to me and says, "I had hoped to be the one to tell you."

"Elizabeth didn't tell me the details of what happened, but she knows this isn't her first kill." I massage my temples as a sharp, throbbing pain forms. "I don't know how she found out, or who told her, but she knows."

Lawrence pinches the bridge of his nose. "Demons and saints..." There's a long pause. Then, he drops his arms back down to his side. "But, *she* doesn't know about..."

I shake my head as he trails off. "She called her a potential slayer, but she didn't name the vampires."

Clara defended herself, as I instructed, and now she will pay the price. She knew the dangers and would not have done so lightly. This way, at least, she will live a little longer, and that will give me time to figure out how to undo this mess.

But that doesn't stop guilt from souring my soul.

I never should have left her alone. I should have escorted her back here before meeting with Elise.

"I need to ask a favor of you."

Lawrence eyes me as if he knows he won't like what I'm about to say. "What?"

"Will you check on Clara when you can?" He opens his mouth to protest but clamps his mouth shut. "Please," I add.

His face softens. "I will see what I can do, but you and I both know I can't make any promises where Elizabeth is involved. It might take some time. I may not even be able to get to her before the trial."

"I know," I say. "Thank you."

CHAPTER
THIRTEEN
CLARA

Hours pass, but Alaric never comes. I strain, listening for any sign of footsteps or voices, but the only sound in this dungeon is the drip, drip, drip of water, and the occasional rattle of chains from what I can only assume are other prisoners.

I count the seconds and minutes by the incessant drip. Not even a single guard enters this level, not since I was dumped in this cell. I wonder if Cassius has told Alaric what happened by now. If not, he's probably wondering where I am.

The light filtering through the cell door remains constant. I have no way of telling time. After a while, my eyes grow heavy from being drained of so much blood and being locked away in the dark for hours on end.

I don't know if I'll make it out of this cell alive, let alone out of this situation. I knew killing the vampire would be a death sentence, but there hadn't been much of a choice. Swallowing hard, I wrap my arms around my legs and rest my chin on my knee.

There's a lump in my boot. I reach in and pull out the dagger.

Holding it up in front of me, I contemplate how I might use it to escape. The blade glints in the low light. I could pick the cell lock, but if I manage to do that, I would still need to get out of the dungeon, make my way through the castle, and… and an entire list of things that would be near impossible, even uninjured.

I slide it into the sheath along the inside of my arm. Reaching up, I press my hand to the wound at my neck. My fingers come away damp, but my skin is whole though still tender. I'm healing faster than any human should. Vague thoughts of the mark come to mind—there really isn't another explanation for it.

I lean back against the stone and stretch out my legs, exhaustion thick in my bones. I relax as much as possible, given the uneven ground.

My eyes snap open and I draw in a sharp breath. I jerk upright, hissing at the stiffness in my muscles—especially my neck. I stare into the dark, searching for whatever woke me.

A shiver works its way down my spine. I'm cold. It's hard to tell if the shock of being injured finally wore off or if this cell is colder now than before.

Once more, I listen for any sign that something has changed, but again, there's nothing. My mouth is uncomfortably dry. I need water.

A shiver runs over me again, but this time it's not from the cold. My pulse kicks up, pounding until it roars in my ears.

I scan the cell again. Nothing is different, nothing out of place. There are no new sounds or smells, so why do I feel like I'm no longer alone?

The corner next to the waste bucket is dark, darker than the rest of the cell. I squint into the shadows, barely able to make out the stone texture of the wall.

A door opening pulls my attention away.

Two—no, *three*—voices speak, but their words are too muffled to make out. One set of footsteps stops, a rattle of keys then the sound of thin metal being dropped on the ground followed by the clank of the cell. Then, the footsteps join the other two again.

On and on it goes for several minutes before one of them reaches my cell. The torchlight at his back shadows the large figure. He stands for a long moment, just watching me. I don't dare speak.

He takes three quick steps in and hisses. My hand twitches, wanting to reach for the dagger. If I lure him closer, I could use it on him...

I quickly reject that idea. Killing another vampire will only make this situation worse, and there's no way I could dispatch all three of the guards.

"Hurry up," the man behind him says. He swings the torch around. The bright light is blinding, and I have to look away. "We don't have all night."

The closest guard drops a metal tray. It clatters, but the bowl manages to stay upright. Then the door slams, and the lock engages. They move on without hesitation. No more doors open after that. Their footsteps fade back the way they came, and I'm once again surrounded by quiet.

I counted four cell doors opening and closing—five including me.

Getting to my feet, I use the wall as I make my way to my meal. It's some sort of grayish mush. I squat, lifting the bowl to my face and sniff then recoil, barely suppressing a gag. It smells like it's a month old and made of scraps no one would want to eat when it was fresh, let alone feed to a person.

I am not that *hungry yet.*

I drop the bowl back to the tray and stand, shoving the slop into the corner with my foot as I approach the bars. I press my face against them and look out as much as possible. Not a single guard in sight.

"Hello?" I call out then wait for an answer.

When none comes, I wrap my fingers around the bars next to the lock and feel around.

Unsheathing the dagger, I look again to make sure I'm truly alone. Then, slowly, I reach my hand out between the bars and feel for the keyhole. Unable to see the lock from this angle, I guide the tip of the blade with my finger but can't maneuver it from inside the cell. I'm not that skilled of a lock pick. After several minutes, my hands and arms start to tingle. I sit back on my heel, running the back of my hand over my clammy forehead.

Giving up, I use the wall for support and go back to the corner farthest from the door and the waste bucket then collapse on the ground. The blood loss must be getting to me.

My stomach chooses this second to grumble loudly. Food might help me get some energy back... I wrinkle my nose at the unsavory gruel.

My hunger is just uncomfortable enough that I can use it to help me stay awake.

It works, for what feels like hours, or possibly days. It's impossible to tell with the never-changing light. Seconds, minutes, hours—they all blend together. Time has no meaning.

I close my eyes and concentrate on breathing slow and deep. After a few breaths, the unsettling feeling of not being alone returns. I'm careful not to move a muscle, waiting for it to pass, but it only intensifies. I peek through my lashes. It's useless. There's not enough light to make out any details. Abandoning all pretense of sleep, I open my eyes fully, scanning the cell. Nothing.

Am I going crazy?

At some point, I fall asleep only to startle awake. The arm under my head is half numb from being used as a pillow, and my legs, knees curled up, are cramped. I rub the sleep from my eyes and push up to sitting.

Alaric hasn't come for me yet, and the longer he stays away, the more I think he won't be able to—but I have to believe he's trying.

Another meal is brought to me, and this time, I am almost hungry enough to attempt to eat. I've been hungrier than this before. It's painful, but it's an ache I know. It's familiar, though it will get worse before my body gives out.

I stare at the ceiling as hot tears form, the pressure building and blurring my vision. Crying will only dehydrate me faster. I press the heel of my hands into my eyes. When I open them again, the space above seems darker. I squint.

The shadow congeals, growing thicker, taking shape until it's an unmistakable black mass.

Demon.

They lower down, hovering inches above. I'm frozen in place. The majority of their body remains a thick cloud of black smoke, but out of their amorphous form, two arms protrude, boney and misshapen, fingers unfurling and becoming talons at the tips. The sharp points caress my cheek.

The touch is… familiar.

Their energy feels softer. It's not warm like Alaric's powers or cold and slimy like Victor's had been.

The demon's mouth stretches. Then, they lower their skull-shaped head within inches of my face. Wintery breath brushes over my cheeks. They are a greater demon, similar to the one that chased me from the forest to Alaric's doorstep, but this one is different somehow.

"You are right, human," they whisper.

I blink up into the face, skeletal and charred. *Demon's and saints…* they can read my mind.

"Yooou muuust staaaay aliiive. It isss not your tiiiime to die. Yooou are needed. Do not be a stupid huuuman. Eat the gruel the vampires give you if you must." Their words become clearer as they speak.

They grip my head in both hands, and there's a blinding flash of red light. Power flows through me, cold like ice but malleable like tilled dirt. I feel it in every inch of my body, every muscle, every fiber. The demon's power borders on searing pain but doesn't quite cross that threshold.

Then, it's gone, and I feel whole again. Every ache and pain is gone. When I test my muscles, I'm still weak, though there is a vast improvement.

"How long have I been down here?" I ask.

"A day and a half."

"I—" I frown. "Is that… all?"

The demon ignores my question, lowering until they slide over me. They purr at whatever it is they find. The boney fingers flex, still holding onto my head. The demon's power continues to flow.

This time, it licks at the insides of my bones, studying me.

"You have been touched by many demons."

"M-many?" I ask.

"Yes, human." The demon's head lifts, their mouth forming what could be a smile if they had any lips. "More than one is rare... more than two has never before happened."

I push up on my elbows. The demon glides backward, giving me space. I press my hand to the side of my head. "I don't understand."

They move around me, wrapping around my shoulders, encircling me but not touching. "If the first demon to get their claws on a mortal does not kill them, the second one will. We do not like our prey to be tainted by another's magic."

The blood in my veins freezes. If I am their prey, why would this demon want me alive? Why heal me?

"Being touched by a third," they continue, "that has made you... malleable. The others have only increased this."

"What do you want from me?"

Another grizzly smile. "For you to live."

"But why?" My voice is barely above a whisper.

The demon releases their hold, floating up and to the far corner of my cell. In a rush, images flood my mind—going down a hidden passage, a dark, winding stairwell, and a demon locked away.

"I know you..." I whisper. "I thought that was a dream."

The demon chuckles and continues to retreat.

"Who are you?" I ask as they seep into the wall.

"Varin." Their voice is a breath that fades, but their name sticks in my mind.

I jolt awake and find myself huddled in the corner, knees pulled into my chest.

Glancing at the far corner, I expect to see the demon, but they aren't there. That area is no darker than any other spot in this grimy cell, yet the sensation of being watched still hovers from all angles.

When I move, my muscles are weak, but there isn't a single ounce of pain. I have been healed.

Both times, the demon had been real.

CHAPTER
FOURTEEN
CLARA

The cell door flies open, startling me from my half-asleep state. It takes two heartbeats to remember where I am. Two tall, dark figures stand in the doorway, backlit by torches. In a blur, they are in front of me. Before I can open my mouth to protest, they grab my arms, hauling me to my feet. Their fingers dig in with bruising force.

The guards march me out into the hallway where two more vampires wait with torches. I have to avert my eyes from the sudden brightness after spending so long in the dark. Though the demon had told me to eat, no more meals had come.

I writhe against the painful grip, which only makes them tighten their hold. We stop before one of the vampires holding a torch.

He sneers down at me and wrinkles his nose. "Get her cleaned up. We can't have her smelling like demon shit when we take her to see the queen," he orders, jerking his chin toward the end of the hall.

My guards nod then pivot, marching me down the long corridor. The pace is brisk, and even at full strength, I would have trouble keeping up. My legs are weak and clumsy. Each time I manage to find purchase with one foot, I stumble and end up with my feet dragging.

When we near a large wooden door with brightly polished hinges and lock, we turn down a side passage that brings us to be a large alcove, similar to my cell. Instead of hay scattered around, the ground is damp with puddles of water in the grooves.

The guards lead me to the center of the room and drop me. I fall to my hands, gritting my teeth at the painful crack of my knees on stone. A hand clamps on the back of my neck and pushes down.

"Don't even think about trying anything." His hot breath wafts against the side of my face.

He presses down harder, bringing my nose within an inch of grayish-green water. I push back until my arms tremble with the effort. He releases me then steps back. A second later a blast of icy water slams into my back, stealing my breath. I nearly collapse from the shock. Another wave is dumped over my head, slower this time. I'm surprised to find the water smells of pine needles and sap instead of sludge or worse.

One guard fists a hand in my tangled hair. Wrenching my head back, he guides me to sit up, while the other dumps more water over me, bucket after bucket until the shock from the frigid temperature slowly wears off, and I lose feeling in my body.

I ignore the quiet chuckles from behind, focusing on keeping my chin up. Not that I have any dignity left to preserve.

By the time they finish thoroughly drenching me, I can't control the shivering that racks my body. A guard flings a towel at me. I grab for it, but my fingers are numb, and my reflexes are slow. It falls to the floor, soaking up a good deal of water.

"Dry off, and be quick about it," the guard orders, hauling me to my feet.

The vampires holding torches keep the light in my eyes, blinding me to their faces. With each passing minute, they seem to grow bolder. The tentative way they approached me, hesitating then using their inhuman speed...

They are afraid of me to some extent.

A sliver of pride tugs at my lips. I am human, weakened by blood loss and a lack of food and water, and it still takes four of them to feel comfortable in my presence.

I fumble with the towel, drying off as best as can be expected but my soaked clothes still cling uncomfortably to my skin.

The same vampires who pulled me from my cell take hold of my upper arms again. They drag me from the alcove, through the door of this wretched dungeon, and out into the hall. There are no windows. Nothing open to the outside.

One of the torch guards walks in front, the other behind so that a vampire is on every side of me. I attempt to look over my shoulder.

"Keep your head down, girl," one vampire snarls, pressing his fingers harder into my arm in warning.

I relax and focus on keeping my feet under me.

We walk for what feels like miles turning around through a labyrinth of halls with no distinct markers anywhere. Sconces are places equal distances apart, furthering the effect. We never leave this level, not by stairs or by an incline. I assume this is a tactic meant to confuse me.

It works.

Beads of sweat drip down the sides of my face, and I'm panting by the time we stop. I lift my head and stare blankly at the door before us. It's similar to the ones that lead into the throne room but a smaller version. The wood is polished to a fine sheen, and in the center is the queen's crest inlaid with silver.

The guard on my right drops my arm and steps up to the door. He knocks once. There's a pause. Then it swings open. Sconces and candles are lit throughout the room. I sigh as warmth rolls out in a wave. It's a welcome change from the constant cold. Holding me at arm's length, my guards guide me inside the windowless room then release me with a shove at my back. I stumble forward and catch my balance after a few steps.

At the far end of a crescent-shaped table, the queen sits in a high-backed chair resembling her ornate throne. Her slender hand rests on Alaric's forearm. On her other side sits Cassius, Lawrence, and six others I don't recognize.

I plead silently for Alaric to look at me. He holds his head high and angled toward the queen, but his eyes remain downcast. His face holds no emotion, and for some reason, that twists my heart.

All four of my guards remain behind me, their gazes burning holes in my back.

The vampire at the end of the table stands and walks to the center of the room, blocking my view of Alaric. She has sharp features, hair the color of snow, and skin equally as pale.

"We have been called here," she says, "because this human is guilty of slaughtering a vampire. The only reason she lives to stand before us today is because she has been claimed by our crowned prince." She pauses and angles her body toward me. Bright pink eyes take me in from head to foot, her ghostly white brows arching. Then facing the court, she continues, "The law is simple; any human who dares kill a vampire for any reason must pay for it with their life."

Murmurs fill the room. The vampires at the table lean in to whisper to one another. Their faces morph from shock and disbelieving to hate-filled.

The pale vampire spreads her arms. "The sentencing will—"

A chair scrapes the ground, the noise reverberating throughout the room. All eyes turn toward Cassius. He rises from his chair, and when he speaks, he looks only at me. "I think the human should be allowed to say for herself what happened."

"What?" the speaker asks. She presses a hand to her chest as if a human speaking to a vampire offends her delicate sensibilities.

Cassius holds up his hands and walks around the table to stand in front of her. "I will not deny that Miss Valmont did kill Kerin. I was there to witness the fatal strike, but she should be allowed to explain the circumstances that led up to the murder."

My heart thumps in my chest at his defense. Why would Cassius defend me and not Alaric? I look between the two of them, my breath caught in my throat.

"*Vampires*," the queen's voice booms. She stands, leaning forward, her long fingers splayed on the table. "You said as much yourself—she is a potential slayer." Lavender jewel-like eyes narrow on me.

Alaric snarls, and I startle from the outburst. The queen holds up a hand to silence him, not taking her eyes off me for a single heartbeat. I don't know if it makes me happy to know he's not as unaffected by this as he seemed, or if I should be worried that he gave himself away.

"This is not a discussion of innocence, Mr. Wellington. This is a formality to decide on the sentence for her crimes out of respect for our prince, but she will not speak."

A lump forms in my throat. What is the point of me being here if I can't even defend myself? Though, knowing me, I would only make things worse. My mouth has always had a habit of speaking before I could think better of it.

Cassius bows his head to her. "My queen, if I may? You know I hold no love for Alaric, so I will not argue for his benefit." He nods in my direction. "Indeed, she killed Victor but only after he challenged her. Alaric, Lawrence, Della, and I were present there to witness that the rules were followed. I myself saw to that, while Lawrence and Della kept Alaric from interfering. The fight was fair, but Victor was demon cursed, and that in itself is a death sentence. It could be argued that the human saved us the trouble of dispatching him ourselves. His death should hold no bearing on her punishment, as per the law."

"That does not excuse her from Kerin's murder," the speaker snaps, backing up a few steps. Her forehead scrunches as her bottom lip wavers, but otherwise, she remains composed.

My gaze shifts from her to Alaric. He leans forward, resting his arms on the table, hands tightening into fists.

"Of course not," Cassius continues, "but she has been claimed by our crown prince. There is not a single vampire in all of Nightwich who isn't aware of that fact, yet Kerin chose to take her blood without permission—an intentional display of disrespect..." he trails off with a shrug. "I have spent time around the human. She never made a single attempt to harm any of us. I believe this was out of self-defense."

Murmurs erupt among the vampire court, deafening to my ears, rising to a din. The words all blend together. It's surreal. It feels like I'm watching this happen to someone else from a distance.

"Humans are not entitled to self-defense," the pale vampire argues.

A high-pitched ringing in my ears drowns everything out, only for everything to come crashing around me until it's too much.

"I warned him, but he still fed on me. He was killing me, so I struck him with my weapon."

Silence descends on the room. Every single vampire stares, slack-jawed. Too late, I realize I've spoken.

Demon shit.

My weapon. I just said my weapon.

Double demon shit.

The speaker narrows her eyes. Then, a slow, dark smirk forms on her face. She caught that. Unease knots low in my belly, spreading through my veins like rot.

"Your Majesty it is little more than an unfortunate situation," Cassius says, moving in front of the woman. "Allow Alaric to have his human but have him keep a tighter rein on her." He shoots a sidelong glance in my direction, scowling.

Elizabeth drums her fingers on the table, watching Alaric for his reaction, but his stony exterior has returned. After what feels like an eternity, she rises from her seat.

The door bursts open. A strong hand grips my shoulder and

squeezes painfully, keeping me from turning to look. My knees nearly buckle from the force.

I watch Alaric for his reaction--confusion, shock, and then anger.

"What is the meaning of this? You are not part of this court." The queen's face reddens.

"My queen, I have come with more evidence against this human," a familiar woman's voice says with a quiver.

The speaker raises her arm and gestures for the new arrival to come forward. "Let them through."

Two women step forward, the blonde woman from the theater and... Elise.

My stomach drops.

"We have evidence against her."

"We don't need—" Alaric starts, but the queen cuts him off with a look.

Elise elbows the other woman, visibly shaking. I don't understand how a human can push a vampire around like that. Elise turns to me, lip curling just enough to show a single, elongated fang before looking away.

"I-I was in the theater with my lover—she was bleeding—it was an invitation, and he was only guilty of staying true to his nature. She slaughtered him without hesitation for it."

Whispers ebb and flow, gaining strength. I catch a few words. "*Kill her*" and "*no mercy*" stick out among them.

They are calling for my death.

Then, Elizabeth breathes a single word that rings out like a bell, loud and clear, silencing the room. "Slayer."

Elise clears her throat. "There is more, your majesty." The queen stiffens, but Elise doesn't wait for an invitation to continue. "When I worked for Mr. Devereaux, I caught this girl trying to kill him several times. She was never punished for it." She shakes her head. "And then I noticed that Rosalie had never returned from the claiming. It's not uncommon for her to go away for days at a time but never months. I think…" Elise chokes on a sob dabbing at nonexistent tears. "I think the human murdered her, too."

The queen turns to Alaric. He is deathly still as he watches me. She has been unnervingly silent for most of this trial. There is something in her posture that sends dread pooling in my belly.

Cassius flicks a hand at the two women, and the guards behind me escort them out. Elise tries to protest, but they are removed as quickly as they came.

"Alaric," Elizabeth asks slowly, placing a hand on top of his. "Is this true?"

My heart sinks.

Demons and saints… I will not survive this.

CHAPTER
FIFTEEN
CLARA

Death will come for me, no matter what happens next.

"Is this true?" Elizabeth asks again.

There is a long pause. Her fingers squeeze, nails biting into Alaric's skin.

He doesn't want to betray me, I can see it in his eyes, but what choice does he have? I don't know what she'll do if he lies to her or defies her.

"Yes." I wince. The word echoes through the chamber. "I defended myself against Victor, and again at the theater, and here, and I will not apologize for that."

My chest rises and falls with each breath.

"And what of Rosalie?" Elisabeth asks. "Did she attack you

as well?"

I lift my chin. "No." There is no reason to lie or hide the truth. "I killed her because she was a vampire, and for no other reason."

The room falls silent and even the speaker is at a loss for words. The only sound is the rush of blood in my ears.

I just admitted to killing four vampires.

Elizabeth brushes the base of the bone crown with her fingertips. The gesture is strange as if she forgot it was there. She slides her hands over her hips, smoothing down the material of her dress. Her nostrils flare. Even she can't hide the rage threatening to bubble over at my crimes.

She presses her lips into a thin line. "There has not been a slayer in over a hundred years. Any human who has taken the life of a single vampire must be put to death to prevent it from happening again. Claimed or not, she must pay for these atrocities. We will begin the draining process immediately," she says.

Alaric pushes to his feet, his cool exterior gone. "No."

Slowly, the queen pivots to face him, and her beautiful features twisted in fury soften. The change sends dread crawling over my skin like a thousand spiders. I fear whatever changed her mood more than my impending death.

Elizabeth reaches up and cups Alaric's face, her hand pale against his skin. She guides his head so he is forced to look her in the eye. The cruelty behind that saccharine expression can only be worse than having every drop of my blood drained.

"For you, my prince, I believe we might be able to come to an agreement." She steps away and opens her arms to the room. "Since this human is not fully marked, she may yet be claimed and marked by another."

Alaric's lips part. I shake my head, willing him not to speak.

I should have kept my mouth shut and never admitted anything, but I was stupid and all too ready to die. Now, I'll spend what's left of my life compelled, all free will stripped.

My stomach churns. I would prefer death.

Elizabeth pulls Alaric down to her eye level. She whispers something in his ear. He jerks back, but she presses a finger to her lips.

"Take her to the dungeon," she says, smiling at Alaric, "until we can find someone suitable."

The speaker lifts a hand. "She will need to be trained," she says meekly.

"Fine, she will be placed in the custody of a vampire who can control her." Elizabeth looks around. "Who here will become the girl's master?"

"I will. I can keep her under control," Lawrence says. His voice sounds odd to my ears. He has watched, silently through the proceedings this entire time until now.

"You?" The queen laughs, shrill and humorless. "No. *You* turned the first human you claimed. You do not have what it takes to keep this beast in line. You will not get another."

"I can control her," Cassius says. "Not to be her new master, but her intern guardian until she is reclaimed. I will compel her into submission and teach her how to be a proper human."

My gaze drills into his broad back, suspicious of his motivations. What reason would he have for helping me?

Alaric snarls at him. The reaction elicits a spark in Elizabeth's eye.

She hums, pressing a finger to the dimple in her cheek. "Yes, that will be acceptable. Train her to behave like the servant she is while arrangements are made for the reclaiming. Any vampires in want of a human may compete. The one who can compel her over any other will be the one to mark her."

Icy fear slices through my chest. Cassius will control me until who knows how many vampires will vie to compel me at once. I would rather rot in the dungeons then become a puppet.

Alaric looks ready to jump over the table and rip Cassius to shreds. Elizabeth must sense it because she places a hand on his shoulder. He lowers back to his seat, but his posture remains ridged.

I squeeze my eyes, swallowing down the bile that threatens to come up.

"The four of you are no longer needed," Cassius's warm voice croons.

There's a shuffle of boots against stone retreating from my back as my guards leave. The door opens, and then they are gone.

I force my eyes open to find Cassius standing an arm's length away, looking pleased.

My head spins with how quickly everything changed.

I'm still alive.

This doesn't make sense, except when I look past Cassius to Alaric... it does. This is as much a punishment for him as it is for me. The difference is, I don't know what awaits him. Separating us is only the beginning.

Cassius takes me by the upper arm. I suck in a sharp breath at the touch on the bruises from the guards. He frowns then moves his hand to my lower back.

"He is no longer your concern, little bird," he whispers in my ear.

Applying gentle pressure, he leads me out of the room. I walk stiffly, my muscles aching. Once we've reached the ground levels, he drops his arm.

After two flights of stairs, I double over, exhausted and panting. I rest my hands on my knees and pull in deep breaths. Cassius rubs a hand over my back in soothing circles.

I swat at him. He avoids my sloppy move with ease and continues comforting me.

"I don't know what you're up to, but if you compel me, I will ki—"

He covers my mouth with a hand. "This is not the place for this discussion."

Straightening my back, I place a foot on the bottom step leading to the third floor.

"You will not be returning to Alaric's room."

I turn to face him as his quiet words sink in.

"Where—" I don't finish. His quirked brow tells me all I need to know.

"Your things will be brought down to our rooms. For now, you are to come with me." He holds out a hand, but when I don't take it, he adds, "This is not up for debate, little bird. What you and Alaric want at this moment doesn't matter. I will compel you into doing as I ask... if I have to."

Putting all further arguments behind me, I follow him with my head down and mouth clamped shut. I don't trust him, but I have questions, and he has the answers.

We reach his room only a few minutes later. Cassius gestures for me to enter. He reaches out to take my hand when I hesitate. I pull away and walk inside.

The door clicks shut, echoing with a finality in my ears.

"What are you up to?" I demand, whirling on him, pointing an accusing finger. He frowns. "Why did you defend me in there?"

"Would you rather I let them kill you?" He takes a step forward then another until he bumps into my finger.

"You know what I mean. What are you up to?"

Cassius doesn't look the least bit intimidated. Not that I expected him to be. He's silent for a long time.

"When was the last time you ate?" he finally asks. "You've lost weight."

"Stop avoiding my questions."

"Bathe, and when you've cleaned up, you can eat and ask me as many questions as you want."

The promise of food and a warm bath is enough to take the fight out of me.

In a blur, Cassius is across the room, taking a folded item from a drawer. He speeds back to my side and places it in my arms. He gestures toward a door. "It's right through there."

I take the proffered clothing and shuffle into the bathing room. My movements are mechanical as I strip down and wait for the tub to fill. The last thing I remove is the dagger and the leather strapping on my forearm.

When there's a few inches of water, I turn the faucet off and step in. The second I sink down, exhaustion wraps itself tight around my bones. Quickly, I wash away the sweat and filth of the dungeon.

No matter how hard I try, my thoughts go to Alaric. I wonder where he is now and if he's all right. I bite down on the inside of my cheek to suppress the gamut of emotions welling up.

He's a vampire and the crown prince—a fact I still have a hard time believing. He can handle himself, but worry still twists at my gut.

I step out of the bath and dry off. Then, I slip the simple cream-colored shift over my head, grab the dagger, and step out.

Cassius leans against one of the bed posters, eyes drawn to the weapon in my hand.

"You were careless, Clara. You never should have mentioned the weapon. The Voice is suspicious of you—" He stops talking abruptly. "Do you still have the dagger?"

I nod. The Voice must be the ghostly pale vampire who spoke for the others.

"If you plan on keeping it in your possession, you would do well to never mention it to anyone besides Alaric and myself." He straightens and motions to the single plate of food on the table. "Eat then sleep."

I scoff, securing the dagger to my forearm. I don't plan on letting it out of my grasp, not even while sleeping. I cross to the bed, grab a pillow and blanket, and then fling them on the ground below the window.

"Use the bed, Clara."

"I'm not sleeping in your bed." To emphasize my point, I sit on the piled-up blankets and straighten them out around me.

Cassius brings the plate to me and sits with his back against the wall.

Aware that I'm being difficult, I shove a piece of bread in my mouth and take a bite of cheese. My appetite returns with a vengeance, jaw aching with the delicious flavors, and I can't seem to eat fast enough.

Twice, Cassius tells me to slow down before I finish. Setting the plate to the side, I cross my arms over my chest. I don't like feeling vulnerable, and I don't like the unknown.

"Why did you defend me?"

"I have my reasons," he says. "but maybe I'm not as terrible as you want to believe I am."

I scoff, not believing a word. "Do you want to know what I think?"

He raises a brow.

"You didn't do this out of the goodness of your own heart. I think you want something Alaric had."

He shrugs, not in the least bit offended. "It might have started out that way back in Windbury. We've always had a rivalry. Elizabeth would give him everything, and he would want none of it. The rest would get nothing." Cassius pauses, light gray eyes searching my face. "I defended you because I find you fascinating, and you wouldn't make it to the reclaiming alive if I'd let anyone else watch over you. Like it or not, I am your best chance at survival."

"I still don't trust you," I say after a long moment.

"I wouldn't expect you to."

A yawn rips free. Cassius pats the space between us, and I scoot down and lower myself. As soon as my head hits the pillow, he begins running his fingers through my damp hair, working out the tangles. It's annoyingly soothing.

"I hate that. Stop it."

He laughs but otherwise ignores me.

I roll to my side and wriggle as close to the wall as possible. "You can leave me alone now."

"Come now, little bird. We will be spending a lot of time together from now on."

For some reason, his words remind me of Alaric. Pressure builds behind my eyes as hot tears work their way up. "I don't want to be your friend."

I have questions, but I'm too tired to remember half of them.

"I will compel you to sleep now," he says as he begins to braid my hair.

"I am capable of falling asleep without your help. I just need you to leave me alone."

He chuckles. "It's so I can heal you."

I press my hands into the floor, lifting myself up to scowl.

"Sleep," he says.

His power slides over me. I push against the compulsion, trying to resist... and failing. A dull throb pounds in my head and my legs as a heavy weight settles over my mind.

My arms give out, and I fall, face first into the pillow.

CHAPTER SIXTEEN

ALARIC

Once the last of the court has taken their leave, I push my chair back and rise. Elizabeth remains seated, leaning back with her long legs crossed. She says nothing as I stride from the room, but I feel the weight of her stare, following me, even after I've turned down the corridor.

My blood boils in my veins. Cassius finally has control over Clara, something I've suspected he's wanted since the day he first laid eyes on her. If he can't be Elizabeth's crown prince, then he'll settle for taking whatever he can from me. Still as childish and petty as ever.

I just hope Clara can see through his disguise to his true intentions. I was ready to give her the final mark to stop the absurd trial and have everything settled. Thanks to Elise, that is no longer possible.

Picking up my pace, I speed the rest of the way to my rooms, hoping Clara is still packing her things and waiting.

Near silent footsteps approach from behind. I stop, my hand hovering over the doorknob.

"I wanted to talk to you," Elise says after several long seconds.

I don't turn. "You have said more than enough today. I have no interest in hearing anything else from you."

She circles me, blocking the door. I strain to hear movement from within, but there's nothing.

"I don't want there to be any hard feelings between us," she says.

"It's too late for that," I snap. "I should kill you for what you did."

Elise presses her fingertips to her mouth to hide her smile. "We both know you're not that kind of vampire, Alaric." She purrs my name in a sickly sweet tone.

"Elise." I growl her name.

She waves a hand, brushing off my anger. "It was the right thing to do. We are vampires. We must protect our kind from humans who break our laws."

"You would be dead if it weren't for Clara, and this is how you repay her?"

"It doesn't matter now," she says with a shrug. "What matters is that I *am* a vampire and *I am loyal*." Her eyes narrow when she speaks, emphasizing the last word.

What she doesn't understand is that no vampire is loyal to anyone but themselves and their desires... not even me. Vampires have been known to betray lovers they've been with for lifetimes.

"You overstepped. You were nothing but a servant in my home. You had no right to act against her, no matter how you felt. She did nothing to you, and yet you continue to hurt her." I lose the distance between us and lower my voice. "If you take action against her one more time, so help me, I will take care of you myself."

The color drains from Elise's face, turning her skin ashen. She crosses her arms, hanging tightly to herself. "I'm no longer your servant to order around, Alaric Devereaux."

"What happened? You used to be kind, and now look at you." I wait, but she shakes her head and doesn't answer. "I don't understand how you became so vindictive."

She refuses to respond. I challenge her with a stare. Elise manages to keep eye contact for longer than I'd expect before averting her gaze with a huff.

Spinning on her heel, she turns and walks to the top of the stairs. Looking over her shoulder, she says, "Maybe next time, you'll be more careful with how you treat others."

And then she's gone.

Elizabeth, Cassius, Elise—they are the epitome of what I hate about this existence. Rash and selfish. Only ever thinking about what they want with no regard to what their plots and schemes will do to others.

The revenge Elise seeks for not returning her feelings is only hurting the woman who spared her life.

"Are you going in, or are you going to stare at the door all night?" Elizabeth asks.

"You were here the whole time." It's not a question.

"That girl will get herself killed if she doesn't learn her place..." She hums thoughtfully. "You should take care of her now before she gets any other ideas." There is a sharpness to her words, something more than the cold, unfeeling tone she usually adopts.

Kill Elise. Moments ago, I had the same thought, but hearing it from Elizabeth's mouth only reinforces my defiance. I loathe the petty side of my nature. While I attempt to make decisions based on logic, it's a part of me nonetheless, and I am not impervious to it.

"Why are you here?"

"Come with me." She holds out her hand, curling her fingers into her palms.

"No."

Elizabeth tsks. "I have a deal you will want to take advantage of."

145

Since the moment I danced with Clara at the Solstice, she knew my weakness.

Elizabeth walks back down the hall and I follow. Whatever deal she offers will weigh heavily in her favor, but I have to know what it is.

We don't stop until we are in the antechamber of her room. She stretches out on the chaise lounge while I remain standing just inside the door.

"You are precious and valuable to me," she starts. A small smile plays on her lips, but deviousness glints in her lavender jewel eyes. "And because of that, I have decided that I will agree to let the girl go free."

I narrow my eyes. Clara has killed several vampires. She is the first slayer in over a hundred years.

"You will free Clara?" I ask when she doesn't continue. "Just like that? No strings?"

Elizabeth laughs, covering her mouth with the back of her hand. "Of course there *are* conditions. She's a slayer, Alaric. She cannot be allowed to go free and do as she wishes. In exchange for her freedom, you must do something for me."

I clench my jaw until it aches.

"You *do* want her freedom, do you not? After all, there's no telling who will become her new master or what they will do to her once they have her fully marked."

I swallow the lump forming in my throat. "What would you have me do?"

Though, deep in my gut, I know what she will ask.

Elizabeth rises from her spot and grabs a decanter of brandy. She fills a glass and brings it to her lips, watching me over the rim as she takes a sip. She deliberately drags the moment out until it's almost painful. Elizabeth has me where she wants me.

Glass clinks against the glass as she sets it down. She prowls forward, the fire in the hearth gilding her figure and throwing shadows over her face.

"It's simple," she says, wetting her lips. "Become mine."

My stomach plummets. Those two words are the ones I dread. *Become hers.*

Allow her to control me and give her the power of my demon. Essentially trading my freedom for Clara's.

If I refuse her, then I will lose Clara to another vampire who will most likely kill her, though I doubt I would be allowed to keep her by my side even if I do agree to this deal.

But I could send Clara anywhere she wants to go, give her what she needs to start a life free of worry.

It should be an easy choice. It is easy.

But I am selfish, and when I open my mouth to agree, no words form.

The stirring of an idea in the back of my mind begins to form and take shape. If I can get to Clara, I could give her the final mark. Clara asked for it on the ride here. Her instincts had been right.

"I will think on it," I say, turning toward the door.

"Oh, my sweet prince," Elizabeth croons. "I know you well enough to see your lies for what they are. You must decide now."

A brush of air and in the blink of an eye, she's before me. Elizabeth reaches up and drags a finger down the line of my throat. Her nail, sharpened to a point, cuts. The scent of my own blood fills the space. My skin knits itself back together almost as fast as she slices.

Elizabeth brings her finger to her lips and licks the smear of red off her finger.

Guilt forms a knot in my chest. I can only hope Clara will understand why I must take this risk. "If you force me to answer now, then I have to say no."

Her brows shoot up. "No? You would still not give yourself to me willingly to save the human you care for?" she clutches a hand to her chest in mock horror. "You are more heartless than I remember." A smile forms. "I love it."

I step away from her and throw open the door.

"Oh, and one more thing, Alaric."

I freeze.

"If you so much as attempt to mark Clara in secret, I will know, and I will not hesitate to rip her head off and leave it for you as a present in your chambers."

My fingers tighten briefly around the doorknob. Then, I throw open the door and leave, without daring to look back at the queen.

Clara is lost to me. There is nothing I can do that will not endanger her further.

Except give up my freedom, something I have fought against for a hundred and seventy-four years.

CHAPTER
SEVENTEEN
CLARA

I feel the weight of the blankets first then the stiffness in my muscles as I shift. An arm pulls me tighter against a hard body. Something brushes against the top of my head. I reach up to shoo Cherno away, but what I touch is cool and smooth and not at all a bat.

"I was wondering how long you would sleep," a male voice rumbles.

Not Alaric's voice.

I bolt upright, flinging the blankets off, and roll off the bed, leaning on the mattress to steady myself. My pulse pounds in my temples from the rude awakening.

Hadn't I fallen asleep on the floor?

Cassius leisurely pulls the blanket from his face, revealing a Cheshire grin as if he doesn't have a care in the world. He stretches and rolls to his side, watching me.

"You slept for two days. I was beginning to think you would die," he says with a yawn.

The demon snake is curled up on my pillow.

"You compelled me," I snap.

"Of course. You needed sleep." Cassius sits up and scoots toward the edge of the bed.

I take several steps back, wanting to put more distance between us.

"You're more of a snake than your demon," I hiss, but Cassius smiles at that. "Compel me again, and I will kill you." My chest heaves as I focus on remembering how the fuck I ended up in bed with this smug bastard.

He snorts. "If you wanted to kill me, you would have done so by now."

"Don't tempt me," I say through gritted teeth.

He rises from the bed, unconcerned, and stalks toward me, forcing me to back up. The back of my legs bump against a table. Cassius reaches up and grips my chin between his thumb and forefinger, bringing his face uncomfortably close.

"Is that any way to thank the man who healed you? You would be back in the dungeon—or dead—if I hadn't spoken in your defense. I risked my position in court for you, little bird."

I press my palms to his chest and shove. He could easily overpower me, but he concedes a step, letting go.

"I didn't ask for your help, and that doesn't mean I owe you anything."

He huffs, straightening his shirt.

At least he had the decency to stay fully dressed.

"I don't expect anything from you, Clara," he says in a clipped tone. "I'm simply reminding you that right now, I am your only ally, and as I told you the other day, I have my own reasons for helping you."

I can't make heads or tails of his motivations. Sometimes, he seems so cold and distant. The next moment, he's friendly, and others, he tries to charm me. It reminds me of our conversation outside of the atrium back at Windbury, where he pretended to be a friend only as an attempt to take me from Alaric and turn me. Could all of this have been part of his plan?

He can't be trusted.

"What are you thinking, little bird?"

"I will never ask you to turn me, so don't bother offering."

He cups my cheek and searches my eyes. I hold my breath. "I will return with more food. Then, we can discuss what is to happen."

He is across the room in a blur and then out the door.

My trunk sits in the corner, a dress splayed on top, ready for me to change into. I push it aside and shift through the other clothes until I fish out something I deem more suitable.

After quickly dressing, I'm not sure what to do with myself and end up pacing the room. My thoughts return to Alaric over and over. I need to find him so we can figure out how to get out of this mess I made.

I stride toward the door, itching to find him. I pull it open and come face-to-face with Cassius. He widens his stance, blocking my path. Taking a step forward, he forces me back inside then kicks the door closed with his foot.

"Clara, you can't leave this room alone."

He may have helped me, but I can't fight the bitterness coating my tongue. It feels like he's trying to replace Alaric.

And I resent him for it.

"You're not my master." I clamp my mouth shut as soon as the words are out.

"No. I'm not, but I am your guardian." His face softens to something that resembles pity. "You're lucky. No other human in the world has a vampire fighting for them as Alaric fights for you, let alone another vampire as an ally." He presses a hand to his chest.

My throat is tight with an array of emotions.

Alaric fights for you…

"It's the only reason you're not being tortured until your body gives out, which would be a very, *very*, long time."

I swallow thickly, unsure if he's threatening or warning me.

He places the tray of food on the desk. He cants his head to the side, eyes narrowing as he studies me. Cassius heaves a sigh and walks to me, taking my hand in both of his.

"Elizabeth would torture you to the point of near death, breaking every bone in your body one by one. Then, she would heal you, just enough, and do it again and again until she considered your crimes against vampires paid for or until she grew bored, but you would not die until she allowed it."

His words chill me to my bones, and I realize just how stupid I've been.

Even after days in the dungeon and the trial, all I've thought about was finding my way back to Alaric. I haven't taken the risks seriously because he always sheltered me from them. We convinced ourselves that if we worked together, we could get away with anything... that we could control our fate.

How long can I continue to defy all the rules before it catches up to me and I have to pay for everything?

I stare down at my hands, curling my fingers into my palms. "I'm sorry."

Cassius pinches the bridge of his nose. "Do you understand?"

I nod. "I will do my best to behave like I'm supposed to. You won't need to compel me." I slip my hand from his and press it to my forehead.

"You don't have to stay here, I won't force you, but we will be spending a lot of time together." When I don't respond, he adds, "Eat, and I will return soon."

I push my food around on the plate, barely able to stomach eating. When I told Alaric I would come with him, I never expected anything like this would happen. We were supposed to deal with the solstice and, once the two weeks were up, leave.

I'm torn by regret.

A swift knock on the door rips me from my thoughts. I glance at the door but don't bother getting up, not sure if I should answer. Cassius hadn't said he was expecting visitors.

The knock comes again, more insistent this time.

Pushing to my feet, I open the door and peek out. Della looks at me expectantly.

"Hello," I say, my voice an octave too high to be natural. She's one of the last people I expected to see.

Della raises a single dark brow. We stare at each other for a long moment.

"I'm here to take you to your new quarters," she says as if I'm an idiot.

Opening the door wider, I look into the hall. "Where is Cassius?"

"Follow me." Della grabs my hand and tugs me out of the room.

"I can't leave without—"

Her head whips around, fangs flashing. "Who do you think sent me?"

Ignoring her irritation, I close the door then follow as ordered. Della's heels clack against the stone as she mumbles under her breath nearly the whole way. I tune her out and allow myself to be led.

Cassius arranged for me to stay somewhere else. He understood I don't want to be alone with him. I hadn't expected that level of respect from him.

Eventually, the halls narrow and all decor fades away to nothing more than dull gray the texture of the stone. We are heading to the humans' quarters.

We finally enter a passage with dozens of doors on either side. I haven't ventured this far with Alaric when we came this way.

Della stops before a door that looks exactly like all the others we've passed. "This is your room."

The door sticks a little when I turn the doorknob. I have to hit it with my shoulder to open it. Della doesn't follow me inside.

The entire space is less than half the size of Alaric's bathing room, with nothing more than essentials. The bed would struggle to fit an average-sized man. Across from the door is a single window, tall and thin like an archer's slit. The opening is only as wide as my hand from the heel of my palm to the tips of my fingers. The only other thing in the room is a rickety dresser with two drawers that looks as if it was pieced together with rejected wood scraps.

I wonder if my possessions will be brought down here or if all I have now are the clothes on my back. I suppose it doesn't matter. This isn't the dungeon, and it isn't torture.

Once I've taken in what will be my new room, I turn back to Della.

"Why weren't you there during the..." I trail off, not sure what to call what happened in the room when I was taken from Alaric. Despite what they call it, *trial* doesn't fit what happened.

"I was sired by one of the court, but that doesn't make me part of it," she says dryly.

I immediately feel bad for asking the question. "Thank you for not... speaking against me. I know you could—"

Della holds up a hand, cutting me off. "If you don't need anything, I'll be going." She turns her back to me. Then, glancing over her shoulder, she says, "I know you might be tempted to, but I would recommend against leaving this room without Cassius."

Her eyes narrow as if she wants to say more, but she doesn't. Instead, she shakes her head. Then, she closes the door quietly behind her.

Blowing out a breath, I plop down on the bed. A small cloud of dust plumes up. The dust particles dance in the thin shaft of light coming in from the window. The smell tickles my nose.

I pull my knees up to my chest. There's not enough room to pace. This won't be as comfortable as Alaric's rooms, but I feel better putting space between Cassius and me.

How has everything gone so wrong?

I think I eventually fall asleep, only to be startled awake by the door banging open. Lawrence steps inside and kicks it closed with his booted foot without missing a stride. Silently, he approaches me where I sit, until I can see the red that rings his irises.

Demon shit. He's furious.

I'm afraid of the anger in his eyes, but annoyance at the rude entrance wins out. It seems every vampire I have ever met will be paying me a visit today.

Every vampire except the one I want to see.

He stops a few feet from my bed and scowls.

"Why are you here?" I ask. I scrunch my mouth to the side. "How did you even know where I was?"

"Alaric asked me to check on you when you were in the dungeon—"

A laugh, loud and sharp, bursts out before I can swallow it back down. I spread my arms to indicate the room. "As you can see, you're a little too late for that." I raise a brow then add, "You were at the sentencing. You even offered to be my guardian. Was that because you wanted to kill me yourself?"

The queen scoffed at his request. At the time, I couldn't have cared less. I want to ask him about it but not as much as I want to ask him about Alaric.

"You lied to me," he states, ignoring my question.

I'm taken aback by the sudden accusation that comes out of nowhere. Did he come here to argue?

"What are you talking about?"

The anger melts from his face, replacing it with a sorrow that takes my breath away. His eyes are glassy for a brief moment. Then, he blinks it away.

"I'm talking about Rosalie. You lied. You *did* kill her, and then, you denied it."

I take in a slow, deep breath through my nose then exhale. Scooting forward, I drop my feet off the bed and fold my hands in my lap.

"I didn't lie," I say quietly. "I never admitted or denied anything."

Eyes widening a fraction, Lawrence snarls. Arinah's power surges, making his eye glow red.

"My loyalty isn't to you," I snap.

His anger is palpable, but underneath it all is a broken heart. He's also Alaric's friend.

I push off the bed and cross the room to when he stands. He's as still as a statue. I clasp his hand in both of mine. He stiffens at the touch but doesn't pull away.

Taking another deep breath, I say, "I am sorry. I know it doesn't excuse what I did, but please understand. I was raised to believe all vampires were vile monsters. It never occurred to me that we are not so different." I shake my head. "I regret hurting Alaric, and you, with my actions."

"I should kill you for it." His threat is hollow and filled with pain with no force behind it. "The only reason I don't is for Alaric's sake."

I step into him, wrapping my arms around his waist and resting my cheek against his chest. It's awkward to initiate a hug with a man I barely know, made even more uncomfortable because he's just standing with his arms limp at his sides.

I have been hugged more by Alaric than anyone else in my life. If there's one thing I've learned from him, it's that vampires seem to communicate more with physical touch than humans do.

After a long moment, Lawrence lifts his arms and returns the embrace. He relaxes into me, and we stand like this for a long time.

"I loved her…" he whispers into my hair.

"I know."

CHAPTER
EIGHTEEN
CLARA

I sit up and stare into the dark void surrounding me. My breath forms white plumes of air. Cold seeps into my muscles, making them stiff and clumsy when I push my blanket away. Squinting into the shadows, I will my vision to focus.

Distant whispers come from all directions in a language I don't know. Finally, a thin sliver of light shines through the slit of a window, allowing me to see.

I don't recognize this place, the small room or the broken down dresser. At first, I think I'm back in Littlemire, but the bed is too small, the window is wrong, and Kitty is not snoring softly at my side.

It takes me several seconds to shake off the cobwebs from

my sleep-addled mind. Disappointment and a prickle of fear accompany the truth as everything comes flooding back.

The corner nearest the window remains shrouded in the pitch dark. I know that there is nothing there but shadows. Still, I can't tear my gaze away as the unsettling feeling of being watched presses down on me. My blood runs cold.

I stare into the impenetrable darkness, unblinking. Shapes seem to sway and move. I can't tell if it's my imagination or if someone or something is there.

The whispers gradually become louder. Then, from the soft melee, three clear words breakthrough. "*Come to me.*"

There's a demon in my room. They come to me at night when I am alone and asleep, and my mind is vulnerable. They dig their claws into my unconsciousness and grab hold before I wake.

"Why?" The question comes out more of a breath than a fully formed word—a single word to ask a multitude of questions. Why would a demon summon me? Why should I go to them? Why am I haunted by demons?

They nod. Moving from the shadows, they float across the room, passing effortlessly through the door.

"I can give you the answers you seek," the demon says before disappearing completely.

Their hold releases. I slump forward, gasping for air. Tears of frustration well up, blurring out the world.

Stumbling to my feet, I run out the door and away from the

demon. I want to find Alaric, to—

I collide with a solid mass. Muscular arms wrap around me in a tight hold.

"Clara?"

I jerk back and look up into Cassius's face. I push against him, twisting, but his grip only tightens. There's a whoosh of air, and the light from the hall is gone. The walls of my tiny room surround me again.

My legs give out from the unexpected speed. I slump to the floor. Cassius follows me, refusing to let go. He pins my back to his chest, holding my arms to my sides, and clamps his thighs against my hips and legs, rendering me unable to move.

"What are you doing?" I hiss, twisting my neck to glare.

"Me?" He returns the look. "I should be the one asking you what you're doing. You were running through the halls crying."

The fight leaves me all at once. I turn away, not wanting him to witness the new tears that spring up. Taking several deep inhales, I work on calming my racing pulse.

His heart beats against my back, and with each breath, the rise and fall of his chest echoes the rhythm. His closeness bothers me. It's too intimate.

"You can let me go." I squirm against him. "I'm fine now."

Cassius gradually loosens his hold as if he doesn't entirely trust that I won't attack. As soon as he releases me, I scoot away. He remains where he is, watching me with a guarded expression. I press my back to the side of the bed across from him.

"I've been suffering from night terrors since..." I gesture toward him. "Since you found me that night at Windbury."

Cassius's brow wrinkles. He draws a leg up and rests an arm on his bent knee. "Then you will return with me and stay until you have a new master."

I shrink back as if it could keep him from getting to me. "No," I snap. "Why do you care? It's not as if this is the first time you found me like this."

Cassius rubs the light stubble along his jaw thoughtfully. A frown pulls at the corners of his mouth.

"It's different..." he says but doesn't elaborate. The stilted tone of his words makes it sound like he cut himself off before he said too much.

He's keeping something from me.

Cassius climbs to his feet. Bending at the waist, he reaches out and takes my hand, helping me up.

"Why are you in my room?"

He blinks in surprise at the harshness of my tone. "You're welcome," he says, "I am here because you are my ward for the time being and I wanted to check on you."

He runs his fingers through my hair, loosening the tangles and brushing it back off my face. I swat at his hands and miss.

Scrunching my nose, I lean away, unable to back up without

falling onto my bed. "Why are you pretending to be nice?"

He drops his arms to his sides. "Despite what you think, little bird, I am capable of being nice, and as I've said before, I have my reasons."

Reasons... I scoff inwardly. Reasons he refuses to tell me. The non-answer only fuels my suspicion.

"Well, you can stop. You're in charge of bringing me to heel, but that doesn't mean anything else has changed."

"Why are you so untrusting of me?" he shoots back.

"Because you are still the same vampire who offered to turn me when—"

A broad grin stretches across his face. "You want me to turn you?" he asks, intentionally misinterpreting what I said.

"No," I bite out. "I have no desire to be a lesser vampire."

"Good. I love a woman who isn't willing to settle for less power than she deserves," he says.

I scoff. "This has nothing to do with power and everything to do with you wanting to take me away from Alaric." I shake my head. "I'm not a thing for you to use in petty games."

His face darkens at the mention of Alaric. "Why do you care? He's a vampire, no different than the rest of us."

"He claimed me, but I choose his mark. I asked for it."

Cassius caresses the side of my face with his knuckles.

"I wasn't sure about you until that day I had Victor go looking for you," he says more to himself then to me.

I rear back, stumbling until the backs of my legs hit the bed. "You... You set that up?" I snap. "You knew he was demon cursed?"

"Suspected," he corrects, admitting what he did as if it were nothing. "I suspected he was demon cursed."

White, hot anger flashes before my vision. "You used me as bait? I could have died!"

Cassius shrugs. "I had a feeling you wouldn't."

A sharp, ugly laugh bursts out of me. "It's a good thing you showed up when you did because I almost died."

"I showed up exactly when I intended to. I wasn't about to leave him in the room with you any longer than needed to confirm my suspicions." Cassius leans in until his face is within an inch of mine. "Besides, did you honestly think I left that dagger where you could reach by accident?" he asks quietly.

That confession takes me aback. "What?"

"Yes, little bird. I left it there for you to use." He nods slowly and pulls his face away.

I ball my hands into fists at my side, fighting the urge to slap him. "What if he'd stabbed me?"

"Whatever transpired between you two before I walked in was the thing that pushed Victor over the edge. He was too far gone to see that he could have used it on you. But you... I knew you would take the opportunity if it presented itself." He frowns. "I had expected you to use it sooner than you did."

I'd been too busy keeping an eye on the cursed vampire to formulate much of a plan.

"You're a bastard," I snap.

"I know." He dips his chin and steps closer. One hand grazes the side of my arm, the other gestures to the bed.

"I'm not going to trust you," I repeat. "I didn't before, and I'm not going to now."

I sit on the bed and pull my legs up. Cassius reaches over and drags the worn blanket on top of me. I might as well be asleep for all the attention he gives to my words.

"We…" I motion between us. "We are not friends."

"That's fine," he says, leaning forward, one hand planted on either side of my head. "I will still be your friend even if you're not mine."

I press a hand to his chest and push him back. Then slow and calm, I say, "No, thank you."

Cassius settles on the foot of my bed, back pressed to the wall. His long legs hang off the edge.

"You can leave," I say.

"I will be staying right here." There's a long pause. Then, he adds so quietly I'm not sure he meant for me to hear, "Alaric's presence seems to keep these night terrors of yours at bay. Perhaps mine will do the same."

I twist to my side, trying to ignore the warmth radiating off him and the hope that his being here really will keep the demon away. It feels wrong to be grateful to him for that. *It should not be him.*

Sliding my hand under my pillow, I find the familiar leather wrapped hilt of the dagger.

Come to me.

The demon from the dungeon had visited tonight. I chew on my bottom lip. The demon didn't attack; they didn't even follow when I ran.

They want something from me... Varin said as much in the dungeon when they healed me.

I think of the scars on my arms and how Alaric couldn't heal those wounds completely. He said that the power of the night-forged silver opposed his own—power that came from his demon.

Even as exhaustion works its way through my body, a final thought occurs to me. A vampire is vulnerable to night-forged silver as a mortal would be to any weapon, so why wouldn't a demon be just as vulnerable to my blade?

My fingers tighten around the hilt.

If the demon wants me to find them, then I will find them.

CHAPTER
NINETEEN
CLARA

I smooth a hand down my shirt and reach for the door. My nerves ratchet up, and I have to remind myself that I'm Cassius's ward, not his prisoner. The hollow ache in my stomach is enough for me to take the chance and leave without him. After all, it's only a trip to the kitchens through the servants' quarters for a little food.

Pulling open the door, I step out into the hall and close it behind me. A half snort, half laugh comes from behind.

I whirl.

"Is this how you sneak around?" Cassius asks with a smirk, his arms folded across his broad chest. He leans a shoulder against the wall, one foot crossed over the ankle of the other. "You're not very good at it."

I step back as he prowls toward me like a large cat.

"Where were you going, little bird?"

"I was hungry. Thank you for checking on me, but I will be fine." I turn my back on him and keep walking.

I find it hard to look at him in the light of the day. A thread of shame curls low in my stomach, twisting it into knots. I allowed him to stay and keep the demon from returning.

His fingers entwine through mine, and with a slight tug, he spins me to face him. "Miss Valmont, I am your guardian. You are not to go anywhere without me by your side."

"Do you expect me to stay in my room and starve while waiting for you to remember I need to eat?" The words fly from my mouth before I can stop them.

Cassius releases my hand and shakes his head. "No, of course not, Clara, but having me with you is safer—" he frowns. I could almost swear that he's genuinely offended by the look I give him. "You are so much more than that."

I roll my eyes.

He takes my arm and hooks it through his then leads me down the hall.

"You shouldn't worry so much about my presence as much as you should be worrying about tomorrow morning."

My steps falter. "W-what's tomorrow morning?"

He gives me a sidelong glance and raises a brow like I should know. When it's clear to him that I don't, he frowns.

"Tomorrow is the reclaiming. You will get your new master before the night is through."

"So soon?" I ask.

I'd expected it to take longer. Elizabeth told Cassius to train me. I'd assumed she meant literally, but maybe she'd only meant for him to keep me from killing any more vampires.

Cassius nods. "Elizabeth wants this over sooner rather than later."

My gaze snags on his. He doesn't need to translate the meaning of his words. We both understand that the queen wants me dead.

Nerves form a rock that settles in the pit of my stomach. My insides twist, and form a pit in my stomach.

"Why so soon?" I ask dumbly.

Cassius gives me a disbelieving stare. "Don't ask questions you know the answer to. Did you think she would allow you to remain unclaimed for long?"

"Alaric has already claimed me." I wipe my clammy hands over my hips. A shiver rakes over my body and my throat goes dry, making my tongue feel thick and heavy in my mouth.

Cassius takes my shoulders and brings me close, gripping my chin between his thumb and forefinger, almost painfully.

Hot tears build, prickling at the backs of my eyes. Though nothing has changed since my sentencing, I can feel my world spinning out of control.

There is something about knowing when my life will end that

makes this all feel more real.

"What is wrong with you? You knew exactly what would happen. This is your life, Clara."

I turn to the window. Hoarfrost covers the edges of the diamond-shaped panes. Outside, a winter bird lands on the ledge for a heartbeat before taking to the skies again. My heart aches, wishing to have that kind of freedom.

But I have willingly walked into a stone cage, trapped with predators hungry for my blood, and the one person I have come to count on has been ripped from my life.

"I don't feel like eating anymore."

"Are you sure? You should eat to—"

I whip my head around to face him. "I said I'm not hungry," I snap.

Pushing past him, I walk back toward my temporary room as fast as my shaky legs will carry me.

I hear Cassius order a passing human to bring a plate of food to me anyway. His footsteps echo down the hall, following me.

When I reach my room, I don't bother closing the door. He's already inside by the time I sit on the floor, leaning against the bed frame.

Tomorrow, I will be reclaimed, and the two marks Alaric gave me will be erased. I shudder. I don't want another vampire to bite me. What I used to fear from Alaric's mark will come to pass, only it will be much worse. That is if I manage to live through the night.

Cassius stands in the center of the room, saying nothing, but the silent judgment radiating off of him irritates me.

After a while, a man comes with food. Cassius takes it and quickly dismisses him. He doesn't offer me the plate but sets it on the dresser. Maybe he knows I would only fling it at his head.

Cassius takes a seat on the floor next to me.

"Why are you still here?"

He shrugs with one shoulder. "I could leave, but I'd rather keep you company."

I let out an annoyed breath and scoot a little farther away. "Your advances are a little too strong. You should learn when a girl doesn't want you around."

"Believe me, little bird, I am well aware, but I think I'll still stay a bit longer." The half-cocked smile drops from his mouth. "What you say and think you want isn't always what you need. Your life is about to change, and I'm the closest thing to a friendly face that you will see before then. No one should spend their final hours locked up in a hole, alone with their thoughts."

I open my mouth to argue then close it. Even Cassius doesn't expect me to live long after I am reclaimed.

That stings more than it should.

I don't want to fight with him anymore, so I face straight ahead and stare at the blank grimy wall, letting my vision blur.

He's right. I don't want to spend this time alone, but he's not the one I want to spend these hours with.

173

I want to see Alaric again. Even for a little while.

Cassius sits silently at my side, never pressuring me to eat or speak anything.

After a while, the silence gets to me. I feel the urge to say what has been on my mind since the moment Alaric and I arrived at this castle.

Somehow, my lack of trust in him makes it easier to admit. "I'm scared."

Cassius closes the distance between us and rests his arm over my shoulders, pulling me into his side.

Vampires and their constant need to touch.

I don't pull away.

We remain like this for a long time. I hate that I am finding comfort in him when he's not the one who should be comforting me.

At some point, he starts talking about places and people I've never heard of. I ignore him, but the steady drone of his voice rumbles though me, and distracts me from my thoughts.

I put my hand on his side and push back, looking at him—really looking. Cassius breaks off mid-sentence, watching me with a perplexed expression.

He hasn't acted insincerely this entire time, never trying to get me to do or think what he wants. He has, as he said, just offered his presence.

"Why did you keep trying to take me from Alaric back at the

manor?" I ask.

His expression darkens, jaw clenching. He takes me in, calculating what to say. I know, at best, I will get a half-truth.

I shake my head and pull away. "Don't bother. If you're not going to tell me—"

"I was there on orders from the queen. She asked me to see if there was a bond between you two and, if so, to break it."

My mouth drops open. I climb to my feet, wanting to put more distance between us. I knew the truth would make me angry, and I still asked for it.

He came to Windbury to break our bond. He set me up to nearly be killed by a demon-cursed vampire. There is nothing good about this man. He is evil—a pawn for his queen.

I run my fingers through my hair and tug. Yet his actions here and last night contradict all of that. He is inconsistent.

Cassius stands with me, advancing. I retreat until my back is against the wall, and we are chest to chest.

"You're a bastard," I say breathlessly. "You can be my guardian if you want, but you needn't bother pretending with me."

Fury distorts his features. His fingers dig into my shoulders. "I'm not pretending with you. I answered your question. If I'd told you anything else, *that* would have been the lie. You need to stop thinking of yourself as pathetic and weak. You will never get what you want without power, and to get power, you must take it."

I frown, not understanding why he's telling me this again.

"You are devious—"

"You must learn to bend so you do not break." He releases me. "Just as I've had to."

I want to curse him, rage at him, but I can't seem to find the words.

After a minute, he backs away. "Eat, Clara, and get some rest. You will need all your energy for the reclaiming tomorrow."

He has gone from scolding me to acting as if we had never fought in the span of seconds.

"A servant will be here in the morning to assist you."

Then he's gone.

I want to hate him, to blame him for everything. But none of this is his fault. Instead, I think of what he said.

He is right. I must learn to bend so I don't break.

I must never break.

CHAPTER
TWENTY
CLARA

After Cassius leaves, I debate whether or not I should sneak out to look for Va'rin. But the halls have been continuously filled with voices. There's no way to leave, let alone make it to the secret passage on the third floor, unseen, so I continue to lay in bed, staring at the high ceiling.

Warmth blooms in my chest. I miss Alaric. I miss the weight of his hand on my hip as I sleep, his warm musky scent, and I miss his presence. I hoped he would have come to visit me before the reclaiming, though I knew that would be impossible from the start.

Dawn was several hours ago, and nothing has happened yet. I haven't moved since I opened my eyes. I'd woken from a light sleep the moment the faintest light peeked through the archer's slit window.

Of course, a vampire's idea of the morning would be different than a human's, but I remain here, on my back, praying to the Otherworld that time would stop or at least slow down as long as I stay still.

Dread pools at what the day will bring when I get up.

The door is thrown wide, and a woman storms in. She sneers when her gaze lands on me still in bed. She fists her hands on her hips and heaves a bone weary sigh.

"Get up, you lazy girl," she orders, marching to the window and opening it. A cold blast of winter air blows in. I suck in a sharp breath, squeezing my eyes against the chill. "As soon as the sun sets, you will meet your new suitors."

Suitors. She either doesn't know what tonight is really about, or she thinks it's some kind of honor. Either way, her word choice sets my blood on fire. These vampires are not going to court me or attempt to win my favor. They are beasts who will vie to see who's control of me is the strongest.

"I would rather not," I grumble, tugging the thin blanket over my head.

The woman grabs my wrist and yanks it, dragging me out of bed and onto my feet.

Demons and saints, she's strong.

"You'll bruise her if you continue to handle her like that. Our queen would not be happy." The woman freezes at Della's words. "You are dismissed. I can handle her from here."

The woman releases me like I was nothing more than a sack of soiled clothing then turns to Della and says, "You have two hours, and not a minute longer. I will return to escort her."

The door slams shut.

"I don't care if I'm about to be reclaimed. I'm not a possession," I seethe.

"If Alaric had fully marked you right away, then you wouldn't be in this predicament."

She picks up a pile of folded material and straightens out a cloudy gray dress. Her hand smooths over the material as she works out several wrinkles.

"Why are you here, Della? Did Cassius send you again?"

She looks up from the dress and says, "Someone had to chase away your *mother*."

"What?" I hiss.

She continues to work out nonexistent wrinkles. "I owed you that much."

I shake my head. There was never any semblance of friendship between us, real or otherwise. "Owe me?"

"Otherworld take me now," she mutters, dropping the dress over the foot of the bed to face me. "How can you be so dense?"

I say nothing.

"You do know that Lawrence is my sire?" she asks.

"Yes."

Della walks up to me and takes my hand, sitting me down on the bed. She sits next to me and takes my hand. "I'll tell you something I've never told anyone before."

I swallow and wait for her to continue.

"I allowed Lawrence to turn me because I loved him. It wasn't until it was too late that I realized I had only been a way for him to pass the time. The moment he met Rosalie, I knew he didn't care for me. At least, not the way I'd wanted him to." Della holds her chin up, but her eyes slide closed. "Now that he can never have her... maybe he will be able to see me again."

I suck in a breath and hold it.

Della waves a hand. "I know it's horrible to be glad that another vampire has died, but maybe some good can come out of everything."

That's... disturbing.

"You... you think you owe me because I killed Alaric's sister?"

Della nods, and a tear glints, caught in her long lashes. Her face pales, and she buries her face in her hands.

I reach out and pat her back, not sure how to feel. I work through what she told me. Rosalie's death is something I've struggled with for a long time.

Della breaks the moment by jumping to her feet and wiping the back of her hand over her eyes. "Enough of this. We don't have much time to get you ready."

"I'd rather you throw me from the window," I say.

Della snorts. "Don't be ridiculous. I couldn't get your head through that tiny opening."

With that, she quickly strips me of my clothes and fits me into the too-tight corset. It's all I can do to keep breathing in this thing.

The dress looks like a storm, dark gray with a thin layer of shimmering material on top. The neckline dips low. It's designed to show off my neck and shoulders. There are no sleeves to hide my scars or my dagger. The skirt is thin and tight.

Della talks as she dresses me with deft movements, instructing me on how to act and when to speak—keep my head up and eyes down and answer questions only when they are directed at me.

She stands before me, a long nail tapping her chin as she examines her work. "Things will go smoother for you if you behave as expected."

I force a smile, but it is more of a grimace than anything else.

"If there is a vampire you think has the possibility of letting you live, don't fight their compulsion. It's not much, but you have some choice in the matter."

I'm about to tell her that there is no vampire I would ever obey when the human woman returns.

Della steps back. "This will have to do."

"Fine," the woman says, turning to me. She jerks her head, indicating that I'm to follow her and walks off without a word.

I take two steps before stopping and running to my bed. I clutch the hilt of the dagger and squeeze my eyes closed for a fraction of a second before holding it out to Della. Her lips part in surprise.

"Give this to Alaric." When she doesn't take it, I add, "We both know I can't take it with me, and he should have it back."

She reaches out, hand hovering over the hilt.

"If you honestly feel like you owe me, then do this and you can consider your debt paid."

Della purses her lips then nods once. As soon as her fingers wrap around the hilt, I drop my hands and race after the human woman.

Della is right. Alaric and I should have made sure I was fully marked. It had scared me then, but why? He is my best friend, a rock against a storm. He is someone I care for.

If only I hadn't been cut at the theater... If only I had stayed in the ballroom and not wandered the halls... If only.

If only.

If only.

I can come up with a hundred things I could have done better, but it will always be easier to see things after the fact.

I follow the woman down the halls, feeling the eyes of palace servants on my back. Their blank faces send a shiver down my spine. It's hard to tell if they are skilled at hiding their thoughts or if their emotions have long since been compelled out of them.

I'm suddenly sick with nerves. I want to run outside and breathe in the cold evening air to get away from the queen and the

182

vampires who want to own me.

Della said to look for one who seems decent. I should have laughed because the chances of that are damn near impossible.

We turn the last corner, and the servant stops, waiting for me to catch up.

"Be on your best behavior," she says, and for a second, I think to be as terrible as I can. The woman takes my wrist and squeezes, her boney fingers digging in. "Don't even think of causing a scene. If you are out of line, make no mistake, the queen will have your head."

There is no exaggeration in her words.

"Now," she continues. "When you enter, keep your head up, look straight ahead, and walk directly to the queen. Bow to her, but do not rise until she gives you permission, and above all, obey her as if she has compelled you."

My skin goes ice cold. The look on the woman's face says she knows her threat worked.

The doors to the throne room lie straight ahead on the right. It's close, but the walk feels like it takes an eternity to reach them. She stops, giving me one last push.

Two guards pull open the doors. I stand frozen in place.

The queen sits on her throne, surrounded by hordes of vampires filling the room, standing to either side to create a straight path to her. Elizabeth stares me down, a smug look on her delicate features.

Somewhere in the distance, someone plays the violin. It's all wrong. It doesn't fit.

All eyes swivel to rest on me. I want to run, painful, agonizing death be damned.

"Get moving, girl," the servant woman hisses.

Finally, I get my legs to obey and take a step forward. The music stops, and the only sound is my heels clicking against the polished marble floor with each step.

I keep my eyes locked on the queen, though I can't help but notice the subtle shift in demeanor in the vampires I pass. Their chins lift, faces angling away. I want to walk faster and end this show as quickly as possible, but in truth, any faster and my shaky legs would give out.

When I finally reach the queen, I bow low.

"Your Majesty," I say in a voice filled with as much saccharine as I can manage. There is no respect underneath the words, and I know she can sense it. She isn't naive enough to think otherwise.

She says nothing for several heartbeats, and I wonder if she is testing me.

"Come and stand by my side. The suitors have waited long enough." Elizabeth pats the arm of her throne.

Slowly, I straighten and do as she bids. The second I've taken my place, a vampire enters then another and another until there is a progression of four men and two women. My heart stops when I see the seventh vampire enter.

The room erupts into a din of murmurs.

I can't breathe.

My heart resumes beating, though now the rhythm is erratic as it pounds mercilessly against my chest.

Alaric.

The queen shifts in her seat. I don't care if she can hear how my pulse races with hope.

"We let him join in the fun, as a way to regain some of his dignity at failing something so simple," she whispers under her breath so only I hear. "Don't get your hopes up. He will try, but he will not win you back."

CHAPTER
TWENTY-ONE
CLARA

I can't pull my attention away from Alaric. Seeing his face only compounds how much I've missed him.

But the happiness I feel comes crashing down around me. His presence here is only to make this process hurt worse for both of us. Alaric has no chance. He will try and be made to fail before everyone. He will be publicly humiliated by having something taken away.

Like the vampires ahead of him, he keeps his chin high and gaze forward. The lines of his features are stony, not even holding a sliver of emotion.

There are seven vampires in all spread out into a long line before the dais. Silence descends upon the room.

Elizabeth lifts her arm, and the large demon bird glides through the air, seemingly to come from nowhere. They soar over the heads of the vampires on silent wings. The demon circles the room once then lands on the high back of her throne. With a flick of her wrist, one guard speeds from across the room to stand right before me, moving too fast for my eyes to track.

The guard leads me down the steps and into the center of the room. Once there, she bares her fangs and says, "Move from this spot and you will not live long enough to take your next breath."

Elizabeth stands at the edge of her dais. She pulls in a single deep breath and commands the attention of everyone in the room.

"Each suitor may approach the human one by one to examine her, but if you touch or attempt to compel her before it is your turn, you will be denied."

I hold my breath as the seven vampires encircle me.

The first vampire steps forward, wearing a half-smile that makes my skin crawl. Tall and reedy, his arms and legs look too long and thin for his body. His sandy brown hair is greased back, making his crooked nose stand out.

He reaches out with his lanky hand, stopping short of running his fingers through my hair. He leans in and inhales deeply. I keep my eyes locked on Alaric, in an attempt to steady my pulse.

Once the first vampire returns to his place in the circle, one of the women approaches. After several seconds, she shakes her head and moves back, allowing the others their turn.

One by one, this continues until all except Alaric has examined me. I wait for him to take his turn, wanting to be near him, to have him make his intentions clear to everyone in the room.

A knot forms in my gut when he doesn't.

"Who among you wish to claim the girl?" the queen asks.

Alaric and two of the men step forward. One is blond with unremarkable features. Nothing about him stands out. His presence is forgettable which could make him dangerous.

The other vampire to step forward is the crooked-nosed man. The gleam in his eye chills my blood and I instantly push the other man from my mind.

The queen looks at the others and asks, "Do any of you wish to try?"

In unison, they shake their heads. Elizabeth nods a dismissal. They back up, melting into the crowd.

"Whoever among you can compel her the easiest can claim her," Elizabeth says. "Mr. Thomas, you may go first."

My pulse races in anticipation and dread as the three vampires surround me. For the first time, Alaric meets my gaze. His face is a neutral mask, but I see the worry in his deep sapphire eyes.

You have some choice in the matter. Della's words come back. I will let Alaric compel me. Whatever he commands... I trust him.

"Come, human," the blond vampire orders.

His voice echoes in my head as his power seeps through his words and latches onto my marrow. It pulls on me, urging me to obey.

I fight it with everything I have as his power clouds my mind. My body takes jerky steps toward him.

"Embrace me," he says. "Think only of me for the rest of your short life."

The order seeps into my mind, making my will weaker by the second. I can feel my body giving in. My thoughts grow hazy behind the throbbing pain.

In the end, I know it's a losing battle. Woodenly my arms fling themselves around his neck. My stomach roils at the touch.

"Kiss me," he orders.

I grit my teeth as I lift up on my toes, bring his face down to mine, but not even the pain can make me follow that order. Sweat beads along my forehead. I close my eyes, using every ounce of willpower to fight. Then, his lips come crashing down on mine. I rear back, pushing at his shoulders.

"No," I snarl.

He releases me. I stumble back, panting and exhausted. I drag the back of my hand across my mouth and back away. "I did not follow that command."

"He failed to compel her entirely," Crooked nose

announces to the room.

Elizabeth nods and waves her hand. "Then proceed, Mr. Hughes."

The second man wraps his fingers around my shoulders from behind, startling me with his touch. He lowers his mouth to my ear and whispers his compulsion.

It's too soon. I'm not ready. I don't get a chance to fight or regain my composure. His power scratches across my skin, and I can feel it take hold of my muscles.

I run from him toward the first and throw myself into his arms.

"Don't let him compel me." The words rip themselves from my mouth, unbidden.

The first vampire catches me, a look of shock on his face that melts into victory. I lift up on my toes and press my mouth to his. He deepens the kiss.

My hands slide down his chest to his sides as I take a step back. He smiles, thinking he won.

I lift my arm and swing. He doesn't even notice what's happening as the blade of his own sword slices through his neck without resistance. His head thumps loudly on the floor, the smile still on his face.

Several things happen all at once. The sword falls from my hand, clattering loudly. His body falls with a heavy thump onto the smooth white marble floor. Massive amounts of blood pour out like a river, and the room erupts into a deafening cacophony of screams and shouts.

Elizabeth calls for the room to silence, but it's several minutes before the noise softens enough for anyone to speak and be heard.

Behind me, the crooked nose vampire raises his voice to the room, "She obeyed my compulsion without hesitation... exactly as a controlled human ought to. There is no reason to continue this."

A low buzzing fills my ears. I can't stop staring at the body. Red is everywhere, swallowing up the room. As the pool of red grows, I step back. It's useless. I am already covered in blood. Splatters cover my dress, and the hem is damp and heavy. I take two steps back, but the river of crimson follows me.

"She will go to Mr. Hughes," Elizabeth says, eyeing the body.

"No," Alaric says.

Elizabeth turns to him, a single brow quirked.

A warm hand slides into mine and pulls me away, breaking the trance. Alaric strides toward the queen, dragging me behind.

"She is mine." His voice booms throughout the room. "She owes me a life debt, and I will not allow anyone to keep me from collecting."

I squeeze his hand, more thankful for his touch at this moment than anything else in my life.

Elizabeth saunters forward with unnerving grace and calm, stopping halfway down the steps to remain above us, looking down.

"You know the rules. If a claimed human is not fully marked within one month's time, they are for bid by any vampire who wishes to vie for them—and that time has come and gone. Besides... she killed Mr. Thomas."

My heart hammers painfully against its bone cage.

A muscle ticks in Alaric's jaw. The room is once again silent, waiting with bated breath for his reply.

"Whether Alexander compelled her to end Jasper is of no consequence. Her life is mine." He takes three slow steps forward. He lowers his voice, and there is an unmistakable growl when he says, "She owes me a life debt for murdering Rosalie in cold blood. I claimed her for that crime."

Behind us, a mix of gasps and snarls breaks out.

Spots dance across my vision as the world sways. I can barely breathe. The stares of vampires prickle against my skin.

Elizabeth growls low, taking a step back in what appears to be surprise, but there's a knowing glint in her eyes.

For a heartbeat, I wonder if she will leap forward and rip my throat out with her sharp nails—anything to keep Alaric from marking me.

The queen scans the room, taking in every detail as if she's looking for a way to deny him. Her nostrils flare. My gaze flicks to the court members who have pushed their way to the front of the crowd. Every single one of them stands with their arms at their sides, expressions blank.

This is all an act.

No one outside that room knew that I killed Rosalie, and I doubt that anyone was told of the other vampires I killed, let alone that I am a slayer. Now, they know of the vampire on the ground behind us as well. Even if I was compelled to murder him, I doubt it would make a difference.

"Fine," Elizabeth bites out after a long moment. "Claim her now, and be done with it, or I will personally take care of her myself." She spins on her heel and waves her hand.

There's a flurry of activity around us. The violin starts playing as if it had never stopped.

Alaric pulls me to him, and the blue depths of his eyes trap me where I stand. He tightens his arms in a swift motion. Unprepared for the sudden movement, I stumble, catching myself, fingers splayed on his chest.

Everything else seems to fall away. My fingers dig into the material of his jacket.

Alaric hesitates, and I realize he's waiting for me to consent. Even now, he's letting me decide if I would rather accept his mark or die.

I blink slowly and mouth, "Do it."

Neither of us has a choice. I do not want to belong to anyone but myself, but if I must choose, then I choose him.

Alaric lifts a hand and brushes my hair off my shoulder. He leans forward slowly. My breaths become shallow as he dips his head to in the crook of my neck. His lips faintly brush along my skin. I can't tell if he kissed me or if it was only his breath.

"It's all right," I whisper.

He says something along my skin, but I can't hear him past the roar of blood in my ears, drowning out the world around us.

There's a sharp sting as his fangs pierce my skin. My face warms. There are too many eyes on us, too many vampires witnessing this intimate moment.

His mouth moves against my neck as if he were merely placing gentle kisses. With each pull of my blood, I can feel his power seeping into me. It's warm and familiar. The same power flowed through me each time he used it to heal my wounds, but this time, it's different, smooth, with no hint of searing heat.

The sensation of something right clicks into place, becoming stronger. It's building, building, building until I don't think I can hold anymore, and it will rip me into a thousand shattered pieces.

And then it's too much... suffocating, burbling toward the surface. My head falls back, but he doesn't stop.

My hands fall away and hang limply. I wait for a scream to rip free of my throat, but it never comes.

He's taking too much. Every ounce of energy seeps from my muscles until my knees give out. Alaric clutches me to his chest, his arms banded tightly around my waist. He's the only thing keeping me from falling.

I want to tell him it's too much, but I can't seem to make my mouth work.

He pulls away. I glance at him through slitted eyes and blurred vision, struggling to keep hold of consciousness.

A warm trickle of blood seeps from the puncture wounds at my neck. It feels scalding hot against my cold skin.

"It is done," he says to the room.

Alaric shifts, curling an arm under my knees. Everything tilts. Then, I'm pressed against him, warm and secure. His arms tighten protectively.

Then, I let the darkness take me.

CHAPTER
TWENTY-TWO
CLARA

I wake with a start. Gasping for air, I wince at the sharp throb pounding against my skull, and press a hand to my head to quell the pain. My thoughts are a hazy mess, and I'm not quite sure how I ended up here—or even where here is.

Slowly, my mind catches up to the moment. This is Alaric's room at Nightwich, and last night, he gave me the third and final mark. My hand flies to the spot where he bit me.

I slide out of bed and shuffle across the room. I'm out of breath by the time I make it to the mirror in the bathing room. A fine sheen of sweat dampens my forehead.

I'm no longer wearing the storm gray dress but one of Alaric's shirts. There's a small sense of comfort in the familiarity of the item. Pulling the collar back, I examine the bite mark. The skin is smooth and healed over, and the two additional scars are light pink. My older scars have faded to little more than slightly raised, pale lines.

There's an echo in my chest, like the ghost of a second heartbeat. I press my palm over my heart, rubbing at the new sensation.

"You're out of bed," Alaric says. There's a soft click as the door closes behind him. "You should rest more, give the power time to settle."

"The queen," I say. The words come out sharp. Spinning, I face him as even more details of last night come flooding back to me.

Alaric's brows shoot up in question.

"She already knew about Rosalie. How…" I shake my head, pressing a palm to my temple.

"Only the court knew, and she didn't expect me to announce it in front of everyone."

"But you did," I say slowly.

He nods. "It was a calculated risk."

Alaric closes the distance between us, his gaze unwavering from the bite marks on my neck. He reaches up and, with the softest touch, brushes the tiny scars with his fingertips. It sends tingles rushing along my skin.

"If this hadn't been the final mark, they would have ripped you to shreds or would have expected me to drink every last drop of your blood."

I swallow, not wanting to think about that anymore.

"I wouldn't have let that happen," he says quietly.

And I believe him.

Alaric shifts his weight, his chest pressing lightly against mine. I lean into him, into his warmth and that slight touch causes desire to rip its way through me. The closer he is, the stronger I feel our connection and the echoing heartbeat.

"How are you feeling?"

Thankful for the change of subject, I close my eyes and take a moment to assess my body. Opening them again, I expel a breath and say, "Good. A little tired, but... good."

Alaric wraps me up in his arms. "I am sorry. It was the only way to squash all doubts." His thumb brushes over the scar. "I'm sorry for this too, Clara."

His long, thick lashes lower, shielding his eyes. He doesn't just mean for the scar. He means for giving me the final mark because that decision was taken from both of us.

Whatever my destiny is now, it's tied with his.

There's a strange feeling running through me, like blood pumping through my veins but separate. It feels at home as if it was always there, and I'd never noticed it before. A part of me has finally woken after hibernating for over twenty years.

I lick my lips and speak words I know he needs to hear, words that are true. "If it hadn't been you, then I would have been reclaimed by another. I do not regret it."

The corners of his mouth twitch into the ghost of a smile. Then, his arms are around me, crushing me to him. I curl into him, needing his touch as much as he needs mine. With one arm banded around my waist, he runs the fingers of his free hand through my hair. I wrap my arms around his neck and inhale his musky scent.

Even though my fatigue and the strange power of his humming through every nerve ending, I am more aware of him than ever before. I bring my hand up between us and rest it on his chest.

Alaric pulls back, giving me a questioning look. I stare at his chest. I can't feel his heart through his muscle and skin, but I can sense every time his heart beats.

"What are you doing?" he asks.

"I can sense you," I explain. He cants his head to the side, so I elaborate, "Your heart... and your breath." I shake my head feeling stupid. *This close up, any idiot could.* "It's more than—I don't know—I think I could feel them even if you were somewhere else in the world."

His quiet laugh rumbles deep in his chest. "I can feel you as well."

I sway on my feet, leaning on him for support, suddenly overwhelmed by processing everything all at once.

"You're exhausted, Clara. You shouldn't be up." He tries to pick me up, but I swat at his hands.

"I'm a little tired," I say. "I'm not going to break."

He chuckles and settles for offering an arm. I rest my head against his arm as we make our way across the room, wanting the extra contact.

"You didn't come for me in the dungeon," I say quietly, immediately regretting the words.

Alaric stops walking. Letting go of my arm, he swings me around to stand between him and the bed.

"Had I gone, you would never have made it out alive." He reaches up and cups the nape of my neck with his palm. His thumb strokes along the edge of my jaw. "I tried to send Lawrence, but even he couldn't manage it."

I open my mouth to ask why he would send a man who hates me, but then something else rises to the surface of my memory, something more important.

"This is going to sound insane," I start, looking at him wryly, watching his expression turn from pained to confusion. I lick my lips and feel the words on the tip of my tongue. "I think... I'm being haunted by a greater demon."

He doesn't speak for a long moment then shakes his head. "That isn't possible," he says slowly. "Greater demons are rare. There was the demon that nearly killed you when you returned from Littlemire..." He rakes a hand through his thick, black hair. "Oliver said the demon vanished after we left. They will migrate, but they aren't known to follow people, let alone haunt them."

"I think what we thought were night terrors was actually this demon," I say. My voice wavers, sounding small to my ears.

I hate it. Saying it out loud feels like admitting I've lost my mind.

There's no taking the words back now. I wouldn't blame him if he regrets tying himself to me.

"Demons and saints, you think I'm insane. I should have—"

"Clara," Alaric says, cupping my face with both of his hands and tilting my head up until I look him in the eye. He ducks his head to eye level, searching my gaze with his. "I'm glad you told me."

He places a kiss on my forehead.

"They didn't feel like dreams," I say.

"Night terrors can have a way of seeming real. They have a way of playing with your mind even after you're awake." He offers me a half-hearted smile. "Yours are the worst I've seen. It isn't that I don't believe you because I do, but what you're describing, what I've experienced... it isn't normal demon behavior. It would make more sense as the result of being around several higher demons for the first time in your life. Without being gradually introduced to so many different powers, there are side effects."

Chewing on the inside of my cheek, I take in his words. He's right. He is bound to a demon. He understands them, where I have only known lesser demons from a distance. It wasn't until he claimed me that I'd been near a higher demon for the first time.

When I was in the dungeon, I was delirious from blood loss. It would make sense for the night terrors to return.

I nod, letting out a small laugh. "You're right."

Alaric watches me, looking for a lie, but there isn't one.

I don't want to think about demons anymore. I want to think about the beautiful, Otherworldly man before me, about how lucky I am that I'm alive and still with him... I want to appreciate this moment between us.

I clasp one of his hands in both of mine then entwine our fingers. Everywhere we touch is a tingle of power dancing under my skin, and judging from his sharp intake of breath, I know he feels it, too.

Alaric's hand slides from my cheek to the back of my neck. His fingers tangle in my hair and draw me in, bringing his mouth down on mine.

Desire, bright and blinding, ignites through my veins like wildfire. He breaks away to trail kisses down my neck, stopping on the final mark. His lips brush the sensitive skin.

It frightens me how much I want this man, how much he means to me. I still can't name exactly what it is I feel, but I know it's different than anything else I've ever experienced, burning hotter than the sun.

"I swear that this will be the last thing that will ever scar you."

My heart warms at Alaric's proclamation. He means every word of it, but I know it's an impossible promise.

Despite the reason he claimed me, he has always tried to

protect me. I still have the scars from the night-forged dagger striped across my arms, the webbing of scars from Victor at the base of my neck just below Alaric's precise, small, punctures, and the three deep lines that run down my lower, left leg.

"You can't always protect me," I say.

He pulls back and smiles. "You don't need my protection. You are human, and that is your greatest strength."

A thin red line forms around his deep sapphire eyes. He grips my hips and pulls me into him.

Then, he's kissing me again, harder this time. His fangs elongate. My tongue brushes one sharp point, just enough to draw a single drop of blood. He moans against me, wrapping his arms tighter against my waist.

Every brush of his tongue against mine, every caress of his hands as they roam over my body just feels right. My exhaustion melts away, replaced with a need I can't fight.

I grab his shirt and tug it free from his waistband. My palms move up the rippled muscles of his stomach, gliding across his skin, bunching his shirt.

He releases me long enough to lift it up over his head and toss it carelessly behind him. A smile forms on his lips, and my heart wrenches in my chest. Then, he grips the shirt I wear and pulls it off over my head. Cool air flows over my hot skin as he presses me to him once more.

His eyes roam slowly down my body then back up to my face.

"Clara..." He whispers my name as he places a series of kisses along the edge of my jaw then trailing down my neck.

Alaric draws back to look at me. His eyes drink me in and set my skin ablaze. I wrap my arms around his neck and press my mouth to his to deepen the kiss.

I can't get close enough—I want to feel more of him. This isn't just the mark. This is what I've wanted since that night in the music room but could never admit to myself.

The back of my legs bump against the bed. Alaric grabs my upper thighs and lifts me up onto the mattress. I release my hold on his neck, bringing my hands to his waist. I tug on the material, but he grips my wrists, halting me.

Breaking the kiss, he steps back and removes his boots then quickly steps out of the rest of his clothes. I can't take my eyes off him.

He tangles a hand in my hair, tipping my face up and gazing at my exposed neck. Bending down, he places several kisses down the column of my throat. I lean back, and he follows me. An arm wraps around my waist as he lifts me enough to move me up the bed.

Alaric kneels between my legs, taking every inch of me in. The sharp lines of his features are softened in the pale light. A thick lock of hair falls forward, obscuring a single eye. I could stare at him forever. His scars stand out against his tanned skin like shards of moonlight.

"You're beautiful," I whisper.

He smiles. "I think I'm the one who's supposed to say that."

He lowers himself, caging me with his body, and his mouth finds mine again. The hard planes of his body press down on my soft ones. I shift in response, and I feel him smile against me.

Alaric's hand drifts down, stilling my movements. I groan, wanting more. Wanting everything.

He presses his lips to my collarbone then down to the space above my heart then between my breasts, making his way down my ribs and stomach then over the swell of my hips. He nips at my inner thigh, moving up. I squirm beneath him, anticipation clawing at me.

He pauses at my core, his warm breath drawing a small whimper from my lips. Then, he places a kiss.

I suck in a breath, and when I feel his tongue against my hot flesh, my hips buck.

"Patience, my dear Clara. I told you this time I would savor every second."

Alaric makes his way back up my body until he hovers over me, the tip of his cock pressing against my entrance.

I run my fingers over the corded muscles, feeling the faint lines of the pale scars that scar his back as they do his chest. When he doesn't move, I lift my hips, urging him.

His hand glides down to mine, bringing it to his mouth. He places a kiss along each scar along my arm as I'd once kissed his.

205

Alaric moves to my other arm and echoes the movement. He holds both of my wrists in one hand. The other glides down my side, coming to rest on my hip.

"Please," I whisper.

Slowly, he presses forward, sinking himself deep. I pull in a breath at the sensation of him filling and stretching me. Once he's fully seated himself inside, he pauses and gazes down at me. The red ring has vanished entirely, but fire blazes in the depths of those two endless pools of blue. There is more than heat and desire in his eyes. Whatever is between us is so much more than just the mark, and I am tethered to it from a place deep inside my soul.

He pulls out then slides forward. I move to rise up to meet him, but his hand still pins me down. He moves in and out, and with each stroke, he threatens to make me come undone. I swallow thickly, unable to think with him inside me. Alaric savors each movement as he'd promised he would.

Tension coils and builds as his speed increases. My back arches, and I tighten around him. A moan rips itself from my lips as my orgasm rips through me. He doesn't slow until I collapse back into the bed, panting.

Alaric leans down and kisses the hollow of my throat, still moving.

"Clara," he says, and I wait for him to say more. Instead, he begins moving again, faster, driving himself home. He's no longer holding back. I rise to meet each powerful thrust.

I wrap my legs around his waist, needing more of him. His gaze snags on mine as he moves in me. Then without warning, I cry out as another orgasm lashes through me. A few more thrusts, and I can feel him thicken inside me. Then, with a groan, he comes.

Gradually, our movements slow, and I lower my legs to the bed, my inner thighs tremor in the wake. Every nerve in my body hums.

Alaric brushes damp strands of hair from my face and places a sweet kiss to my forehead then to the corner my mouth before shifting to lie next to me.

For a long moment, Alaric stares into my eyes as if he can see down into my soul. I feel the weight of his gaze caressing each place and curve of my face like a feather-light touch. My cheeks warm, and I have to look away, unable to hold the intensity.

I never knew being with someone could feel like this. It's almost overwhelming.

Alaric gathers me in his arms, holding me tight, his warm breath brushing over my cheek. I'm suddenly overcome with exhaustion, but I feel the need to share a truth with him I hadn't dared think before now.

"I thought I was going to die in there," I say against his chest, listening to the steady rhythm of his heart beating.

He chuckles.

That is not the response I expected. I bend my neck back to look at Alaric because there's nothing funny about that.

"That's impossible," he says. The sexy grin playing on his lips is almost enough to make me forget what we're talking about. "Remember, I told you?"

I scrunch my brow.

"If you are to die, then it will be by my hand and my hand alone." He places a kiss on my mouth. "I meant it, and I would sooner cut my own heart out than harm you."

My pulse jumps as I lay my head back down in the space between his arm and shoulder.

His words echo the look in his eyes from moments ago. It feels less and less like a silly promise between two almost-friends and more like a vow of something that could irrevocably break me if I dared to give into it.

CHAPTER
TWENTY-THREE
ALARIC

Clara sighs contentedly in her sleep, scooting closer when I shift. Since the day Elizabeth turned me, I never had any desire to claim a human, let alone to mark one, yet, somehow, Clara has managed to change that.

I glide my hand over the smooth skin of her back and close my eyes.

A knock on the door is irritatingly loud. I debate ignoring it altogether when whoever it is knocks again.

I disentangle myself from Clara's limbs, get up, and quickly dress. Sliding open the drawer of the night table, I pull out the returned dagger.

Elizabeth might have "given me permission" to attend the

reclaiming, but I'd had no plans to until I felt the weight of it in my hand. Clara's message had been clear. She'd given up and had no plans to defend herself against a potential new master.

Carefully, I place the dagger atop the pillow next to her.

Another knock sounds, louder this time. Clara wakes with a scowl on her face. She tilts her head as she takes me in, frowning when she spots the weapon next to her. She props herself up on her elbows and looks from me to the dagger and back.

On impulse, I lean forward and place a kiss to the top of her head. "This belongs to you."

She smiles, sleep tugging on the expression.

Another knock on the door breaks the moment. I turn away, hurry toward the door. Jerking it open, I'm ready to scold the servant on the other side but by words catch on my tongue. A vampire stands, chin held high and a single delicate brow arched. Her lips press into a tight line as her rich brown eyes scan me from head to toe. She's a few years older than Clara, though not by much. The power radiating off her is weak.

"Our queen has requested your presence. She would not like to be kept waiting."

Elizabeth. I clench my jaw so hard I'm lucky my teeth don't crack under the force. I push down my anger. Instead of a reply, I offer a nod of acknowledgment. This is a simple message. I can't fathom why a lesser vampire would be the one to deliver it instead of one of the many human servants.

"May I come in?" Her question catches me off guard, but before I can refuse, she glides past me, stopping in the center of the antechamber. She stares at the closed doors to the bedroom and says, "I'm here to see Clara."

There's no reason I can see for an unknown vampire to see Clara, especially not without my presence.

She lifts her chin and scents the air. Her eyes narrow, and if I didn't know better, the look on her face is disapproving. *Who is this lesser vampire who thinks she has the right to judge me?*

Possibilities why this vampire is here, boldly entering my rooms, rush through my mind. One possible reason stands out—Elizabeth sent her to kill Clara as my punishment for defying her in front of the court, not caring that I would kill her.

If this woman so much as touches a hair on Clara's head, I will end her life.

Before either of us can say another word, the bedroom doors open, and Clara steps out. She's dressed in her usual attire: suede leggings and a fitted shirt, though she remains barefoot.

In a blink, I stand before her. Gripping her shoulders with both hands, I say, "I must leave you now. I've been summoned."

Her brows crease.

I slide my hands down her arms, feeling the dagger strapped to her left forearm, and look back over my shoulder at the lesser vampire. Clara leans to the side, her gaze following mine.

She jerks back out of my grasp and gapes, wide-eyed. "What are you doing here?"

The venom in her voice is unexpected. There's no fear, only anger.

"I have come to talk with you, dear. It has been long enough."

Clara knows this vampire. But when—or how—would she have met her and developed such strong feelings toward her? The look on her face is far deeper than simple annoyance. There is something personal between them.

"We have nothing to talk about. You were alive all these years and never once bothered to see how Kitty and I were doing."

Her sister?

I close the distance between Clara, taking her hand. I look into the lesser vampire's face. *Really look*. She shares the same shade of brown hair, the same rich, brown eyes with flecks of amber. This woman's features are sharper, harsher, but they could be sisters. Everything clicks into place, and I understand. This woman is Clara's mother, claimed years ago.

I pull Clara to the side and guide her chin to face me. The fact that her mother is alive has to come as a shock. The only emotion I can sense coming from her is anger.

"Would you like me to remove her? I can post a guard at the door."

She sucks in a breath and holds it for a long moment, eyeing the woman. Releasing her breath, she shakes her head, not taking her narrowed gaze off the vampire. "No, I can handle this."

I release her. I must go now. Defying Elizabeth further at this point will make things worse. Reluctantly, I move away, trusting Clara to know if she can handle the situation on her own, and knowing she is armed.

They stand face to face. Clara fists her hands on her hips, her knuckles white from the strain, and levels a glare at the woman who seems unfazed by her hostility.

Cherno glides down from their spot in the rafters and lands on my shoulder.

As I close the door behind me, the vampire's voice drifts out. "I wanted a better life than your father could ever hope to provide, so I agreed to the claiming—not that I had any choice. How can you blame me? Look at you now—marked by a vampire."

I wince. That conversation will not go well if that's how she plans to approach Clara.

She wasn't surprised to see her mother alive. I frown, realizing only now how much I've missed in the time we've been separated. In everything that's happened since arriving at Nightwich, we've had little time to talk. She has gone through so much, and I know very little about any of it. Her mother is proof enough of that.

That is something that will need to be remedied later.

"I have nothing to say to a woman who abandons her family as if they mean nothing." There's a hitch in Clara's voice.

The door closes with a soft click, shutting out the rest of their conversation.

I rush through the halls, having delayed longer than Elizabeth will deem acceptable. A sinking sensation fills my veins as I approach the open, ornate door.

A servant busies himself with straightening up and wiping imaginary spots from the glasses on the long table against the wall.

Stepping one foot inside then the other, I enter. The human turns and dips his head, keeping his gaze locked on the floor. He motions for me to sit on the sofa. Cherno inches closer to my collar as I take my place.

"Her majesty will be out momentarily," the servant says.

Then, he scurries to grab a goblet and brings it to me. Empty. I'm about to speak up when he lifts his hand over the rim.

With a flick of his hand, he slices his wrist, cutting deep. Blood pours into the cup, but my eyes linger on the mesh of pale scars that cover his forearm. There are many. It's clear that he's been in Elizabeth's service for a long time. This human is the one she chooses to serve her important guests.

Every inch of him moves and works as if his mind was compelled out of him, but there's an awareness to his eyes that says he is still his own man, that he chooses to serve the queen.

When the glass is half full, the man draws back and fills another. Once that, too, is half-filled, he wraps his wrist in quick, efficient moves. Then, he bows, turns on his heel, and walks out of the door.

Minutes pass, and I sip the blood even though I don't need to feed. I took more blood than necessary from Clara last night. Refusing to drink would be an insult, and I don't wish to push my luck again so soon.

This is the first of the many games I will be forced to play before this meeting is over.

Clara's blood will be replenished already now that she has my final mark. I will never take her blood like that again, even if the mark allows me to do so daily. She is not a food source, and I would never want her to feel as if she were.

I finish the last of the blood and set the cup down on the side table.

Elizabeth is making me wait. She would never summon me without being ready. She's testing my patience, seeing how far she can push before I push back. I could wait here all day if I had to, but I decide that this game has gone on long enough.

Rising to my feet, I make my way toward the door as if to leave.

"Leaving so soon, Alaric?" Elizabeth croons.

Keeping my expression placid, I turn to her. She was watching me the entire time.

Elizabeth wears a glittering black dress similar in style to the one Clara wore last night. She is mocking me with it.

"I am sorry to keep you waiting."

Elizabeth glides over to the selection of glasses and an assortment of drinks, ignoring the human's blood prepared for her. She plucks an empty glass and pours in a red liquid, too thin to be blood. The warm scent of the fermented fruit tells me it's wine.

She has never consumed anything other than blood in the past or, at the very least, mixed with blood.

This attempt at seeming more human to me isn't fooling anyone. It's a wasted effort. She must see that because, after a single sip, she taps her nails against the side of the glass, taking me in from head to toe.

"That was quite the stunt you pulled last night," she says, moving closer with every step. "I am surprised you would risk those outside of the court knowing you would rather mark a murderer instead of doling out the justice we deserve."

"Don't pretend you give a shit about Rosalie's death. You're glad to be rid of her. You always made sure I knew she was a disgrace." I bite out the words between clenched teeth. My jaw aches with the effort to hold back the snarl threatening to break loose. "The ability to save her was the only way I would ever let you turn me into this."

She tilts her head and drags her teeth over her bottom lip. The movement ends with her fangs bared. "I didn't know you had it in you to defy me like that."

"I don't know why you refuse to understand. I am playing by your rules and taking every right you have bestowed on us all.

You've tried for years to persuade me to participate in your asinine claiming ritual, and now that I have, I will not allow anyone to take the human I had every right to claim and mark. Not even you."

She tilts her head to the side. "But, she *wasn't* marked."

"She is now."

Elizabeth reaches up and cups my cheek, smiling fondly, but the expression quickly turns into a glower. She runs a sharpened nail down the side of my face with a slow, deliberate stroke. She presses harder and deeper until the scent of my own blood is thick on the air.

I don't flinch. Already, the skin knits back together.

She brings her hand to her face, blood coating her finger and dripping down the back of her hand. Elizabeth lifts her cup without breaking eye contact, dipping her finger into the wine, stirring it around. She brings her finger to her mouth and sucks.

With a Cheshire grin, she takes a sip. "Mmm, that's better," she says, moving away from me. She tips the cup up and drains it. Her tongue darts out and licks at a stray drop from the corner of her mouth. "Your plan won't work."

"I don't have a plan," I say as she sets her glass down hard on the side table, next to the rapidly cooling chalice of blood. "But even by your laws, I have done nothing I was not entitled to. I gave her the final mark before another reclaimed her."

Elizabeth crosses her arms under her chest, rolling her eyes. With the fire in the hearth on her other side, the edges of her profile glow orange and red.

"I will let you keep your silly human *if...*" she trails off, giving me a sidelong glance. "You agree to finally be mine and take your place as crown prince."

I laugh, harsh and humorless, before I can think to stop it. Elizabeth whirls, snarling. Cherno leaps off my shoulder and takes to the air. He spirals erratically around the room and settles on top of an empty, gilded birdcage near the bedroom door.

Looking her dead in the eye, I say, "I will never be yours."

"You were once," she says almost wistfully.

"Was I?" I snap.

I am weary of this conversation. Every day, it's the same thing—her attempts to seduce, threaten, and cajole me in some way to play the part she has designed for me, a fate I want no part in.

"Or was I doing what I needed to keep Rosalie safe?"

If my words hit home, she doesn't show it. The rapidly changing moods are a part of her facade meant to keep me guessing... to lure me into obeying her every whim.

Elizabeth returns to stand before me, her face unnervingly calm. If anyone saw her for the first time, they would think she was sweet and worth protecting from the world.

"I will be more than happy to kill the little bitch for her crimes, if you prefer." She bats her lashes. "I made the vampire laws, and I can change them. It is only by my grace that your murderous little human still lives, and it is only for your sake."

I swallow thickly but don't respond. Begging is precisely what she wants.

Elizabeth pulls back. "You have one week to decide if you would rather see your human killed or if you will submit to your fate and finally become mine." She pats my cheek over the nearly healed cut and smiles like I am a misbehaving child. "I hope you enjoyed your night with her because it will be your last. She is to stay in the human quarters from now on."

I snarl, snapping at her hand. She draws back, just avoiding my bite.

"Or would you prefer she stay in the dungeon? I do not have to let you see her again, so consider it a gift that I let her live."

I rein in my anger, swelling the bile that pushes its way up.

All those years of letters urging me to participate in the claiming, her threats against Rosalie, and refusing to let Clara and I leave... it was all leading to this moment.

She knew I would never claim a human and discard them, as so many others do. She knew it would never be a casual decision on my behalf.

And with Clara finally marked—finally tied to me—I will still end up losing her, either by agreeing to become Elizabeth's puppet, bowing to her every command or by her death for my continued refusal.

CHAPTER
TWENTY-FOUR
CLARA

As soon as the door closes behind Alaric, I regret not asking him to send her away.

"Come now, darling. Let's put the past behind us. We are together now, in this world."

I drop my arms, my anger instantly replaced by shock. Shaking my head, I say, "We aren't in the same world at all."

Mother smirks, jutting out a hip. She's nothing like the woman I remember. She was never warm, but she was also never this *cold*.

"I suppose you're right. You decided to aim quite high with your choice."

I take a step back, feeling like she punched me in the gut.

"Was it your aim to be sired by the crown prince?"

"I-I never asked to be claimed, nor did I want to be." I stutter, finally managing to recover. "In case you forgot, *your family* thought you were murdered by the vampire who claimed you, and for you to insinuate that I am little more than a social climber—" I cut off, my emotions thick and choking. Tears burn the back of my eyes. *Demon shit, it hurts to have the mother I loved and missed think so little of me.* "I never knew who or what Alaric was until we arrived here."

She gives me a look that I haven't seen since I was seven years old and caught sneaking a snack when I was supposed to be in bed and lying about it. Her slender brow arches as she dips her chin.

She thinks I'm lying.

When I don't relent, Mother heaves a sigh and rubs her temple with two fingers. "Clara, I'm trying, and I need you to try." She drops her arms as if her intention has been clear from the start. "We can get to know each other again."

I pace the room, working off some of the anger threatening to choke me. I need to think clearly.

"You can try all you like, but don't ask me to pretend that the last thirteen years never happened." My throat feels thick and dry as I fight the tears of frustration rising higher, nearly choking me. "Father lost himself in his drinking and gambled away everything we had." I look down at my hands. "I learned to hunt and steal just so Kitty and I wouldn't starve, and even then, there were times we almost did."

221

Pulling in a breath, I hold it, doing my best to push my emotions back down. I turn around to face Mother again. It's impossible to read her. The arrogant, condescending expression is gone, but in its place is one that's more suitable if we were talking about last week's weather.

"Kitty and I mourned you every day." That simple sentence is all it takes for my emotions to push their way to the surface. "Didn't you think to check on us, to make sure we weren't struggling? Did we ever cross your mind even once?"

She opens her mouth.

I hold my hand up, shaking my head and stopping her before she can speak a word. "I already know the answer to that. If you had thought about us, you would have come home. You needn't bother wasting your breath trying to build something you never wanted." I drop my hand and level a glare on her. "So no, *Mother*, I don't want to have anything to do with you. You had your chance and you threw it away to be selfish. You betrayed your family."

She steps forward then, arms stretched out as if intending to wrap me up in a hug and tell me that everything will be fine, but her efforts have come too late.

Years too late.

"Don't come here anymore. Don't seek me out. Don't send anyone to talk to me in your place. I never want to see you again."

Tears build, swelling to the edge, ready to spill over the second I blink.

Turning on my heel, I stride across the room and out the door, slamming it behind me. I jog down the long corridor toward the stairs that lead to the human quarters. I blink, and my tears finally fall in hot streams down my cheeks.

Knowing I shouldn't stray far from Alaric's rooms, I stop at the top of the stairs and lean on the stone banister, gripping it until my fingers ache.

It's stupid to allow her to crawl under my skin. She hasn't been my mother since the day before she willingly left with a vampire.

The mother I loved is dead. She died thirteen years ago.

I brush my hands over my cheeks, wiping away the tears when the door opens.

My heart stutters, afraid she will come looking for me to continue that useless conversation. I search frantically for a place to hide without going downstairs and end up ducking into the closest alcove with the strange bust of the unknown woman.

Crouching, I cling to the pedestal and peek around, watching to see where she'll go. It's like salt in a wound to watch her leave without even looking for me. She doesn't scent the air, doesn't look to see if I'm even around.

She just leaves, head held high, as if she doesn't have a care in the world. I could have remained standing in the middle of the hall, and she wouldn't have noticed.

One more traitorous tear slips out. I roughly brush it away with the back of my hand. I don't move even after she's gone or when my legs begin to cramp from the half-crouched position.

I turn my gaze on the bust, examining the lines of the flawless stone. This is the statue from my dream, but this time, I'm awake. I lick my lips, wondering what would happen if I moved it, to see if it really was a dream or—

"What, or rather, whom are you hiding from, little bird?" Cassius whispers into my ear from behind.

I jump, nearly hitting my head on the curved arch that houses the statue.

"Are you following me now?" I snap, irritated he caught me off guard.

Cassius laughs and snatches my hand, dragging me out into the open. I stumble forward, bumping into him. He hooks my arm in his and presses it tightly to his side.

Cassius starts walking, pulling me along. I dig my heels into the floor but can't find any leverage barefoot.

"Let me go, vampire."

"I told you; we will be spending a lot of time together from now on. That doesn't stop just because Alaric finally finished marking you."

"I'm sure he's capable of watching me without your help," I grind out, pushing on his arm with my free hand.

He stops walking, loosening his hold on me. I rip my arm free and look up at his face. His dark gray eyes cloud over. He watches me with those large, sad eyes. "Is that why I found you hiding alone in the hallway?"

Cassius grabs for my hand again, but I pull it out of reach.

"Stop looking at me like that, and leave me alone," I snap. I don't want his pity. I want to be alone. I turn, heading back toward Alaric's room, but he catches my wrist and swings me back around. "If you keep pulling me around like that, I will punch you in the throat."

"I'll try, but I won't make any promises," he says, chuckling. "Anyway, I have something better to show you than dusty, old sculptures of people no one remembers."

"I'm not interested," I say. "Learn to take a hint."

Cassius smiles widely, showing off his fangs. "You can hint all you want, but that doesn't change my duty." He tugs me closer, lowering his voice and winks. "But I can make it work in your favor."

I narrow my eyes, suspicious and yet curious at how he thinks he'll be able to do anything that I might consider helpful.

"Trust me, little bird."

I snort. His eyes and smile widen at the sound. "You know I don't trust you," I say. "We already had this conversation, and after what you did—"

Cassius presses a finger to my lips, silencing me. If he tries to tell me to put the past behind me, I might be tempted to draw my dagger on him. My fingers twitch.

Instead, he says, "I know. I know I will have to earn your trust, and I am also well aware that it may never happen, but I might be the only other vampire in this city who doesn't thirst for your death, so you might as well come with me." He motions toward the empty room. "Unless you would rather remain locked up in the room for who knows how long?"

"Fine. Show me whatever it is," I say. Pausing, I eye him up and down with a heavy sigh. "And this better not be a trick, or I will—"

"Kill me?" he asks in a tone that almost sounds... hopeful.

"Yes," I say slowly.

"I count on it." Cassius grins.

Vampires are so strange. I press my hands to his chest and push him back a step.

I let him lead me back through the hall and down the main stairs then through the corridors.

As we walk, I lose myself in thought, going over the conversation I had with mother. I wish I'd said more; I wish I'd said less. There are a thousand ways that could have gone, and none of the ones my mind can come up with would leave me satisfied.

Halfway down a flight of stairs, I stop to look around. The stairwell is dim with a musty dampness to the air, and the lighting is spaced farther apart, making this area darker than the main halls. Ahead of us is pitch black.

"Where are you taking me?" I move up one step, backing away from Cassius.

"You'll see." He jerks his chin and pulls a torch from the wall. "I wouldn't want to spoil the surprise."

He continues walking. After a few heartbeats, I follow, not wanting to be left alone in the dark.

The torch in his hand blinds me to our surroundings.

When we come to a stop, he looks over his shoulder and offers me a large grin before pushing open an old door. The wood is cracked and warped from age.

A smile tugs on my lips. I know this place.

Using his vampire speed, Cassius enters and runs around the room. Light flares to life, bathing everything in an orange glow. The floor is mostly open, with weapons stored against one wall that glint with the light of the flickering flames.

Cassius stands in the doorway, looking like he found a stash of hidden treasure. "Well?"

When I don't answer, he takes my hand, pulls me in closing the door behind us.

"Why did you bring me here?" I ask.

"You don't seem surprised."

I press my lips together to stifle a laugh. "No. Alaric brought me here when we first arrived. We trained... until everything happened."

Cassius deflates, and I almost feel bad. He crosses his arms, muttering under his breath, "Of course he did." He straightens, his smile reappearing, though this time, it doesn't reach his eyes. "I suppose it doesn't matter. We're still going to use this room."

He circles me as he talks. Stopping behind me, he rests his hands on my shoulders and brings his mouth close to my ear. His warm breath glides across my skin.

"I am going to train you, little bird. You can't expect to protect yourself against every vampire like you did with Victor or by being compelled into killing one. Or..." Cassius pauses dramatically. "By luck."

I shrug him off, stepping out of his grasp.

"Alaric is already training me," I say.

It makes me uneasy having him step in to take Alaric's place in anything, even this.

True, we haven't actually trained since the first few days here, and so much has happened since then. I hardly see him anymore, and I have to wonder if that will change because of the mark.

Cassius watches me closely.

I shift under the weight of his gaze. "Why are you doing this? This doesn't seem like... you."

He steps closer. "You hardly know me, Miss Valmont. How can you presume to know if this is *like me* or not?"

He has a point.

"Then why *are* you doing this?" I ask again.

"I have my—"

I cut a hand through the air. "Forget it. If you're going to give me the same non-answer, you might as well save your breath."

He shrugs, unbothered. "Do you want me to train you or not? Because I can guarantee that Alaric's mark isn't enough to stop others from trying to kill you."

I bite down on the inside of my cheek, debating. On the one hand, it would be stupid to refuse. On the other, he's not Alaric, and that bothers me more than it should.

Cassius circles around to the weapons, picking one up, examining it then setting it back down.

"All right," I relent. Weariness from the day settles heavily between my shoulders. I don't want to argue anymore with anyone. I turn and trudge toward the door. "You can train me, but I'm tired and want to—"

"Dodge," Cassius's voice booms from the far end of the room.

I scrunch my brows, not understanding as I turn back toward him. It takes entirely too long to process the lightning-quick movement of his hand as he lifts something. Firelight glints off polished metal.

I feel the whoosh of air and the sharp sting on my ear before I can react. The thunk of a weapon comes from behind as it embeds itself in the wooden door at my back.

Clapping my hand to my ear, I drop down into a crouch, hissing through my teeth. I look at my hand. Blood coats my fingertips.

Cassius's boots stop inches in front of me. He kneels and roughly tilts my head to the side, prodding at my ear to assess the damage.

"You can't trust anyone, and you must always be ready," he scolds.

"We've already established that I don't trust you." I suck in a sharp breath as he presses his palm to my ear.

Red light encircles his eyes as he pulls his power to him then into my injury. Like the last time he healed me, it burns like hot metal on skin, though the pain seems distant, less intense than last time. Cassius releases me before I can pull away.

He holds his hand out to me. I take it and let him pull me to my feet. I tug on my hand. "You have a really bad habit of holding on too long."

"And you have a bad habit of walking away when we aren't finished," he retorts, relinquishing my hand.

With a hand on my lower back, he guides me from the training room and out into the hall. We walk in silence as he leads me the way I'd come with Alaric that first day. Instead of continuing to the third floor, he guides us out into the servants' wing.

Cassius gestures toward a door. "I will come for you every morning, and we will train for three hours before breakfast."

"No," I say when I recognize the door. "I'm with Alaric. He marked me."

"I am sorry, Clara, but you are to stay here." He averts his gaze, and to his credit, he seems genuinely sorry. "Queen's orders."

I shake my head, mumbling under my breath, "The mark was supposed to fix things."

"Usually, it would," he says. Lowering his voice, he inches closer, too close. I feel suffocated by his presence—trapped between him and the wall. "Elizabeth may have allowed Alaric to fully mark you and to stay with him last night, but that is where her generosity ends. The consequences of doing other than what I tell you to will send you back to the dungeon, and that's if you're lucky enough to live."

"This is your reason," I say, and it's not a question.

Cassius nods, reaching around me to open the door to the tiny room. Without another word, he turns away, and in the blink of an eye, he is on the far end of the hall.

He pauses, looking over his shoulder before disappearing around the corner.

CHAPTER
TWENTY-FIVE
CLARA

Tap, tap, tap.

The sound is so quiet I almost dismiss it as the familiar sounds of the servants' quarters at night, when it's busier than the day. The night is nearly over, but there's still an hour before dawn.

After a moment, the sound comes again. The lock rattles. Then, the door inches open, creaking lightly on the hinges.

I slide my hand under my pillow and wrap my fingers around the hilt of the dagger, being careful not to make any sudden movements.

Peeking through my lashes, I keep my breath slow and steady. It's so dark I can't make out much more than the size and shape of the man inching toward me.

I prepare to attack—tension coiling in my muscles.

"Clara?"

My eyes snap open as I release the dagger and sit up. The sudden movement startles Alaric into taking a step back.

"You're here," I say dumbly.

A dozen questions flitting through my mind, and I manage to state the obvious.

He smiles. The watery moonlight washes over the sharp features of his handsome face and the small, unassuming bat perched on his shoulder. Cherno lets out a small chirp.

I hold out my hand, beckoning Alaric to my side. He doesn't hesitate. His fingers entwine with mine, his grip firm but gentle. Alaric climbs onto the tiny bed, situating himself next to me, our backs pressed to the wall.

Cherno crawls from his shoulder to mine and presses their face into my neck. I reach up and pat the top of his head. "I missed you, too," I say.

The little demon stays there for a moment longer before leaping into the air. They circle the room once then glide out of the window, leaving the two of us alone.

Alaric pats the poor excuse for a mattress and gives it a disapproving look.

I laugh, leaning into his side and resting my head on his shoulder, soaking in his presence. The mark responds, and if it were a living thing, I would say it purred.

"I wasn't allowed to return," I say after a long moment. "He said I had to stay here from now on."

He presses his lips to my temple and asks, "Who?"

I suspect he already knows the answer. Part of me doesn't want to say, knowing it will annoy him, but I don't want to lie.

"Cassius," I say eventually. He lets out a low growl. I gently squeeze his arm and say, "He won't harm me."

That seems to temper his anger. Slightly.

"I did try to come sooner, but I couldn't get away until now." His fingers trail up and down my arm in soothing strokes. "Elizabeth is forcing my hand."

A long silence stretches out, heavy with things unsaid. She's using me against him. He won't tell me because he doesn't want me to feel guilty or attempt to fix this mess. Not that I would have the faintest idea of where to start.

"I won't allow her to—" Alaric presses his lips into a tight line.

I pull away and look him in the eye. "What would happen if you give in to her?"

"I can't." He releases me, glaring at me for suggesting it.

I swallow the lump in my throat at thinking these thoughts, let alone pushing the issue. "What will happen if you don't?"

He doesn't speak, though the muscle ticking along his jaw is answer enough. I drop my head, understanding. Saying he would be miserable would be an understatement.

Alaric shifts at my side, his arm flexing under my fingertips.

He leans into me. The gesture sends a sensation of ease through my muscles. I wonder if he feels the bond too—the pull—or if he simply understands that this somehow comforts me.

"She knows you'll protect me, so she'll never stop using me against you until you either prove you don't care what happens…" My stomach knots. I pull in a breath, waiting for a sign he doesn't feel that way. "Or I die, and maybe not even then. You should consider—"

"No. Don't ever suggest that again," he snarls. "I would rather die than become her consort."

My heart aches for him and the impossible situation he's in. As long as I'm here, alive, I will be a weakness. I bite down hard on the inside of my cheek. Could I let him go, or am I too selfish, too?

We've tried to play the part of vampire master and claimed human while avoiding it, and in the end, we became precisely that. Now that it's real, it has accomplished nothing. We are still in the heart of Nightwich after the two weeks of solstice celebrations with no hope of leaving.

I tighten my hold on his arm, squeezing. Alaric places a chaste kiss on the top of my head and pats my hand.

My gut feels hollow as the sense of an impending event grows, hovering over me like the movement of a shadow just beyond my line of sight. I don't know what it will be or when it will come crashing down over us.

We sit in silence. I hate feeling powerless to help him. He has done everything in his power to protect me and continues to do so.

He deserves the same from me. I just wish I knew how.

I flick my gaze up and take in the sharp features of Alaric's face—the tight press of his mouth and the slight crease between his brows. There are countless things we could talk about, but I think he needs this silence.

It pains me to admit it, but Cassius was right. I need power, and I will do whatever I must to gain it.

"I should leave," he says after a while.

Reflexively, my hold tightens even when he doesn't move. I force myself to release him. Straightening, I twist to look him in the eye and ask, "Will you come back?"

He lifts his hand and runs his fingers through my hair, stopping when his palm cups my cheek. I lean into the touch. "I will always return to you."

Something inside clenches because what he says reminds me of his words from last night. The feeling is so overwhelming I don't know how to respond. Warmth travels up my face and stings my face the longer he watches me.

"I can stay for a little longer."

When I can't take the intensity any longer, I shift and sit back, pressing my side into his. Alaric drapes an arm over my shoulder and pulls me into him. I breathe him in, letting my eyes slide shut.

My eyes fly open at the sound of three swift knocks on the door. I blink, looking around. Alaric is gone, and I'm in my bed, covered by the threadbare blanket, eyes burning from exhaustion. The morning light is barely visible. I don't remember falling asleep, but it can't have been for long.

Alaric's visit feels like a dream. I collapse back down on the flat, lumpy pillow, wanting to fall back asleep and remember the feeling of his hand on my face.

The door bursts open. I roll to my side, sliding my hand under my pillow, reaching for the dagger. Cassius strides in, stopping a few feet from the bed.

I relax back into the mattress and cover my head with the pillow. "What kind of monster enters a room like that?" I groan.

His clothes are simple compared to his usual style but no less immaculate, and his long pale hair is pulled back into a braid.

"Get up," he orders, ripping the pillow from my grasp and tossing it. It hits the wall, falling to the floor with a muffled thump. Then, he does the same to the blanket.

Cold winter air wraps around me, and goosebumps form almost painfully over my entire body.

I roll over to my back and glare up at him.

"Get your ass out of bed."

"The sun isn't even up yet."

Cassius takes two steps forward, the front of his legs pressing against the bed frame. He folds his arms and looks down his nose. "That is the point, little bird."

He reaches for my hand, but I jerk away, sitting up and scooting away from him. He waits.

I know I should listen, but I'm so tired, and my lumpy bed looks so comfortable right now, even without the blanket and pillow.

I can feel my eyelids grow heavier at just thinking about a few more delicious minutes of sleep.

"All right," he says, relaxing his arms. "I can see you won't get up."

A small smile creeps over my lips as I start to lower back down.

Cassius's hand wraps around my wrist. In a swift movement, he pulls me up and flings me over his shoulder. I sputter, unable to form words as he strides from the room.

"What are you doing?" I snap, planting my hands on his lower back to lift my upper body, so I'm not hanging upside-down. "I'm not even dressed."

My protests do nothing to slow his pace. If anything, he speeds up. The walls pass in a blur, making me dizzy. I let my arms go limp.

"You're wearing clothes. Everything that needs to be covered is covered."

It's too early to go this fast. "Cassius Wellington, you unhand me this second and return me to my room."

"If you want to be dressed when you practice, then you should learn to get up before I arrive." His grip on my thighs tightens as we descend. My stomach rises and falls at the change of direction. "Did you think I was lying when I said I would make you practice for three hours before breakfast?"

Actually, I hadn't put any thought into what he'd said. As soon as I saw Alaric's face last night, I'd let everything else from the day fall away. Forgotten.

I take a step back, panting. My bare feet pad on the cold stone floor. A heavy bead of sweat drips down the side of my temple. I reach up and swipe at the wisps of hair clinging to my damp face.

Cassius closes the distance as fast as I create it, not giving me an inch of leeway.

My arms and legs shake from the effort, and my nightgown clings indecently to my body, making it difficult to move.

He swings. I fall to my knees to avoid the strike. His arm passes just over my head, creating its own wind, barely missing me.

Unlike Alaric, he doesn't pull his punches, more than willing to strike to make his point. My bruised ribs are a testament to that.

The second my knees connect with the hard stone, I know I've lost the fight. It's a terrible position to be in. My body is pushed to the limits, movements slow and messy.

Cassius plants his foot on my side and pushes, knocking me over with little effort.

I land hard on my side and roll to my back. He straddles my ribs, standing over me, saying nothing.

When he doesn't move or continue the fight, I push on his legs but have no strength behind it.

"You're a bastard," I snarl.

Unfazed, he jerks his chin and says, "Get up and try again. I'm not letting you go until you can deflect."

"I deflected," I argue.

"No, you avoided. Waving your arms around won't help you. It only uses up energy, energy you will need."

I push up to my elbows and scrunch my nose. "Need for what exactly?"

Cassius crouches down, leveling his face with mine, baring his fangs. "Get up. I won't ask again."

My body is exhausted. I don't think I can stand, even if I wanted to. I'm tired, my mind is sluggish, and all I want to do is close my eyes and sleep, even if that means doing so on this dusty old floor.

"What is it with you vampires and teaching me to fight?" I grumble.

Cassius clamps his mouth shut, and a long, tense moment

passes between us. Then quietly, he says, "Do you want to be killed?"

"Of course not," I snap. I understand why Alaric wanted to teach me, but for the life of me, I can't figure out Cassius's motivation.

"Then get up." He straightens and backs up.

It's a struggle to push to my feet. After my short break, the fatigue has set into every fiber of my being.

Cassius motions with his hand, letting me know he's about to start. Even with that warning, I don't have it in me to get my body to cooperate and move in a coordinated way.

I step back, but my knees buckle, and I land hard on my rear.

He sighs and rubs his forehead. "I suppose since it is your first day, I will go easy on you."

I can't help the sharp laugh that bursts from my chest. If this is taking it easy, then I'm the mother of demons.

He crouches at my feet and takes one leg in his hand, pushing up the hem of my gown.

Blood speckles my knee from my fall. I take a deep breath and relax back, knowing what will come next—the fiery burn of his power as he heals every wound he's inflicted.

The second he steps away from me, I jump to my feet and run out the door. My stomach growls, but instead of heading to the kitchen, I hurry toward my room, determined to get dressed before getting something to eat.

Cassius chuckles as he catches up to me in seconds. "You won't lose me that easily, little bird."

I do my best to ignore him as he remains at my side. I steal a glance as we near the main floor of the castle. Two voices, as familiar to me as my own, float down the hall.

I stop in my tracks. Cassius's hand grips my elbow gently. Alaric and Elizabeth pass, arm in arm, by our shadowed stairwell.

They speak, their faces close and voices low. I bite down on my lip to keep from calling out to him.

Alaric's chin lifts a fraction and angles toward me. The expression on his face is cold, distant, and unfamiliar. An ache blooms in my chest, deep and uncomfortable. He looks away, leaning in closer to the queen and whispers something that elicits a delicate laugh.

I don't understand what message he is trying to send with that look. Everything about his body language contradicts his words from last night.

I watch the way Elizabeth clings to him and the intimate way they interact within a few strides. The sting of something ugly sloshes its way through my veins, forming a pit in my stomach.

I'm no longer hungry. I don't move, even after they've gone. It takes a long moment before I recognize the emotion.

Jealousy.

"Clara," Cassius says. He steps in front of me, blocking my view.

242

I turn my head, not wanting him to see the turmoil of emotions that must be written on my face.

He takes my hand and hooks my arm through his. Normally, I would pull away, but every ounce of fight has left me, and I can't summon the energy to care as he leads me away.

CHAPTER
TWENTY-SIX

CLARA

I stare at the stone ceiling, too exhausted to do anything more than sit on this lumpy bed and breathe. After Cassius escorted me back to my room, I had every intention of sleeping, but my mind refuses to settle.

The scene replays in my mind over and over. Alaric so close to the queen, the way they touched, the way they leaned into each other... He told me he hated her, but the brief glimpse I had said otherwise.

Knots form, twisting my insides. I hug my pillow tightly to my chest.

Is he deceiving me... or her? And if he has a plan, why wouldn't he have told me last night?

There's an ache inside me, not just in my muscles but bone deep. It's a loneliness I've never felt before, hollow, dark, and empty.

I don't miss home. I don't miss hunting or stealing or scavenging to put food in our bellies. Of course, I miss Kitty, but knowing she's safe is enough. I'm glad that part of my life is over.

I want to be where I am now, which is utterly insane considering all that has happened—thrown in the dungeon, nearly reclaimed by another vampire, and all of the games where I am in the center of it all.

I am the pawn, the sacrifice that everyone is using.

How can I want this?

How can I want to be with a vampire? A man I should hate but who has taken my heart without me noticing. A man I love who has no reason to ever return those feelings.

While there are things I would change, I would still choose to be here with Alaric. No games. Just being at his side.

Three soft knocks on the door pull me from my thoughts.

"Go away," I call out.

Silence greets me, but I know exactly who it is without having to hear his voice. The knock comes again, and this time, I ignore it.

With an annoyed growl, Cassius throws open the door and slams it closed behind him. He marches into the room with a large plate balanced in one hand, heaped with what looks like at least half a roasted chicken, bread, a thick bunch of grapes, and a single strawberry.

"I said *go away*." I fling the pillow at him.

He bats it away with his free hand. It drops to the ground with a soft thud.

"You can send me away all you want, but I'm not about to let you starve." Cassius shoves the plate of food under my nose.

My stomach clenches at the aroma. I push his hand away. "I'm not hungry."

"Demon shit," he snaps. "Eat it, or I will force it down your throat. I don't care about your hurt feelings. You need to keep up your strength."

I don't doubt for a second that he will follow through with his threat.

With a huff, I snatch the plate from him. Several grapes break free from the vine and roll off to the mattress, followed by the lone strawberry.

I cross my legs and set the plate down in my lap. "I'll eat. You can go."

Cassius shakes his head. "I'll leave when you've finished."

Irritation prickles over my skin. I don't take my eyes off him as I rip into the meat with both hands.

The steam burns my fingertips. Bite after bite, I shove seasoned chicken into my mouth. I don't even wait to finish before stuffing more, filling my cheeks.

I wait for him to be disgusted and leave, but it doesn't work.

Cassius relaxes against the wall, arms crossed, and one perfectly shaped brow arched as he watches me.

Halfway through eating, my hands are dripping with grease. It takes a while, but eventually, I manage to swallow the food in my mouth.

My gaze darts around, looking for something to wipe my hands with, but all I have is the blanket beneath me and my clothes. Neither option is ideal.

"Forgive me. I didn't think to have a bath sent up. I assumed you knew how to eat like a civilized person."

I do feel better, at least physically, now that I've eaten. As much as it pains me to admit, he was right.

Rubbing my hands, I wipe as much food off as I can. Regret and embarrassment seep up my neck, stinging my face.

I glance up ready to apologize, when a ball of cloth bounces off my face. At the same time that Cassius snatches the plate from my lap.

A thought occurs to me as I run the napkin over my face then hands, eyeing him. The snake that was always nearby at Windbury has been scarce.

"Where is your demon?" I ask. Come to think of it, I've hardly seen Cherno since arriving, and when I have, they haven't spoken a word. "Actually, why is it I hardly see any demons around?"

"Asmod is one of the stronger demons to grace Nightwich," Cassius says. "Elizabeth's demon, Kharis, draws on the power of any demon while they are within the confines of these walls. You will most likely never see a demon unless their vampire needs the proximity of their power."

He plucks the napkin from me and swipes at my cheek, dislodging a small bit of meat I'd missed and wiping the rest of my face like I was a child, then straightens. Cassius searches my eyes. He frowns then turns away, walking to the door.

"Get some rest while you can. I will not go easy on you in the morning just because you decided to mope about things outside of your control."

There is so much I don't understand about him. Nothing I say or do gets under his skin. I suppose I should be grateful because other than Alaric, he is my only ally.

Cassius stood up for me during the trial and has taken it upon himself to train me.

But he has also lied and attempted to manipulate my situation for Elizabeth…

I breathe deep and blink into the darkness that envelops the room. Straightening, I wince at the twinge that developed in my neck after falling asleep sitting up.

My eyelids droop as I consider lying down and going back to sleep when I hear the sound that woke me.

Clara...

Clara...

... Clara...

The soft whisper of my name pulls on my consciousness.

Clara...

The slow rhythm of my pulse speeds up. Scooting forward, I drop my feet to the floor. I grip the edge of the mattress and peer into the dark.

"Who's there?" The words come out weak and dry, scratching my throat. I wait in the answering silence. My fingers twitch, wanting to reach for my dagger.

Then, I feel it.

The lightest tug within my chest. I rub my hand over the spot. I focus on it as it grows stronger.

Is this... the mark?

The possibility that Alaric is using our connection to lead me to him has my pulse vibrating in my veins. I push up from the bed, finding my legs stiff and aching.

Carefully, I pluck the night-forged dagger from under my pillow and strap it to my arm. Then, crossing the room, I slip into my suede boots near the door.

I peek out into the dimly lit hallway. The usual bustle of activity has yet to start for the night. Quietly, I step out of my room and close the door behind me. I keep close to the wall, hurrying toward the stairs leading up to the third floor.

The worn leather soles of my boots pad softly against the stone. I stick to where the shadows are thickest. Halfway down the hall, the sensation shifts. I stop trying to lead it where I want to go and focus on where it's pulling me—which isn't up to Alaric's rooms, as I assumed, but down through back halls.

Is it possible that he's waiting for me somewhere else?

With each passing second, the pull intensifies. I pick up speed, taking the stairs two and three at a time, hurtling down toward the lower level.

The sense of urgency continues to build with every step until I'm nearly crawling out of my skin with anticipation. I jump the last three steps, landing in a crouch that jars my knees and taking off in a run.

There's a single torch lit at each end of the hall, but I don't slow until I pass the training room.

What I had assumed was the end of the hall turns out to be a sharp corner that descends farther beneath the castle. I wrinkle my nose at the overpowering musty air and mildew wafting up.

I hesitate, not wanting to enter the inky darkness below.

Why would Alaric lead me this far?

I glance down the stairs then back the way I came, not sure I want to go down, but the tug in the center of my chest twinges, urging me to continue. I suck in a deep breath and take one step then another.

My eyes strain against the insufficient light to see the details, but I can't make out more than the next step. It slows my progress, which only seems to increase the impatient pull.

There's an eerie familiarity about this place. I can't shake the feeling that I know where I am, even though I've never been this far down before.

The darkness is so thick I expect to walk into a barrier. Finally, the gentle glow of another candle set against the wall on a step comes into view. I pick it up and use it to guide me down, down, down. It is several minutes before I reach the landing. There is nothing here but a single metal door straight ahead.

Grasping the handle, I pull. It opens without resistance. The hinges are quiet. Almost as if they've been taken care of regularly. Cool, damp air washes over me. The scent of mold and rot stings my nose. It's silent with a steady drip of water somewhere deep inside.

I step out into the long hallway. Along one side are several doors with small barred windows near the top. The metal hinges and locks shine like new against the rotted wood. Cobwebs adorn nearly every corner, thick and wispy, moving with every breath I take.

I pause at each door to look inside, but they're all empty.

"Alaric?" I call out, attempting to whisper, but my voice echoes. I cringe at the volume.

If he's here, he doesn't answer.

Goosebumps erupt over my skin. Closing my eyes, I feel for

the pull to lead me back the way I came. I wait and wait. After several long seconds, I give up. I feel nothing.

The pull is gone.

Pivoting on my heel, I turn to leave.

Chains clank, followed by softly spoken words too low for me to make out.

My heart thuds against my ribs, afraid he's locked away, unable to call out, but needing me. Before I know what I'm doing, the tug has returned, pulling me toward the cell at the end of the hall.

I press my palms to the door. The wood is soft and worn with a thin layer of dust. On instinct, I turn the handle, but it resists, locked.

"I appreciate you trying to free me, but the queen isn't in the habit of leaving prison doors unlocked," the voice within rasps.

I jump back as if the handle shocked me. *Night-forged silver.*

Alaric isn't the one on the other side.

This place... It feels...

Shaking my head, I back up several steps and look at where I am with fresh eyes.

On a wall, doused in darkness, is a thin slit, only noticeable because it's a shade darker than the shadows that cloak it.

This is... Oh, demons and saints!

I came through the main entrance rather than the hidden passage. My blood roars in my ears. I would run, but I'm not entirely sure my legs would carry me.

"Where is Alaric?"

"Why would you think he is in a place like this?" the person on the other side asks.

I spin, facing the door, brows scrunching together. "Why would he lead me here if he wasn't?"

The voice laughs, and a dull ache throbs in my head.

"What makes you think he has anything to do with you being here?"

"I—" Clearing my throat, I try again, "Because he led me here through our connection from the mark."

The prisoner chuckles. "Stupid girl, the mark doesn't work like that. Your prince is lost to you."

"Demon shit!" I shake my head, backing up until I hit the wall.

"If he is not lost to you yet, then he will be soon enough."

My hands ball into fists at my side. "There's no way you could know that."

"Free me, and I can help you."

I open my mouth to retort then clamp it shut as the words sink in. "Why would I free a prisoner? You obviously did something to deserve being locked up."

"Ah, so then, you are an ally of the queen?"

"I... Of course not." I scoff.

"Then free me." Their voice grows closer to the door.

"I don't think I should." It finally clicks. This place... I've been here before. I blow out a breath, relieved I finally understand. "This is a dream."

"You are right." They release a heavy sigh. "This is a dream, but before you go, at least come in and give me a drink of water. The guards keep it out of reach." The voice sighs.

A choking laugh rips from my throat before I can stop it. "I'm reckless, not stupid."

"I am chained. There is nothing I could do to hurt you." For emphasis, the prisoner rattles their chains. "Look for yourself. If this is a dream like you suspect, then where is the risk? And if it's not, then you've help bring relief to one of the queen's prisoners."

I scrape my teeth along my bottom lip.

It *feels* real, but Alaric assured me that it was a dream... A place like this can't possibly exist.

I inch forward and lift up on my toes to look inside. It's dark, with only the light from the hall shining inside.

Whoever it is sits in the corner. A shadowy arm, shackled in silver, reaches for the light, stopping with the length of the chain pulls taut.

It's just a drink of water.

Pulling the dagger from its sheath, I pick at the lock. It only takes a moment before the springs inside give, and it snaps open. I blow out a breath then step inside.

"It's been so long since I've seen a human face," the voice, vaguely feminine now, says. "Come closer."

I move deeper into the cell stopping halfway inside. There isn't a bucket, no bowl or spoon, no way to give them a drink.

"How are you alive if you haven't seen anyone in a long time?" I ask, but I know the answer before the final word leaves my mouth.

The prisoner is not a vampire, human, or even a shifter. Darkness churns around them. *This is a demon.*

The realization hits me with such force my vision wavers. I stumble back. My boot catches on the uneven ground, and I land hard on my rear.

"Do not worry, girl. These chains that bind me are night-forged silver. I cannot escape until they are broken. I am eternally bound to this castle."

Wisps of power reach forward from the charred, dry skin, brushing along my boots. I can feel them willing me closer. I stand, but I remain rooted in place.

"What do you want with me?"

The demon stretches out their arm as far as the chain will allow, unfurling their fingers. I take a few steps closer to see what it is. A small silver band. "To give this to you."

"I want nothing from a demon."

They chuckle. "This is not *just* a piece of jewelry but night-forged silver. The metal has the power to destroy, yes, but it can also create objects of great power that you can wield, if you so choose."

"Why me?" I ask, knowing how ridiculous this is—talking to a demon in my dream. They could answer with anything, and this would still only be a night terror.

"You have been touched by several demons. Their powers linger, flowing through you even now."

I swallow. "You... you said that before..." This is the demon from my dream in the cells. "Varin?" I press my palm to my throbbing forehead. "But how... when you're locked up here?"

I blink, realizing too late how close I inched while we talked. Close enough to embrace... if anyone would ever want to embrace a—

The demon snarls, "You foolish girl, this isn't a dream!"

Faster than lightning and twice as dark as any shadow, the demon lunges forward. Their body collides with mine. I suck in an icy breath as they pass through me as if they were nothing more than fog.

The world tilts, and I have to squeeze my eyes shut, hitting the ground hard again.

When I open my eyes again, the demon is sitting where they started in their twisted skeletal form. They watch with red eyes that seem to glow in the low light.

Not a dream.

I look down, and on my right middle finger is the silver band, warm against my skin.

I need to leave.

"I will never free you," I snap, scrambling to my feet.

I pry the ring from my finger and throw it into a dark corner. Then, I race from the cell, slamming the door. The lock clicks back into place, and I run to my room without stopping.

CHAPTER
TWENTY-SEVEN
ALARIC

Another day, another summons. It's the same thing, the same conversation.

Elizabeth sits with her legs dangling off the arm of her oversized chair, sipping on a glass of blood. She watches me through pale lashes that sweep over the rim of the cup, eyes never leaving me for a second.

For two days, I have not returned to see Clara. Every time I think there might be an opportunity, she is either gone, or Kharis is flying around nearby.

"Do you know why I asked you here tonight?" Elizabeth asks.

Holding back an irritated growl, I answer, "Yes."

She swivels in the chair, setting her feet delicately on the

ground before standing. Each movement is smooth and graceful —
all part of her act. Her loose tendrils of flaxen hair trail down her
back to mid-thigh. "Then, will you finally submit and become my
consort?"

"How many times must we do this?" I ask. Weariness seeps
into my voice. I am tired of this never-ending dance.

"As many times as we need to." She brushes her fingertips over
her collarbone, hooking the thin chain of her necklace around a
finger, twisting and untwisting. "You seemed so genuine the other
day…" Her lavender eyes darken to crimson as her demon's power
coalesces within her. "Or was that for the benefit of someone other
than myself?"

In a blink, she is across the room, standing inches away. Her
heavy perfume fills the space between us, thick and cloying. She
reaches up and presses a hand to my cheek. I avoid jerking away as
her touch sends waves of revulsion that churn my stomach.

She has been a vampire for hundreds of years and has yet to
learn that she cannot manipulate the feelings and minds of others,
molding them into whatever she wants. She might have the power
to compel obedience, but it will never be real.

"I did try… but it's no use. I do not want the life you offer." I
take her hand and slowly pull it away, lowering her arm. "Please,
Elizabeth, give this up. I do not want to be your prince. I've never
wanted that. Plenty of others would kill for this. You don't need
me. Cassius—"

"I don't want him. You are the crown prince, fated to be by my side. It was foretold by the oracle witch almost three hundred years ago. I have waited long enough for you to take your place. It's time you stop avoiding your responsibility."

"I don't care what some witch may have told you. I do not want this."

"You say that..." she purrs, running a finger up my chest and hooking her hand around the back of my neck. "Like you have a choice."

"There is always a choice. It is a matter of deciding which consequences you can live with."

"Bow to me, and you have my word that the human will not be harmed... no matter what crimes she commits."

She could be lying, or she could see keeping Clara safe as an opportunity to keep me under her thumb.

I shift back on my heels to create distance between us, but she holds on, moving with me. Elizabeth rises on her toes and presses her mouth to mine. To the world, it would appear to be a simple kiss—but it's far more than that. Her fangs snag against my lip, drawing blood. Her power wends its way around me, invading my mind, tuned into my own.

The cuts on my cheek and neck.

And every other drop of blood she drew in every meeting. It was more than a threat, more than a failed seduction. She drew on my power, drop by drop, all so her demon could connect to Cherno and overpower them, seizing control.

Red sparks up and down my arms as I pushing against her, struggling to force her out, but she is stronger, resisting my efforts.

The room is cast in a soft red glow. No matter how hard I fight, I am pulled down by the undertow of her power. Waves of it crash around me, swallowing me up into its depths. Darkness constricts on my consciousness, leaving pinpricks of my own will.

Slowly, I relax my muscles. The less I fight, the less she pushes. I rein it in, slowly… carefully breaking our contact.

I keep my mind silent, void of thoughts, burying all emotions and anger into the dark recesses of my mind. I gaze at her face, imagining it to be anyone's but hers.

She has won. Now, she must believe it.

I feel the words rising to my tongue like bile. They twist my gut. "If you want me, then I am yours, my queen."

Elizabeth narrows her eyes. We remain perfectly still for a long moment. Tendrils of her power brush against mine. I pull mine back, allowing her all the room she desires. She untangles her fingers from around my neck and releases me. A slow, sinister smile creeps up on her lips.

Agreeing to obey her commands is not the worst I will have to endure. However temporary, I retain the majority of control over my mind and body, but this is only the first step in losing every last sliver of freedom.

"What of the girl?" She arches a single delicate brow.

"What girl?" I ask, completely void of emotion.

Elizabeth tsks. "We both know who I'm talking about." She's testing me. One wrong word could ruin everything. "What would you have me do with her? Kill—"

"What you do with her is of no consequence to me," I say flatly. "Give her to Cassius. He is always begging for my scraps."

She barks out a sharp laugh. "How delightfully spiteful." She takes my hand in hers. "How I've missed this side."

I don't reply.

Elizabeth leads me deeper into her room for one final test. I follow, dreading spending any time with her. She drops my hand when we reach the center of the room and moves about as if I'm not even here.

She pushes the straps of her dress off her shoulder, letting the material pool around her feet.

The room has remained the same since I last stepped foot in here, down to every last detail. It is a room I'd hoped to never see again. A low fire burns in the hearth. Elizabeth slips a thin nightdress over her head before finally turning back to me. My blood chills in my veins from her expression.

"You may go," she says, "but return before nightfall."

I bow at the waist and say, "Yes, my queen."

As I turn from her, I don't dare to breathe until I've closed the bedroom doors and have left her rooms behind me.

Outside in the hall, I rake my fingers through my hair. I may have more power than any other court members, but it means nothing when she can still force her will over me without effort.

I mourn the freedom slipping through my fingers like sand. I am doing this because I cannot win against her and also for Clara.

Moving as fast as I can, I rush to my own rooms, wanting to put as much distance between me and the unpleasant future to come. I will pretend to be complicit, to be under her control, but my resistance will not last forever, and one day, she will control my every thought.

I have always known Elizabeth would get her way in the end. She always has. Though I'd hoped to grow tired of living before it came to this, I hoped to no longer have a reason to resist, but as long as Clara lives, I will fight.

I push open the doors to my room, unsurprised to find it cold and dark. The door shuts with a quiet click. The drapes are drawn, and no fire burns in the hearth. It's dark and fits my mood.

"Alaric?" Clara's voice is a ghost of a whisper.

I whirl at the sound of my name.

Clara emerges from the shadows to stand in a thin shaft of light, wearing a black cloak over dark clothes.

Seeing her face is a relief, but it also breaks a piece of my soul.

She inches forward, cautiously.

"How long have you been here?" I ask.

Clara sucks in a sharp breath.

"You need to leave."

CHAPTER
TWENTY-EIGHT
CLARA

Alaric closes the door behind him and stops halfway into the room. He hangs his head, heaving a sigh, letting his shoulders slump.

I lift my hand, reaching out then curling my fingers back into my palm. Something is off, and it sends a sense of foreboding through me when seeing him should feel like a relief.

"Alaric?" His name slips out from between my lips.

He whips around, startled. I expect him to close the distance, to smile, but his face remains an unreadable mask.

"How long have you been here?" he asks. The coldness in his question takes me aback. "You need to leave."

I take a tentative step forward, uncertainty tugging on the corners of my heart. "Several hours. I snuck up here once the halls quieted. When you didn't show up yesterday..."

I've been afraid Varin was right. I chanced a visit because I have to see for myself if they lied. Looking at him now, I can't be sure.

"Where have you been?" I ask when he doesn't say anything.

He recoils. The movement is subtle, but I catch it.

"What are you doing here?" He takes a step forward and another, stopping an arm's length away.

The unease coils tighter, settling between my shoulders. "It's been two days. You said you would come back, but when you didn't, I thought..." My throat constricts, and I can't voice the words. He feels distant, and the space between us might as well be a chasm. "I hate it here. When can we go home to Windbury?"

I never considered Windbury home before this moment. Now I realize it is, more so than Littlemire ever was.

Alaric lifts his hand, and for a brief moment, I think he might pull me into him. My breath catches as I wait to feel his touch.

Instead, he shrugs off his jacket, draping it over the back of a chair. His hands grip the backrest, fingers tightening.

Alaric rubs his forehead and says, "We don't."

I inch closer, stopping at his side, and reach for him. He pulls away and looks me in the eye.

"We will never return to Windbury."

The words are harsh and unexpected. I suck in a sharp breath. It's a simple statement, but I can't accept it.

I take a step back and shake my head.

"Stay with Cassius," he says darkly. "He will be your guardian as long as you wish him to be."

Irritation flares. I press my lips into a tight line to keep from snapping at him.

"I do not *wish him to be*," I grind out between clenched teeth. My temper rises, refusing to be held down. "I never did."

Alaric looks me up and down. "He has been training you well."

Cherno cuts through the air between us. I flinch and glare at the demon as they land on the fireplace mantle.

I return my focus to Alaric. He stares blankly at the wall, avoiding my gaze.

Though we never trained more than a handful of times, I can't help but feel that doing so with Cassius has been a betrayal on my part, that I took something that was ours and moved on without blinking.

"I never asked for him to train me." I shake my head, trying and failing to contain my rising voice. *We're fighting. We shouldn't be fighting.* "He's only my guardian because he's following orders. He insisted—"

Alaric holds up his hand, stopping my rush of words. I feel a slight pulse of his power caressing me.

"I know. I was merely stating a fact." A ghost of a smile turns his mouth upward then quickly disappears. "You will more than likely need it until you two leave."

Leave with Cassius? He says that as if Cassius was the one to mark me.

My throat grows thick with emotion. Scanning the room, I retreat.

"Is… is someone here?" I ask. It's the only thing that would explain this change in Alaric.

"No, we are alone."

Confusion and hurt bubble up, and my eyes grow warm with building tears. "Then why are you saying these things? Is this part of a plan?" I spread my arms wide, palms up. "If so, let me in on it, so I can play my part."

"There is no plan, no trick. It is simply what is best for you."

I blink, and the first hot tear escapes, burning a wet trail down my cheek. "Don't I get a say in what I think is best for me?"

Alaric's eyes soften as he opens his mouth then snaps it shut. "No," he says thickly. "You are only a human."

He turns his face away.

"Stop it." I ball my hands into fists, my nails dig painfully into the delicate skin of my palms. "You said our fate would be what we choose." I swallow hard as another tear escapes. "Why would you mark me at all if you planned on giving me away like I'm nothing?" I fling the words at him. I want him to feel the lies he fed to me as much as I want this moment to be the lie.

"You are not nothing," he retorts with the same level of anger. Alaric thrusts his hand through his thick, black hair, tugging on the strands.

The silence is suffocating, filling the space. It grows more oppressive the longer we stare at each other. His tongue darts out, dampening his lips. My gaze trails from his mouth to his neck, watching the knot of his throat bob.

"Cassius wants you, Clara. Now go back to him."

Those words cause a physical pain in my chest, and all the air leaves my lungs in a sharp exhale.

In the background, I barely register the squeak Cherno makes and the skittering of their small feet.

"And... what about you?" I ask, my voice cracking on the last word. "You said... you wanted me the last time we were together."

I returned to Windbury for him. I chose him over the rest of the world. I came with him of my own free will to this demon-cursed place because I thought—

I squeeze my eyes tight for three heartbeats before looking up at him again. Coming here had been my choice, and now, regret is a bitterness coating my tongue.

"I don't want you," he says, voice gravelly and low. "I never did."

My heart is breaking, crumbling, and it leaves a hollow pit in my chest. I'm stunned into silence.

The door opens, but I can't take my eyes off the man who is breaking me in a way I never thought possible.

"Alaric, I—" Lawrence stops. "What is going on?"

I don't turn to look behind me at the vampire as scalding tears fall freely.

"Alaric," Lawrence says, pulling Alaric's attention from me to him.

Alaric gives a single shake of his head.

I swipe at my face with the back of my hands to hide the evidence of my tears, though I doubt it matters. I can feel how swollen my eyes have already become and the prickle of heat across my cheeks.

Suddenly, I can't breathe. I don't want to be here while they have a silent conversation over my head.

I want Alaric to look at me one last time, to tell me this has been some terrible plan he doesn't want to continue. Even when he claimed me, things between us were never like this.

Spinning on my heel, I push past Lawrence, making him leap out of my way. I run from the room, but the wide, open hall does nothing to alleviate the crushing feeling that presses down on my shoulders.

"What have you done? You fool, go after her," Lawrence all but shouts at him.

If Alaric replies, I don't hear.

I push myself as fast as I can until I am down in the servants' quarters, panting hard, pulse wild. Bursting into my room, I slam the door shut. The small, nearly empty space feels more foreign to me than it ever had before.

Gradually, my breathing slows, returning to normal. A small part of me clung to the hope that Alaric would listen to his friend and come after me, but that part is mistaken, and it hurts more than I want to admit.

I feel lost...

Hopeless.

A fresh wave of tears wells up. Dropping down onto the uneven mattress, I curl into a ball.

I bring my knees to my chest and stop fighting the ache in my cracked heart.

CHAPTER
TWENTY-NINE
CLARA

I understand everything Alaric said to me that night in his room. I'm willing to accept it, but there's a voice in the back of my mind screaming that something is wrong.

He set me free, never expecting to see my face again. If he didn't want me here—if he truly felt this way—then wouldn't he have refused my company outright? When I told him I would come, I felt his relief.

Every day for the past week, I go out of my way, attempting to cross paths with Alaric... much to Cassius's annoyance. If this end is real and not some part of a plan, then I want to know what changed, and why.

He marked me. He came to my room and promised to return,

so I can't help but feel that the man I spoke to wasn't really him.

All the air leaves my lungs in a painful whoosh, and before I can inhale, my legs are kicked out from under me. I land with a brutally hard thud on my back. The practice pole flies out of my hand, clattering on the stone floor and rolling out of reach.

Cassius places a foot on either side of my ribs and squats down, straddling me. He fists the front of my shirt and jerks, pulling me into a half-sitting position as he lowers his face within an inch of my own.

"Focus," he snarls. "Wherever your head is, you need to come back."

With some effort, I pry his hand free from the material of my shirt. He releases me, and I flop back on the ground.

"I don't care," I say.

Cassius upped our training from once to twice a day—first in the morning for three hours before breakfast and then after lunch for another two.

I'm exhausted… and my heart aches.

Cassius narrows his eyes. "Why do you look like you haven't slept in a month?"

With the amount of training we've been doing, I should sleep like the dead. But each morning, I wake more exhausted than the day before—and those are the mornings when I do manage to sleep.

My night terrors with the demon Varin in the oubliette have

increased, except they aren't night terrors. They are real. As soon as my eyes close every night, Varin calls me down to their cell. When I open my eyes, I'm standing before them, my outstretched hand reaching for the night-forged silver band.

When I refuse, they ask for me to free them, but I will never do that. This world doesn't need another greater demon haunting it.

The demon reaches out with their twisted, elongated fingers and brushes my cheek. Their power flows through me, silky and cool, as they attempt to possess me long enough to free them.

Cassius flicks my nose to bring my attention back to him. He shifts so that he hovers over my knees and pulls me up to sitting. Bothered by his continued closeness, I lean back on my hands. He watches me curiously. I squirm under his study, uncomfortable with how his gray eyes dance over my features as if he's reading my thoughts.

"What's on your mind, Clara?"

His concern irritates me. I grit my teeth. "Stop pretending to care. What makes you think I would ever open up to you? We're not friends."

"So you've said…" He shrugs. "You don't have to be my friend, but you can't stop me from being yours," he says in all seriousness, not in the least bothered by my tone.

Friends with a vampire. I used to think that was impossible… until Alaric.

But being friends with their kind hasn't turned out well at all.

273

For immortal beings, they are more temporary than one would expect.

My mood sours further, but instead of stoking my anger, it's doused like a bucket of ice-cold water over a candle, and all I can feel is the ache in my hollow chest.

"You're getting steadily quicker. I didn't expect you to improve so quickly," Cassius says. Perhaps he recognizes that his friend tactic isn't going to work. "Imagine what getting a decent night's sleep will do to help you along."

I snort.

He still crouches over me, keeping me from moving. Sitting here is only allowing me to dwell on Alaric and the questions that have no answers. Frustration builds. I need to let it out, or it will consume me.

I lift my hands and place them on Cassius's shoulders, shoving as hard as I can. He topples back, and I pull my legs up. He hits the ground, and I scramble, grinning as I get to my feet at the same time he leaps to his.

He doesn't waste a moment starting up the carefully choreographed sparring sequence we've developed. Seamlessly, we switch as I stop blocking and strike out with my own punches and kicks. He adapts without the slightest effort.

The moves feel awkward, but I've watched him enough to have a basic understanding of what to do. He leaves an opening to his face. I strike, and he blocks. Again and again, I don't land a single hit. Sweat drips down the dip of my spine and the sides of my face. Loose wisps of hair stick to my skin.

I let out a growl of frustration and kick.

I miss. The lack of contact sends me off balance.

Cassius reaches out and grabs me by the waist, keeping me from falling. He holds me in mid-air, grinning. "You need to learn to fine tune your movements, but I'm pleasantly surprised by how much you've picked up. We can call it a day and work on your technique tomorrow."

"No," I snap, maneuvering out of his hold and straightening. I don't need him to placate me.

I swing my fist, missing.

Every time I fail to land a hit, it fuels my determination to keep going, to put every ounce of frustration into each movement.

I tell myself that if I can land a hit, then Alaric will let me in on his plan. I know things don't work like that, but if I can do the impossible, then—

Cassius steps inside my circle of space and aims a fist for my face. I tilt my head and strike. My fist connects with him just below the ribs. His eyes widen, and I drop, sweeping my leg and connecting with his. He falls hard.

I stand above him, panting, my fists balled at my sides, and I glare down at him, furious.

"You let me land those hits," I accuse. Cassius remains on his back, returning my look with a neutral one. I crouch next to him and offer a hand. "I don't need you to go easy to make me feel better."

He sits up.

When he doesn't take my hand, I start to rise, but he grabs hold of my arm in a lightning-quick move and pulls me back down to his level.

Cassius stares at me, lips parted. The way he's looking at me makes me feel self-conscious.

"Get up, or let go," I say.

"I didn't *let* you land your hits out of pity."

"Then what was it—trying to get on my good side or trying to make me feel better?"

"When have I ever given a shit about your feelings, little bird?" He raises a brow. "That was your own doing. As I said earlier, you are getting faster."

He stops talking, but there's a heavy weight to the air around us, and I have the feeling that, as usual, there is more that remains unsaid.

I tug on my arm when he refuses to let go. His hand cups the back of my neck and drags my head closer.

"I've never noticed the gold flecks in your eyes before."

I groan at the terrible line. It's close to the things boys back in Littlemire would say when they wanted to flatter the girls they wanted to court. Cassius is an idiot if he thinks terrible flirting will work on me.

His gaze flicks to my mouth then back up. My heart stutters.

"They are the same as they've always been." I roll my eyes and squeeze his wrist, prying it from my neck. When he releases me, I stand and retreat several paces.

Watching him sit on the floor with that childlike expression unnerves me. I brush off invisible dust from my clothes in an attempt to busy my hands.

"I'm hungry," I say even though I'm the furthest thing from it right now.

"You are getting better, markedly so over the past week," he says again.

I round on him, a little surprised to find him standing so close.

"Stop that." I jab a finger into his cheek. "I know you hate him, but you don't need to point out that he hasn't wanted anything to do with me for at least as long. I don't need your reminders."

Cassius walks over to the poles, still leaning against the wall from the beginning of our session.

"You should stay with me," he offers as he moves about, putting the room back the way it was.

I press my hand to my forehead, thrown off by his constant subject changes. "Why would I? In case you forgot, I'm already claimed."

Cassius is back in front of me in a blink, a gust of air sipping around us from his lightning-fast movements. "Has he forgotten? Because it seems as though he's finally accepted his roll as the queen's consort and doesn't give two demon shits about what becomes of you. You need to stop dwelling and move on."

The words sting and somehow ring true. They are the words I spent hours thinking about as I lay in bed, unable to fall asleep. My face burns with anger.

"You go too far," I say, meaning to bite out, but my voice is barely more than a whisper.

"No, little bird, I haven't gone far enough. You need to wake up to the reality of your situation before you get yourself killed because you can't stop thinking about a man who is lost to you." He bares his fangs.

What he says echoes Varin's words.

"Go fuck a demon," I snap and turn on my heel, storming out of the training room.

I storm through the hall and into the servants' quarters. Passing the door to my room, I keep going, wending through the corridors, putting more space between me and that insufferable vampire. I want to hide, to find a place where no one can find me.

A little too late, I slow down and take in my surroundings. Not paying attention was careless. Both Alaric and Cassius have drilled the need to be aware into me.

This wing of the castle is empty. Cream curtains frame the windows that have the same decretive diamond-shaped panes. Occasional paintings decorate the walls, the paint faded and chipping. I wonder when the last time this area was used. Dust particles dance and swirl in the last of the afternoon light shining in through the windows.

A cold hand wraps around my wrist. I know without looking that it's a vampire. I twist my arm and jerk. The hand lets go.

I open my mouth to snap at Cassius to stop following me like I need to be watched or have my training tested every second. I've had enough of him for one day. I spin around and come face to face with someone I don't expect.

"Mother?" I croak out.

CHAPTER
THIRTY
CLARA

She rubs her hand, giving me a disapproving look as though I was playing outside in the mud and tracked it into the house.

"What do you want?" I snap.

Mother glowers. "I want to talk with you."

"We've already tried that, and I have nothing more to say to you." I turn sharply from her and start to walk away.

"I was wrong," she says. Those three words echo through the hall, ringing in my ears. "I never should have left like I did, and I never should have dismissed you when you told me what happened." Her words grow softer as she approaches cautiously.

She places a hand on my shoulder. That simple touch releases the gates on the emotions that have been compounding for the past several weeks.

I can't find the words to respond.

"Clara, I never meant to hurt you. I thought... without me there, Gerhard would be able to provide a better life for you girls. There would be more money for food, and pretty dresses, and your dowries."

My throat thickens. For the first time since learning she was still alive, I feel like she is finally being honest with me. I squeeze my eyes shut and count to three, composing myself, then, I turn to face her.

"It didn't quite go like that," I say.

She nods. "I see that now."

"We missed you," I admit, "every single day."

A light draft riffles the stands of my hair, lightly brushing them against the side of my face.

"I missed you too, my dear girl. I'm so—" She stops in mid-sentence, her brows scrunching together. Her mouth opens and shuts like a fish out of water.

"Mother?" I reach out to her.

A small bead of blood forms in the corner of her mouth, staining her teeth. The drop slides down her chin.

I take a step back, staring at a dark spot on her chest through the light green of her dress. The spot grows, blooming like a macabre flower, spreading until red stains the front of her dress.

She collapses to her knees and crumples into a heap on the floor, but my gaze doesn't follow—snagging on the man behind her.

The vampire from the reclaiming, the one who compelled me into beheading his competition.

"If you know what's good for you, you will refrain from screaming or making any other loud noise intended to alert others." He pulls out a white handkerchief as he speaks. His eyes glow red, never leaving my face as he wipes down a long, thin blade before placing it into the top of a cane and twisting it back in place.

I back up. My instincts scream for me to run, but if I take my eyes off him for even a fraction of a second, I will be dead before I'm aware of what's happening.

He drops the handkerchief on top of Mother. It flitters down, landing in the red nimbus forming around her. It soaks into the cloth until every stitch of white is saturated in dark blood.

He steps over her unnaturally still body, prowling toward me.

"Mr. Hughes…"

An unpleasant smile forms, stretching his thin lips. "Please, call me, Alexander."

"What do you want from me?"

He adjusts his jacket and cuffs. "I couldn't help but notice that your master is nowhere to be found for the past week."

Alexander moves lightning-quick, grabbing my wrist. He looms over me, flashing his fangs.

"I wonder if you are even claimed or if that was all an act, like everything else *our dear prince* does." His voice is full of disdain. "He struts around pretending as if he's stronger than the rest of us when he is far from it."

Strutting? This man talks about Alaric as if he's never met him before.

"He's powerful enough to not have to prove it to anyone," I mutter under my breath. Realizing too late that I spoke out loud, I clamp my lips together, pressing in a tight line.

The vampire snarls and tightens his hold on my wrist. Alexander pulls me behind him, dragging me farther from the populated area. I have to jog to just keep up with him. I don't struggle, waiting for my chance to strike and run.

When we reach the end of the hall, he continues up a narrow staircase. Cobwebs cling to the banister telling its story of how long it has been forgotten. I suppress the feeling of dread crawling its way up my throat.

I'm breathless by the time we reach the top. There's a small landing with a single door. The vampire shoulders it, splintering the wood around the lock. He jerks my arm, flinging me inside. I stumble forward, barely catching myself. I take a second to let my eyes adjust to the low light. The door slams closed, trapping me with him.

Inside the cramped space, furniture is stacked against the wall, covered with heavy, white sheets. A tall window faces out on the valley to the south.

Alexander didn't bring me here to talk. He brought me here to kill me and dispose of my body, ensuring no one will find me... at least not for a long time.

Let them underestimate you, and let them live to regret it. Alaric's words come back to me, and I cling to them, using them to steel my spine. I have been claimed and marked by Alaric. I have been trained by Cassius to fight vampires. I might have a long way to go before my skills are honed, but today, I landed a hit on a vampire and knocked him on his ass.

I don't need to be rescued.

Drawing in a deep breath, I blow it out slowly and look Alexander in the eye, giving him the same smile that so many vampires have given me. "You need to let me go now, or you'll regret it."

He throws his head back and laughs.

"I'm marked," I say. "I don't give two demon shits if you believe it or not."

He ignores me and removes his jacket, flinging it onto a covered chair. Dust explodes into the air, thickening the musty scent of this room. He unbuttons his cuffs and rolls up his sleeves.

The actions minor his earlier ones. They seem to be a tick, and I wonder if he is aware of them.

"If you don't believe me, then try compelling me," I offer. Turning to the side, I look out the window to the sprawling land below—not giving him my back but letting him know I'm not concerned.

Alexander grips my arm and spins me around to face him.

"Bow before me, human."

His power sprawls out from him with each word and wraps around me. It's a strange prickly sensation, nothing like Alaric's, or Cassius's, or even Varin's power. It wraps around me, but no part of me twitches, wanting to do as he commands.

I lift my chin a little higher and smirk.

"So it's true then." He glowers. "I guess humans can't lie all the time."

I keep my mouth shut. Humans lie as often as vampires. There is little difference between us.

He circles me slowly as if he's seeing a human for the first time. A twisted part of me revels in the fact that I'm throwing him off balance.

"You humiliated me at the reclaiming," Alexander says when he's in front of me again.

I cant my head to the side, remaining quiet. A sense of calm washes over me. I am not afraid of this vampire, not like I was afraid of Victor back at Windbury, not like I used to fear their very existence.

"You let him mark you," he spits out.

"You say that like I had a choice in any of it." I turn slowly as he circles me. "You were there. You saw what happened."

"You are responsible for his actions, so his marking you was a humiliation on both of your parts."

I frown, giving him the best pitying expression I can muster. "Did it injure your pride that much?"

In a blur, the back of his hand strikes my cheek, snapping my head to the side. My skin burns, and the slightest tang of blood hits my tongue. If he thinks a hit will make me quake before him, then he will have to think again. I've endured worse, and I'm stronger for it.

"You belong to him... for now."

I scoff. "I belong to no one but myself."

Maybe I'm wrong about his motivations. All he's done is talk. If he wanted to kill me, he would have done so by now.

I step around him and hurry toward the door, but he moves fast and cuts me off.

"It's too late," I say, "and there's nothing that can change that. Even if he's not around, I am still bound to him."

"Not so fast," he says.

I inch to the side, but he matches my movements seamlessly.

"Eshroth," Alexander calls out.

There's a quiet chattering noise, and then a large spider crawls onto his shoulder from his back. Bile burns its way up my throat, and I stumble back several steps. No spider should be that large, but I suppose it's not really a spider at all, but his demon.

He doesn't seem to notice my reaction.

"There is still something that can be done about that pesky mark of his," he says casually. Those words are enough to draw my attention from the creepy demon back to him. "We can make it so it's as if the mark was never there."

The back of my heel bumps up against a stack of wood, sending spare pieces of planks or framing clattering to the floor.

Undo the mark?

He lifts the spider from his shoulder and stretches his hand out to me. I lean away.

Alexander sighs then, with a dramatic eye roll, yanks on my hand, and sets the spider in my palm. My muscles strain to pull out of his grip, but he continues to hold me.

The spider's long, needle-like legs dance over my skin. They move up my arm to my shoulder. I want to slap them away. I've never liked spiders, but I never feared them before. Seeing one this size is... unsettling.

The demon sniffs, and I feel the tiny scratching of two legs that prod at the bite marks on my neck and shoulder. The demon turns and skitters back down my arm into their master's hand, chirping the whole way.

The vampire glowers at whatever they say.

Alexander's mouth turns up at the corners. "Interesting," he murmurs, relinquishing his hold on my wrist. I take several steps back until I bump into the wall. He looks like he's planning something I know I won't like. "You've been getting yourself into more trouble than I could have guessed for a human *Alaric* picked out. Who knew he has such... curious tastes."

"I have no idea what you're talking about."

The vampire lists his lips. "I am quite pleased Elise persuaded me to try again to reclaim you."

"If you want to kill me, then get on with it," I say, tired of his endless droning.

I need him to make a move. If I draw my dagger too early, then I will have lost before I begin. I need to catch him off guard.

"Oh, no, my pet," he says, placing his spider demon back on his shoulder. They scurry away, back to wherever they were hiding earlier. "I have no plans to kill you. I will bind you to me, overriding the mark."

I shake my head, not understanding. "The mark is for life."

"Normally, it would be, unless..."

I don't ask what the condition is because that's what he wants.

He pulls me away from the window and presses my back against his chest. I hadn't planned on throwing myself out, but the way he's looking at me makes me reconsider.

"You and I will take the oath, and it will bind you to me, like the mark binds you to Alaric." He paces the room, stopping when he's at my back. "The oath is stronger, and it is for life. Our bond will be unbreakable. You will live as long as any vampire, and you will only die in the ways a vampire can die. You will essentially have the powers I have, except of course, you will not have your own demon, nor will you be able to overpower me."

"That's... impossible," I whisper.

"You and I will be bound. *Forever*." He runs his fingers over the scars of my neck, thumb caressing the nape of my neck.

"You're insane if you think I would willingly bind myself to you. I would rather die."

He leans forward, putting his mouth next to my ear, his hot breath fanning across my cheek. "Consider it. What human wouldn't want the long life of a vampire? Added strength and speed, never aging, never suffering a single day from human ailments, and none of the side effects like needing to drink blood."

I step away, but his hand slides up and tangles in my hair, keeping me in place.

"Me," I say. "I don't want that."

Especially not when it would mean being bound to the

vampire who compelled me into decapitating someone.

I've had enough. Flexing my fingers, I run through what I need to do in my mind. Then, I shove my elbow back into his gut. Alexander's hand loosens, and his breath is forced out in a pained whoosh. Then, I'm free.

He snarls, bumping into the frames behind him. "You'll pay for that, girl!"

I whirl in time just as he backhands me.

The hit forces me to the side. I stumble. There's a deep thunk, and blinding stars explode before my eyes as my head cracks against stone.

CHAPTER
THIRTY-ONE
CLARA

Fiery hot needles prickle across my cheek in time with my pulse as my face already begins to swell. My vision wavers in and out of focus. Hissing through my teeth, I press a hand to my head to stop the ringing.

Alexander lunges, and I roll away, but I'm too slow. He grips my arm, hauling me to my feet, preventing me from drawing my dagger.

Using his hold to steady me, I widen my feet and sink down into my stance as Cassius taught me to do.

Alexander drags a sharp nail over my heart. I suck in a raspy breath, and he digs deeper, past the skin and into the muscle, drawing a whimper. His lips curl at the sound.

I grab hold of his shoulder, bringing my knee up into his groin. His mouth drops open as he doubles at the waist, stumbling backward, but his momentary distraction doesn't last long. He strikes out with both hands, fingers curled into claws.

I spin away, but his nails slice through my sleeve, tearing into my arm and sending a searing wave of pain across my skin.

Spinning away, I stumble into the wall. I need to get to the door, but Alexander is careful to keep himself positioned between me and my escape.

A wave of dizziness throws me off balance, and I use the wall to prop myself up, gasping for air more than I should. The vampire bares his fangs and stalks forward, stopping just out of reach. Keeping his gaze locked on me, he drags a nail down his forearm.

"Stop fighting me, pet. Do as I say before you bleed to death."

I press tighter against the wall. The sight of him cutting his own arm startles me. He inches closer, watching my every movement.

When he's within reach, I push off the wall and ram him with my shoulder. He grunts and uses his weight to pin me to the wall.

Shit, shit, shit.

He takes both of my hands and holds them above my head. Pain explodes along my right arm where he cut me. Blood continues to seep from my wounds, the tangy smell of copper filling the air. His is already healing.

"If you're lucky, you might just live through this process." He hums thoughtfully to himself. "Unless I change my mind and kill you instead." He leans in and drags his tongue along one of the deep gashes on my arm, watching me from the corners of his eyes. "If you live," he whispers, "I will chain you up in my room for the rest of eternity and feed on you."

Demons take me. I will not let that happen.

I spit. The wad of saliva lands below his eye. The shocked expression on his face sends a spark of pride through my veins. The vampire reels back, horrified. His perfectly quaffed hair sticks out wildly.

"Yes," he growls. "It's a good thing we will be taking that oath. You are in need of a master to teach you how a proper human ought to behave."

I don't bother replying. If Alexander hasn't guessed by now that I will fight him until one of us kills the other, then he hasn't been paying attention.

As Alexander wipes his face, I sprint around the edge of the room, racing toward the door. A cold hand with a steel grip catches my arm. I stumble to a halt as he squeezes down on my wounds, digging his fingers in.

"Tilt your head," he orders. Power reverberates in his words as he attempts to compel me.

I laugh. At first, it comes out as a strangled chuckle, quickly becoming hysterical.

"I will never obey you," I say.

Alexander clicks his tongue as if reprimanding a petulant

child. "Fine. Then, I will make you bleed."

I'm about to retort that he already has when he swipes a hand across my abdomen, scoring my flesh with his nails.

Hot and cold wash over me in waves. I gasp, pressing my hands to my stomach to stanch the bleeding. He releases me, and I crash to my knees. I peel my hands away to assess the damage, but doing so only makes the pain more real.

Alexanders hums pleasantly to himself, drawing my gaze up. He watches me with a bemused expression, sucking on each finger, tasting my blood.

He lifts his foot, setting it on my shoulder, and knocks me flat on my back. Positioning himself over me, Alexander sits on my hips. He leans forward, placing one hand next to my head on top of my hair, locking me into place. His other hand runs up my sliced arm, across the gash over my heart, and then down to my stomach.

Alexander smears blood over what remains of my shirt as he plays with my wounds. Each poke and prod sends waves of nausea roiling through me.

I twist my hips, lifting them off the floor and wrench to the side, dumping him off of me. He lands at my side, shock written over his expression. I pull back my arm and aim. There's a sickening crunch as my fist connects with his nose. It's enough to sap most of my remaining energy. I'm not sure how much fight I have left. If I don't end this soon, I will never leave this place.

I push up from the floor and scramble past him. Alexander

grabs my ankle and pulls. I land hard, barely catching myself before my face smashes into the stone.

He drags me backward. I scream as the cuts on my belly rub across the floor. I'm almost relieved when he flips me onto my back, but it doesn't last. His long fingers wrap around my throat, squeezing. It doesn't cut off my air supply entirely, just enough that black spots blot out my vision.

"Nothing beats fresh blood with the sweet taste of adrenaline. It's so rare to find a human willing to fight but doesn't fear me," he pants. He presses a finger into the cut on my chest then brings it to his mouth. "You will be mine, and then, we will have eternity to play."

I stop struggling as his grip on my throat tightens. Several heartbeats later, he makes a disgusted sound and releases my neck, disgusted that I've stopped resisting. I gasp in the stale, musty air of the small tower room.

His plan might be to bond us with the oath, but I'm slowly bleeding out, inching closer to death with every passing second. I will die if he keeps this up much longer—not that I ever stood much of a chance. I may have landed a few blows, but he is at full strength.

A soft cackle sounds in my head, humorless and dry. The sound wraps around my mind.

What have you gotten yourself into this time?

I groan, not needing to fight Varin off as well.

You can go back to the Otherworld, demon, I snap back at them mentally.

If you had accepted my help, you would not be in this mess. You might not have had to die.

I'm not dead yet.

Anger flares, and I shove the demon from my mind, block it out, and focus on the monster on top of me.

Alexander continues to carve my skin, completely focused on what he's doing. I don't know if he thinks I passed out or am on the edge of death, too weak to fight anymore.

"Enough games for now," he says.

He slices one nail across his own chest, reopening his wound, then tangles his fist in my hair, and forces me to sit up, pulling me toward his chest.

I slide my hand over my stomach, inching toward the sheathed dagger strapped to my arm. When my right hand is firmly around the hilt, I flop my left arm to the ground, drawing his attention. His head moves a fraction, his eyes following.

This is my only chance.

"I will never be bound to you," I grind out through clenched teeth.

I bring my knee up, hard and swift. The move doesn't do more than shift both of our positions, but that's all I need.

He rears back, scowling. Then, I bring my right fist up and plunge the blade into his side. The point strikes between ribs, meeting no resistance.

The hand gripping the back of my head goes slack as I pull the night-forged dagger out.

Alexander gasps, pressing a hand to his side. He looks at the red staining his palm. I push him over and scramble until we've switched positions, and I straddle him. Then, I plunge the dagger into his chest with every ounce of strength I have left. He reaches up, clawing at my face. I twist the blade then yank it out, and he falls back.

Gripping the dagger in both hands, I bring it down again.

Again.

And again.

CHAPTER
THIRTY-TWO
CLARA

I plunge the dagger deep into his chest until the hilt prevents it from going farther. I drop my head, letting my shoulders slump. I refuse to let go, too afraid to look away—afraid he will sit up and rip out my throat.

I am not dead yet…

I am not dead…

My breath comes in shaky, uneven bursts as warm blood still trickles down my arm… my chest… my stomach.

I am not dead.

The pain of my wounds comes back, rising like a pool of water. I can't see through the tears burning the backs of my eyes.

"Clara…"

The sound of my name vaguely registers, sounding like a faraway echo.

A hand lands on my shoulder. The touch is so unexpected I rip the dagger from Alexander's chest and swing.

Cassius leaps back, barely avoiding my strike. I blink and focus on his horrified expression then release the dagger. It clatters on the floor. The sound is loud, deafening silence.

"Fuck," Cassius mutters, running his hand down his face. "What happened, Clara?"

I look down. My hands, my shirt, and the dead man I straddle are stained in a mixture of my blood and his.

"I…" I curl my fingers into my palms and hug my middle. Whatever kept me going is beginning to wear off.

Cassius crouches at my side, hands hovering as if he's afraid to touch me. Seeing his uncertainty makes me wonder if this scene is even worse than I think.

I offer him my uninjured left arm, and he helps me to stand. He doesn't speak but continues to hold onto me, letting me lean on him. He reaches up and smooths his hand over my head in a ghost of a caress.

With that touch, I feel everything all at once. I was attacked for being Alaric's marked human, and he was nowhere in sight. Tears well up and fall without warning, tears of frustration, anger, pain, betrayal… and relief that somehow, I didn't die.

"We need to get you cleaned up. There's enough blood here to call half the vampires in this castle."

I grip his hand hard, not sure when I'd taken it. I feel so weak, and that thought makes me giggle. Weak? But I've managed to kill five... or is it six vampires now?

"Clara?" Cassius asks, an unsure expression on his face. "Did you damage your brain in that fight?"

"I'm fine," I say, reining in my laughter. "I just feel like I'm dying."

He tsks, wrapping an arm around my waist, careful to avoid the gashes on my stomach, and scoops my legs up.

I relax into him, tired and aching.

"How did you find me?" I ask.

The muscle of his jaw feathers before he answers. "I knew what direction you went, and when you never returned to your room, I came looking for you. When I found your mother, I knew you couldn't be far. You weren't hard to find with as much as you've bled." He looks down at me with an unreadable expression.

"Are you angry with me?" I ask. Though, I'm not sure why because I don't care if he is.

"No, little bird, I'm not," he says. "Now hold on. I need to get you somewhere safe to clean up before anyone else finds you here."

Fisting my hands in his shirt, I dip my head, resting it on his shoulder, and close my eyes.

He moves with a sickeningly fast pace, not slowing until I hear the click of a door moments later. I peel open my eyes and take in his room.

Cassius marches over to the cushy chair next to the fireplace. The heat of the fire instantly washes over me. I hadn't even realized I was cold until now. Shivers rack my body, and I can't seem to control them.

He sets me down on my feet and points to the chair. "Sit. I need to heal you."

I expected him to be furious that I wandered off and killed another vampire.

"Why are you being nice?" I demand. I don't trust him. He's been ordered by the queen to keep me alive from what I can tell, but the training and the rescue...

"You'll bleed to death. It will be slow, but it will happen."

"You could heal me without my cooperation," I point out, unsure why I'm arguing the point.

"Is that what you want?"

"No."

"Then sit down, and tell me where you're hurt. There's too much blood for me to see without undressing you completely."

I lower myself onto the chair, sinking into the cushions, then point out my numerous injuries.

Closing my eyes, I breathe through the ache.

"I meant, why do you train me in the mornings? I already

know the queen ordered you to keep watch over me, so why bother pretending to care?" I ask.

Vampires can't be trusted, but even thinking that squeezes at my heart because the thought is directed more toward Alaric than Cassius. I trusted him, and I'm beginning to think it was a mistake.

Cassius says nothing as he pulls the material of my shirt in a way that both keeps me covered and exposes every slice on my skin.

"It's not that bad," I mutter. "I can wrap them myself."

"It is, and it will bring every vampire on this floor to this room if you don't let me heal you."

I lift my shoulder of my uninjured arm and give a half shrug.

"These wounds are worse than anything sustained in training. This will be painful," he warns.

I steel my jaw, bracing for what's to come. "I've been healed while awake before. I understand."

"Because of the mark, I can't compel you to sleep."

"I know," I snap, irritated with his warnings, wishing he would get on with it already.

Tilting my head up, I focus on the texture of the ceiling, the unfinished beams painted white to match the walls, and the knots still visible in the wood.

Cassius lays his hands atop the open wounds. I flinch, my heartbeat kicking up. Every part of me is raw and aching. I don't look forward to the added pain of healing.

Several endless seconds pass before the warm light of his power radiates under his palms. I pull in a breath and hold it, waiting, but all that comes is a deep ache. It's uncomfortable but not painful. I release my breath and relax.

Cassius's hands move to my arms next, my chest, and then to the scratches along my shoulders, healing the worst of it first. His eyes are focused, not looking up from each area until he's finished.

"How do you feel? Are there other injuries you didn't tell me about?" When I don't move or say anything, he presses the back of his hand to my forehead. "Clara, talk to me."

I blink, not understanding why he sounds more worried now than he did minutes before. I sit up and go through the motions of flexing my muscles and bending my joints. "I'm fine. I feel like I haven't slept in a year, but nothing hurts."

"You didn't seem bothered by the process."

"I wouldn't say it was pleasant... Perhaps it didn't bother me because everything else was worse?" I offer.

He seems doubtful but doesn't press the issue.

I jump when someone knocks.

Cassius glares at the visitor through the door, then rising to his feet, he says, "Go in the bathroom and get cleaned up."

My heart hammers in my chest as I wonder if it's Alaric at the door. "But—"

"Go now, Clara." He rips off his shirt and tosses it into the fire.

I don't understand his sudden mood shift, but I really do

need to wash this blood off me. I turn and make my way to the bathroom, stopping just inside the threshold. I strain to hear the voice of whoever came by, but they are talking too low. Giving up, I sit on the edge of the bathtub and wait.

Minutes later, Cassius walks in wearing a new shirt and frowns.

"Was that him?" I ask. I don't have to say Alaric's name for him to understand.

"I told you to get cleaned up."

His tone grates on me. "I don't have my clothes here. They are in my old room."

"Then, I will send for them later, but for now, you need to wash. Help yourself to anything you can find here."

I need clothes, not towels or bedsheets. I can't imagine that he would have women's clothes lying around. Even considering wearing something of his twists my gut. There aren't many options other than washing my clothes and laying them out as I bathe.

"You didn't answer my question," I say. "Was that Alaric?"

He grinds his teeth then bites out, "No."

If that had any semblance of truth to it, there would be no anger, no hesitation. Anger and sorrow mix in an ugly combination of feelings. He was so close to me, and I missed him.

"This is why I don't trust you," I snap.

"Let him go, Clara."

"You let *me* go."

Cassius stalks closer, his speed and posture sending me on the defense. I jump to my feet. Cassius takes me in from my fists to my defensive stance then backs up a step.

"Do you understand why so many vampires seek you out and not any of the other hundreds of humans in this castle?" he asks.

The question is unexpected. I pause, scrunching up my nose and think. "Is it because I'm chosen by the demons and saints of the Otherworld?"

"Clara, this isn't a joke."

I fold my arms over my chest and, not having a genuine reason to offer up, shake my head.

When I don't answer, he says, "It's because they don't respect him. Elizabeth is offering Alaric more power than any of us could dream of, and yet he refuses. He doesn't want it, and not a single one of us understands why."

I swallow thickly. My head starts to pound but not from the day's events.

"I must leave for the evening. That is no small mess to clean." He turns and walks away, stopping in the doorway to look back. "Please stay inside until I return."

Then, he leaves me alone.

CHAPTER
THIRTY-THREE
ALARIC

The door opens, just enough for Cassius's face to show, his body blocking the view of the room.

My nostrils flare as the sharp tang of human and vampire blood wafts from inside. "What is going on in there?"

"You shouldn't be here," Cassius says blandly. "What do you want?"

"Is Clara in there?"

Cassius arches a golden brow. "You know better than to ask that."

"Tell me if she's here." I pause before adding, "Please."

Cassius looks over my shoulder where Cherno flies in erratic circles in the air then back to me. "She is."

I press against the door, intending to push past him.

He doesn't budge.

"You are Elizabeth's consort first and a human's master last," he says. Lowering his voice, he adds, "Coming here will only put her in more danger. You need to stay away from Miss Valmont."

His words are a reminder that keeps me from forcing my way in to Clara. I straighten and adopt a blank mask. "I have a message," I say. "There's to be a court meeting at midnight, per our queen's decree."

Cassius shifts, giving me a sliver of sight into the room. I don't see Clara or evidence of the blood I smell.

"Has Elizabeth demoted you to her little errand boy now? That's quite the status fall, even for you."

"Be careful," I say, bringing my face close to his and flashing my fangs, "You would do well to remember your place. I might never have wanted this position, but I am here now and will soon have even more power at my fingertips." Stepping back, I straighten. "I am giving you this message for a reason."

Cassius studies me with a pensive expression. Finally, he says, "Then, tell me the *real* reason you're here."

I remain silent for a long moment before saying, "I want to see her."

"We both know why you can't do that. Do not be a fool."

I snarl. "She bears my mark, not yours or anyone else's. And so help me, if you touch her—"

Cassius grins wickedly. "Again, *my prince*." He spits the words

307

as though they're an insult. "That is no longer your concern."

I grip him by the front of his shirt and bring my face within an inch of his. "Do not touch her."

"That is up to Clara." He pushes my hands off and smooths out the wrinkles from his shirt. "Did you know she killed another vampire? Another court member and he wasn't even demon cursed."

Whatever I was about to say or do evaporates. I gape. "Who?"

"Alexander Hughes."

"The one from the reclaiming..." It takes everything in me to not demand the details. The blood... it is hers, but there's another's mixed with it.

Cassius nods. "She is unharmed, but you will need to do something if you don't want to see her dead."

Elizabeth lifts herself up on her toes and cups my cheek, giving two pats before placing a kiss on my mouth.

"This was a pleasant surprise," she says, pulling away. "It is good you have finally accepted your fate. Things will soon be as they always should have been."

"You are right, my queen. I have been stubborn." I put every ounce of repentance into my words that I can summon.

Elizabeth smiles, cat-like and victorious. She snaps her finger, and Kharis swoops out of the shadows. They glide through the room and snatch Cherno from my shoulder with their taloned feet. The raven swings around, cutting the air with their broad wings and flinging my demon into the empty, gilded birdcage. The cage door closes and locks. Cherno presses against it and hisses, falling to the bottom of the cage.

Night-forged silver coated in gold to make it look harmless. It's the perfect size for a creature as small as Cherno, meant to keep them, and me, weakened.

My lip pulls back in a snarl at Kharis.

"Now, now, don't look so sour. This is only temporary. I will let them go once everything is in place."

Reining in my fury, I nod obediently. "Of course, my queen."

I have chosen to stand by her side in exchange for Clara's life. Eyeing the cage, I have to wonder if she knew this moment would come by her design or if she had only hoped it would.

I stick out my elbow, offering it to her. She loops her hand through, and I tuck her arm into my side. Together, we walk down the halls toward the throne room.

It's empty, save for the eleven remaining court members. We were twelve for so long, and then, she created Victor. But Clara had killed him... and now Alexander.

I watch her from the corner of my eye and wonder if she notices. Her face is unreadable as I escort her to the throne and remain standing at her side until she motions for me to sit.

The court is restless, murmuring quietly among themselves. I catch a few words here and there. No one knows the purpose of this meeting except for Elizabeth—and her secrets have never led to anything good.

She looks at each member of her court in turn. The moment her lavender eyes land on them, they fall silent.

Lawrence catches my eye, frowning. He tilts his head a fraction, confusion about this unexpected meeting clear in the crease of his brows, but I have no answers for him. I turn away from my friend to watch the man who has been a thorn in my side since the day Elizabeth turned him. Cassius holds his head high and places every ounce of his attention on the queen.

"Thank you all for coming. While the matter we are to discuss tonight is not dire, it is one that must be dealt with sooner rather than later to keep the peace we have become accustomed to," Elizabeth begins. Her smile is far too broad.

Other than the typical petty squabbles among ourselves, there has been nothing out of the ordinary happening to call a meeting. The shifters have all left and live far enough away that there is no reason for our groups to have conflict.

Elizabeth holds her hand out to me, and I take it. Together, we stand.

"But first, I have an announcement." She pauses, drawing out the moment until it is painful. "Our prince has decided to finally accept his place as consort. The crowning ceremony will be in two months' time, where he will be oath bound to me."

My blood turns to ice.

There's a pregnant pause before the court breaks into subdued applause.

Oath bound to Elizabeth. I want to rip my hand away, to refuse all of this right here and now. That was not part of the deal, but speaking out against her now would be a death sentence for Clara.

I would rather cut out my own heart and feed it to the demons of the Otherworld than suffer a bond with Elizabeth. Whatever I do from here on out, I must do with care, or Clara will be the one paying the price.

She retakes her seat and looks ready to dismiss everyone. Surely this could not be the reason she called the meeting.

Elizabeth motions with her chin for me to sit. I do, keeping my mouth pressed into a tight line.

"Now, down to business," she says once the room quiets.

I blow out a relieved breath. That announcement was a last-second addition... except that doesn't explain the cage made specifically for Cherno. The details of her plans are beginning to take shape. I have fallen into every single trap she has laid out.

"Now that my consort will finally be crowned, he no longer has need for his marked human."

My gut twists. Clara is the purpose of this meeting, after all.

"The reclaiming ceremony did not go as expected, and to prevent another such bothersome event, I will allow one of you to claim her."

"But she is already marked," a woman, hidden by several other taller members, says.

"Yes," Elizabeth says, a fake pout on her lips. Her delight at this situation only serves to feed the dread freezing my blood in my veins. "The vampire who will become her new master must be willing to oath bind themselves to her."

What she means is that Clara will not be bound to me.

Murmurs erupt with most of the court shaking their heads. A few even take a step back, revolted by the idea that they would be unable to claim another human ever again. Not many vampires willingly bind themselves to a human, and only on rare occasions will they do so with another vampire.

The urge to stand up and defy her nearly takes over, but I force myself to remain precisely as I am—keeping very still, my hands resting loosely on the arms of my throne, my face void of any reactions.

Cassius steps forward, and my vision turns red.

"I have been her guardian since the masquerade. I have developed a rapport with the human. I'm confident I can persuade her to take the oath with minimal effort." He looks around at everyone, daring them to challenge him, his gaze stopping on Elizabeth—purposefully avoiding mine.

No one speaks up; no one else offers. He is above them all, only below Elizabeth and I in power. There is no doubt in my mind that is the reason for this. If he can't have my position, then he will take everything he can from me.

Elizabeth's fingers graze the back of my hand, drawing my attention. She watches me with cool curiosity. I have no idea if I've given anything away.

This farce of a meeting is all about Clara, giving Elizabeth the chance to announce her victory over me to the entirety of this court. Publicly giving me power then taking something from me simultaneously—showing us all that she is the queen for a reason.

"Yes," she says, finally turning back to Cassius. "The human is yours. Oath bind her to you." Her gaze flicks to me. "But do not kill her. No matter what her crimes are, she will be safe from punishment, but you are expected to bring her to heel. However you do it, get it done. She cannot remain wild."

I stop listening as the queen brings this meeting to an end.

Clara will be oath bound to Cassius, and I to Elizabeth.

Elizabeth either knew I was planning to give in, at least in appearance, even before I consciously made the decision, or she intended to force my hand.

Though less than a half-hour in length, every second of this was a carefully crafted performance—a test to see how much control she has over me.

I turn my face up and take in the sharp angles of her profile. She gives me a sweet smile that could mean anything.

Though it remains to be seen if I have passed or failed.

Continue the series in

THE VAMPIRE OATH

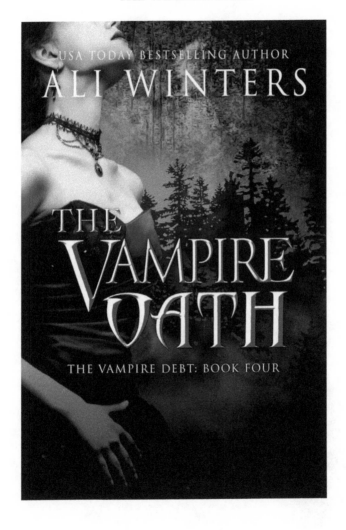

USA TODAY BESTSELLING AUTHOR

ALI WINTERS

THE VAMPIRE OATH

THE VAMPIRE DEBT: BOOK FOUR

ACKNOWLEDGEMENTS

Writing is a solitary occupation and yet, it takes so many people to breathe life into a book. And this book was no exception.

So in random order:

Thank you to Krys and Erin for having my back, my fellow atomic indies, my ARC readers, beta readers, husband, SmartFood spicy popcorn, my pups, and of course, you, my readers—thank you for your love and support.

ABOUT THE AUTHOR

Ali Winters is the USA TODAY Bestselling author of several series filled with romance, magic, and adventure.

Her first love will always be fantasy, but she fully admits to being obsessed with coffee and T-Rex, and has a weakness for love interests that walk the line between gray and villainy.

Ali was born and raised in the PNW but now currently resides in the wastelands that time forgot, with impossibly cold winters, and summers that are too short. She spends her days with her husband and alpha of her two dog pack. (They have assimilated her as one of their own and since she's the only one with opposable thumbs, have made her their leader.)

When she's not consumed with creating magical worlds for readers to get lost in, she can be found walking, reading, designing graphics, and creating art in various mediums.

Visit Ali on the web at www.aliwinters.com
Facebook.com/authoraliwinters
instagram.com/authoraliwinters

To learn more about The Vampire Debt
www.thevampiredebt.com
To subscribe to Ali's monthly newsletter for new releases,
exclusive sneak peeks, and visit
www.aliwinters.com/newsletter

CPSIA information can be obtained
at www.ICGtesting.com
Printed in the USA
LVHW091814220321
682103LV00005B/1169